THE SONGBIRD

MARCIA WILLETT

ISIS
LARGE
PRINT

First published in Great Britain 2016
by
Bantam Press
an imprint of Transworld Publishers

First Isis Edition
published 2017
by arrangement with
Transworld Publishers
Penguin Random House

A catalogue record for this book is available
from the British Library.

ISBN 978–1–78541–368–1 (hb)
ISBN 978–1–78541–374–2 (pb)

THE SONGBIRD

When Mattie invites her old friend Tim to stay in one of her family cottages on the edge of Dartmoor, she senses there is something he is not telling her. But as he gets to know the rest of the warm jumble of family who live by the moor, Tim discovers that everyone there has their own secrets. There is Kat, a retired ballet dancer who longs for the stage again; Charlotte, a young navy wife struggling to bring up her son while her husband is at sea; William, who guards a dark past he cannot share with the others; and Mattie, who has loved Tim in silence for years. As Tim begins to open up, Mattie falls deeper in love. And as summer warms the wild Dartmoor landscape, new hope begins to bloom . . .

SPECIAL MESSAGE TO READERS

The extract on page ix from *Sands of the Well* by Denise Levertov is quoted by permission of Bloodaxe Books.

Every effort has been made to obtain the necessary permissions with reference to copyright material, both illustrative and quoted. We apologise for any omissions in this respect and will be pleased to make the appropriate acknowledgements in any future edition.

To Canon Michael and Jane Lewis

And to Roddy

This longing to show, to share,
Which runs full tilt into absence

from *Sands of the Well*
Denise Levertov

My thanks to Dr Tony Born and the District Nursing Team at South Brent Health Centre, and to the Crisis Team at St Luke's Hospital, Plymouth.

PART ONE

CHAPTER
ONE

All through the spring, early and late, the thrush sings in the ash tree below the cottage. It's the first thing he hears, when he comes carefully down the narrow precipitous staircase to make coffee, and the last thing, as he leans from the small window into the quiet luminous evening, unable to abandon the unearthly magic and get into bed.

There are no leaves yet on the trees. They hold up bare, misshapen arms and bony, twiggy fingers against a pale, translucent sky; yet he can never see the thrush hidden within these interlaced, fantastical patterns. He stands watching, seeing how the gardens tip down to the two fields — sown with barley, edged with thorn and ash — and across those fields to the lane beyond, which curls and climbs up to the old farmhouse.

Tim's is the last in the terrace of cottages, converted from stables to provide accommodation for Victorian servants; modernized again more recently. The old stable-yard, flanked by two open-fronted barns where cars are parked, is separated from the courtyard behind the main house by a five-bar gate.

It is many years since Brockscombe was a working farmhouse. Bought by a naval captain with his prize money from the Napoleonic wars, it has grown into a graceful family home, with white stucco and long sash windows, standing end-on to the lane and surrounded by fields sold long since to neighbouring farms.

Sometimes, when he's walking in the grounds, Tim thinks he sees ghostly figures waving at the upstairs windows — and his heart jumps with terror. But surely the ghosts are simply reflections: of racing clouds and the branches of the trees tossing in the wind? And why should he be afraid of ghosts? Is it because he fears he might soon be of their number: lost and alone, untethered from this friendly, familiar world?

It was Mattie who sent him to Brockscombe Farm. Pretty Mattie, with her honey-brown eyes and dark, curling hair.

"I'm leaving next month," he told her as they made tea in the small kitchen of the London publishing house where they worked, she as a publicist, he in the marketing department. "Taking a six-month sabbatical then moving on. I need somewhere to chill for a while. A cottage in the country but not too remote. Got any ideas?"

She looked at him thoughtfully, as if she could guess his secret. Suddenly he longed to tell her the whole truth but she asked no questions.

"You must go to Brockscombe," she said. "To Cousin Francis, William and Aunt Kat and Charlotte. It's perfect there for a sabbatical. Just west of Exeter."

He laughed. The set-up sounded so odd. "What's Brockscombe? Who are they, Cousin Francis, William and Aunt Kat and Charlotte?"

4

She laughed too. "Brockscombe is a beautiful old Georgian farmhouse owned by Francis Courtney. He's in his eighties and he lives there on his own. He was an MP and now he's writing his memoirs. I'm not exactly sure how he's related to William and Aunt Kat but they are cousins and they share one of the cottages in the grounds. Charlotte is my big sister. She's married to William's son, Andy. He's in the navy, first lieutenant on a frigate based in Plymouth. Charlotte wasn't very impressed with the naval quarters on offer so they moved into the cottage next door to William and Aunt Kat last autumn just before she had baby Oliver, which is really good because Andy's ship will be at sea for the next few months so she's got lots of support. Kat's Andy's cousin, too, of course, but he always calls her Aunt Kat and now we all do. It's all a bit off the wall but great fun. You'd like them."

"It certainly sounds . . . unusual."

"There's another cottage," she said. "It was empty last time I was there. You'd be private. Up to a point." She looked at him again, intently, consideringly. "They won't be tiresome and nosy," she assured him. "Well, not much, anyway."

They laughed again; it was so good for him to laugh, to ease the fear.

"I'd like to meet them," he said.

"Well, I can arrange that. Would you rather go alone or shall we go down together and I'll introduce you?"

Once again fear chilled him, disabling him. "I think that might be good. To go together. If you're sure?"

"Sure I'm sure," she said casually. "It's time I went down to Devon to see everyone. Let's make a plan to drive down, if you're happy to risk my old car."

Cousin Francis, William, Charlotte and Aunt Kat: Mattie briefed him on the drive from London. So vivid were her word pictures that Tim was able to visualize them clearly as the M4 reeled away behind them. William, separated from his wife, Fiona, is in his middle fifties, an accountant: short, cheerful, with a tonsure of curly pepper-and-salt hair and bright blue eyes. Aunt Kat, in her early sixties, a former international ballet dancer and choreographer: tall, graceful, unconventional. Charlotte, just turned thirty-two, a web designer; energetic and capable, and determined to be the perfect mother to her baby, five-month-old Oliver, as well as looking after her and Andy's golden retriever, Wooster. Cousin Francis, thin, angular, tough, emerging from his lair from time to time to sit in the sunshine and have a chat. As she recalled past meetings, told anecdotes, described their idiosyncrasies, Mattie brought them so clearly to life for Tim that, when he finally met them, it was as if they were already old friends.

How easy she made it, how simple. Driving him down, booking him into a local pub as if she knew that he'd need his own space; introducing him to William and Charlotte and Aunt Kat, who welcomed him warmly and naturally. He was taken to meet Cousin Francis, a tall, frail but indomitable old man with a penetrating gaze, who agreed that Tim could take the cottage on a six-month shorthold tenancy. So it was arranged.

"Stay in touch, Tim," Mattie said on his last day at the publishing house. It was almost a question. "Charlotte will tell me how you are, of course, but it would be nice to know if it's really working for you."

"Of course I will," he answered. "I'll email."

Email was OK: he could manage that without committing himself too far.

Six weeks later he is here at Brockscombe: he loves the tranquillity, the extraordinary beauty of the old house, the stable-yard and the surrounding countryside. It is as if, at last, he has come home. He smiles wryly at the thought: rather late in the day.

"But better late than never," he says to himself.

He's talked to himself quite a lot in the recent weeks, ever since that diagnosis of the very early stages of a rare degenerative disease; trying to stave off negative thoughts, anxiety, loneliness.

Now he has a plan. He has supplied himself with Ordnance Survey maps and he has begun to explore this wonderful county in which he so fortuitously finds himself. Sometimes his journeys take him across the moors, sometimes to the sea. Often he gets lost in the deep, secret lanes, but now he rises each morning with a sense of purpose, with a plan, to distract him from his fear. And now, for the first time in his life, he seems to have the family he's always longed for — thirty-two years too late.

Charlotte flips open her iPhone and reads Mattie's email:

"How are you all? Lovely pics of Ollie. He's gorgeous. Just showed them to everyone. Proud auntie. Don't forget to be nice to Tim. Everyone here sends love to him."

Charlotte experiences a tiny spasm of irritation. She doesn't need to be told to be nice — to Tim or to anybody else — and especially not by her little sister. Anyway, she's glad Tim's around. It's fun to have someone of her own age to talk to sometimes, and he's very amusing, though quiet and thoughtful, too.

"I don't know quite what's gone wrong for Tim," Mattie told her, "except that his relationship with his girlfriend broke up rather suddenly. He says he needs a new direction but he wants time to think about it."

Charlotte checks on Oliver, fast asleep in his cot, shuts the door quietly and goes downstairs, twining up her long fair hair into its comb: an hour if she's lucky. She could do some more work on the website she's designing for a local hotel or she could catch up with the ironing. There's quite a pile but that's partly her own fault for volunteering to do William's for him this week.

"You are such a star," Aunt Kat said, admiringly. "As if you haven't got enough to do with darling Ollie and Wooster."

But the thing is that she *likes* to be busy. It's better to wake up to a day full of different activities than to be gazing into emptiness. She said as much to Aunt Kat, who answered that some people were perfectly happy simply gazing. Charlotte occasionally wonders what Aunt Kat does when she drives off in her little car, dashing here and there, but she doesn't ask. And Ollie adores Aunt Kat. Despite her lack of domesticity — "Simply not a nurturer, darling," — she is great with the baby.

Charlotte opens the front door and wanders out into the courtyard with Wooster at her heels. Last autumn she and Andy painted the old wooden tubs they found in the stables and planted them up with bulbs: snowdrops, daffodils, crocuses and tulips. Now, in the late March sunshine, the daffodils make puddles of golden light all amongst the flagstones and purple crocus glow against the surrounding grey stone walls. The big open-fronted barn to the north of the yard is empty except for her own little car, and a line of washing hangs in the sunshine in the south-facing barn where logs are stored.

Wooster wanders round the courtyard, lifts his leg halfheartedly against the gatepost, whilst Charlotte perches on a wooden bench and glances between the high stone walls, across the five-bar gate, to the big house: no noise, no movement.

"It seems rather a pity to think of your cousin Francis in there all on his own and you out here," she said to William some months back. "All that space going to waste. You and Aunt Kat would be company for him."

She likes Francis, who often sits in the courtyard and chats to her, and who seems to understand the loneliness and responsibilities that go with being a naval wife.

William looked faintly uncomfortable — but she notices that he tends to edge away from discussions about Cousin Francis — muttered something about the old fellow being perfectly happy with his little team popping in to minister to his needs: Moira, the retired district nurse who checks him out each morning and evening, and drives him to any appointments; Stella, who cycles up from the little hamlet to clean and cook, and her husband, Rob, who keeps the grounds under control.

Even so, Charlotte feels there is a distinct lack of organization. The two cottages she and Tim now rent were empty for months after the elderly occupants, who also once worked for Cousin Francis, went to live with their younger families. If William and Aunt Kat moved into the house and the cottages were marketed properly there would be a good income to be had, and by the look of the house it could do with a facelift. Yet William and Kat seem content to let things ride. They live peacefully together, rather like an old married couple, though there is nothing old or married about Aunt Kat, or Irina Bulova as she is known professionally.

"She danced all over the world in all the leading roles," Andy told Charlotte. "And then she turned to choreography. She had a Polish lover who was a composer. He composed music specially for her — a kind of jazz ballet — and her work became iconic. He moved to New York and she went with him. He died very suddenly, very tragically, about two or three years ago and that's when she came home. She came here to recover. Dad adores her. We all do."

And here she is, driving into the courtyard in her tiny car, waving to Charlotte, parking in the barn. The driver's door opens and a long elegant leg shoots out.

Every movement Kat makes is graceful, thinks Charlotte enviously. How does she manage it?

Tall, slender, her storm-cloud hair knotted casually, Aunt Kat emerges into the sunshine, her thin face alight with a wide smile.

"Time out?" she asks. "Having a breather?"

She bends to murmur words of love and appreciation to Wooster, whose tail thumps gently as he accepts her compliments with regal tolerance.

"I ought to be doing some work," admits Charlotte, "but I couldn't quite bring myself to go back inside."

"Of course you couldn't." Aunt Kat sits beside her, raising her face to the warm March sunshine, closing her eyes. "Days like these are gifts from the gods. You should always seize them with gratitude."

"Have you been shopping?" asks Charlotte idly.

Foolish question: Aunt Kat never seems to do the ordinary, humdrum kind of shopping. One never sees her with carrier bags bursting with the rather dull necessities of life. A bunch of flowers, yes; a delightfully unusual toy for Oliver; a pretty piece of china. "Found it in the market, darling. Couldn't resist."

It is William who buys the bread, cheese, eggs, milk; plans the menus.

"He is a gastronomic retard," Aunt Kat says cheerfully. "Can't bear the least hint of anything spicy so it's best to let him do the cooking. Good prep school food."

Charlotte glances sideways at Aunt Kat's lean body, long legs, and wonders if she eats anything at all.

"I went to see someone who wants me to do a talk," Aunt Kat is answering, eyes still shut, her hand stroking Wooster's ears. "At a ballet studio in Newton Abbot. Sweet of them to ask me."

"You're still famous," smiles Charlotte.

Aunt Kat opens her eyes and beams at her. "For all the wrong reasons. All those lovers, dashing off to New York with Gyorgy, my choreography. I was always just a bit avant-garde. It wouldn't be remarkable now, of course."

"You'll always be remarkable," says Charlotte, still smiling. "You can't help yourself. It's a gift."

"Darling," says Aunt Kat, clearly moved by this tribute, "that's very sweet of you. I tell you what. I shall go inside and make us some coffee and bring it out and we'll drink it in the sunshine."

"Oh, yes, please," says Charlotte gratefully. William might choose the food but it is Aunt Kat who buys the coffee and it is seriously good. "I'd love that."

She, in turn, closes her eyes and relaxes. It is blissful to sit here with Wooster in the sun, in the rural silence, and anticipate Aunt Kat's coffee. The website can wait.

Kat makes coffee, whizzing the beans, setting out two pretty mugs and some milk for Charlotte. She chooses some biscuits and arranges them in a little dish. It's good for Charlotte to have a moment in the sunshine without the demands of Oliver or work. Kat smiles as she waits for the coffee machine. She likes to be Aunt

Kat to Charlotte and Andy and Mattie — and Ollie as he gets older. This is her family. She's feeling stronger, happy, in love with life again, though she's beginning to miss her theatre friends, the world of dance. Just now, though, it's good to have Andy and Charlotte and the baby around — and now Tim. She loves to be with young people. It was right to come here, to William, to Brockscombe, after Gyorgy died. She couldn't bear the old haunts, the well-meaning sympathy of old friends. She needed change and peace in order to regroup: to mourn. It was wonderful to be with William again, after all these years, to be able to support him after the break-up with Fiona and the death of his mother. His father, Kat's uncle, died some years ago and her own father — a Polish fighter pilot — died whilst she was still a child. As children, she and William spent the summer holidays together and the bond between them is a strong one.

They are happy here together, although there is always the uncertainty of the future: what happens to them all when Francis dies?

"I don't trust Francis' boys," William would say.

"But surely they can't just throw us out," Kat would answer.

William would snort. "We're on six-month shorthold tenancies here. Nothing is certain."

She'd jolly him along, as she always did, and they'd talk about having options, of looking for another house, though neither of them wants to break up this little family group. But now, as she makes the coffee, disquiet nibbles at the edges of her happiness. Could it really be possible that one day — even quite soon — they might all have to leave Brockscombe?

She thrusts the thought away, pours the coffee into a big pot and carries the tray outside to the courtyard, where Charlotte is waiting in the sunshine.

CHAPTER
TWO

There are flowers there again today. The little stone statue of a child, just a few feet high, is almost hidden at the edge of the woodland. Once there was a clearing here, but the bushes have grown tall and moss has covered the paved area around the plinth, so that Tim first came upon the statue quite by chance. He guesses that it is Pan: small stone fingers curl around his pipes, an arm upraised, one chubby knee lifted as though the little figure longs to dance.

Tim is touched by the way daffodils have been carefully threaded into those curled fingers; a spray of laurel, plucked from the nearby bush, is tucked into the crook of the elbow. He wonders who might have done it: who it is that loves the little statue enough to honour it with flowers.

The first time Tim chanced upon it there were snowdrops wilting in Pan's stony grasp and a garland of ivy looped around his neck. Today the daffodils are freshly picked and Tim glances around to see if there is anyone nearby. Occasionally, as he walks in the grounds and woodland that lie to the west of Brockscombe, he has the sensation that he is being watched. He stands still, looking around him, but the only movement is

15

made by the dashing away of a rabbit, kicking up the fallen leaves, and the sudden flight of a jay. There is a stile in the hedge just here. He climbed over it once, into the field beyond. The sheep raised their heads and watched him curiously for a few minutes before continuing to graze but there seemed no obvious footpath, no finger posts, so he climbed back again and went on his way through the wood.

Today, as he stands listening to the birdsong, he sees a silvery glint amongst the dank, dead leaves and crunchy beech mast. He bends down and picks up a small toy car, a model of a Jaguar. It reminds him of the toys he had when he was a child and, as he runs it to and fro on the palm of his hand, the wood seems to dislimn and vanish away and he is once again a child, lying on the carpet in the warm sitting-room. Toys are scattered about him and his father kneels beside him. How tall his father is, how strong. Today he is happy. Though he is not yet four, Tim knows that his father is not always happy. Sometimes he is very quiet. "Don't bother me," he'll snap if Tim grasps his arm, asks him to play. He'll jerk his arm free, unbalancing Tim and sometimes knocking him over — though he has learned not to cry. That makes things worse and his mother will come hurrying in and then they'll argue in a terrible, quiet sort of way, with low angry voices that are more frightening than if they shouted.

Mummy sometimes shouts: "Don't touch that, it's hot." "Don't climb on the chair, you might fall."

He understands this kind of shouting. In an odd way it makes him feel safe. But this fierce, whispered shouting gives him a horrid, knotted-up feeling inside and he wants to do something, anything, that will make them stop. Once he threw one of his little cars and broke a cup and his father cried out so loudly, smashing his fist down on the table, that his mother picked Tim up and ran out of the room. It was a little silvery car: the model of a Jaguar.

Now, as he smooths away the traces of damp mud from the shiny metal, it occurs to Tim that it might be a child from the local hamlet across the field who comes to put the flowers in Pan's hand: perhaps he has dropped the toy. Tim glances around again, wondering if the child might be hiding behind the trees, watching him to see what he will do, frightened to show himself. Afraid that he is trespassing.

Gently he places the car on the plinth beside Pan's small foot. He touches the rough, pitted toes and then turns to leave. As he walks away he wonders if he might ask the others if they know about the flowers: yet some instinct inclines him to secrecy. Aunt Kat occasionally walks in the grounds but he's never seen her on these overgrown paths; Charlotte is confined to the lane where it's easier to push Oliver in the buggy and Wooster doesn't get too muddy; William doesn't walk at all. He sings with a local group and works in his garden. Francis is rarely seen outside though he occasionally appears in the courtyard, leaning on his stick and ready for a chat, but he leaves the grounds and the woods to the care of Rob, the gardener.

So who is it that visits Pan and garlands him with flowers?

William turns into Church Close, passing along by the churchyard, just as the clock begins to strike eleven. He is nearly late for his meeting with Fiona — nearly, but not quite. He is experiencing the familiar mix of anxiety and resentment that, since their separation, is implicit in his relationship with his estranged wife. It is she who has asked to meet him this morning, rather than coming as she usually does to Brockscombe to see Charlotte and Oliver, and he is curious — and nervous. It is nearly five years since Fiona was head-hunted by a London practice of architects following her brilliant designs for the conversion of some waterside flats in Salcombe. Ambitious, longing for change, missing Andy, who had left Dartmouth Naval College and was away at sea, she was unable to understand why William should be so set against the move to London.

"I'm a countryman," he told her. "You know that, Fi. I'd hate to live in London. Anyway, my work is here. I know my accountancy firm looks small beer beside a big shiny London architects' practice but it's mine. I have a loyal, hard-working staff and faithful clients. I don't want to leave them all and go to London."

So she started with a weekly commute, but the relationship soon began to deteriorate. Her new colleagues, new life, challenging projects, all engulfed her and she made very little effort to conceal her growing impatience with his parochiality. Through her eyes William could see how small his world and their house in Ashburton now appeared to her, and how empty life was for her without Andy around, bringing

18

home his friends. William felt unable to measure up, to compete. He felt guilty that he couldn't face sacrificing his life for hers, resentful that she should so readily cast away all they had built together, and in the end they decided to make the break. Not a divorce — for Andy and economy's sakes — but an amicable separation. The house was sold, the proceeds split between them, and William moved to Brockscombe. Andy spent part of his leaves in London, part in Devon, until he got married.

Fiona liked her daughter-in-law but William knew that she was disappointed that her son had chosen a local girl who would keep him even more firmly rooted in Devon. Andy, based in Devonport, often at sea, had less time to spend on leave in Fiona's small spare room in London, though he and Charlotte visited her as often as they could — and then Oliver was born.

Fiona's focus changed with the birth of her grandson. She adored Oliver and tried to make her smart little flat more child friendly.

"Though it's quite impossible," Charlotte told William. "We can't squash the three of us into her tiny spare bedroom and she only has a shower-room; no bath."

Once Andy and Charlotte moved to Brockscombe, Fiona began to visit more often, staying at the Cott Inn at Dartington, driving to Brockscombe to spend time with her grandson.

On this occasion, however, William didn't know she was here: her text asking him to meet her arrived unexpectedly just after he got in to his office in

Ashburton. He replied that he was seeing a client in Totnes and suggested coffee before his meeting.

Now, William hesitates in the shadows at the end of Church Close, looking at the café across the High Street, seeing Fiona before she sees him. She's chosen one of the tables in the window and she is peering up and down the street, looking for him.

It's an odd sensation, watching her through the plate-glass window as if she were a stranger, as if he is spying on her. Her collar-bone-length shiny dark hair, held back with silver clips, those quick decisive movements of her head — everything about her is so familiar. They remind him of times past, and they still have the power to move him. As he crosses the road she sees him approach and she waves. She looks animated, really pleased to see him, and he is even more unsettled.

"Hi, Wills," she says, half rising, leaning forward to kiss him. "Thanks for coming out at such short notice."

"That's OK." He stands awkwardly, ill at ease. "Why didn't you say you were coming down?"

"Well, sit down," she says, smiling a little as though she has guessed his unease and is amused by it. "Don't tower over me. I've ordered an Americano for you."

William's irritation rises. To begin with, at five foot seven he never towers over anyone and, secondly, he feels faintly nettled that she feels so confident in her knowledge of him that she can order his coffee. He has an urge to be childish, to say that he doesn't drink coffee any more, but he sits down and looks at her, raising his eyebrows.

"So why the secrecy and silence?" he asks.

Fiona frowns a little and bites her lips; then she laughs, a little self-deprecating snort.

"It's tricky to start," she admits, "but I'll just come straight out with it. I wanted to see you on your own without the others knowing yet. I want you to ask your cousin if I can rent the cottage at Brockscombe."

He stares at her, his mind jumping between scenarios that fit this extraordinary suggestion, just managing not to say: "What on earth for?"

His expression makes her laugh again, but her amusement is forced, embarrassed.

"I know, I know," she says, raising her hands as if to ward off his unspoken question. "Sounds a bit crazy. I get that. But the thing is," she pauses, looks away from him out of the window. "I'm re-evaluating my life, Wills."

He watches her, calm now and very wary, and waits for her to go on. She looks at him again until his silence forces her to speak.

"I'm getting older, I suppose, and it changes your perspective, doesn't it?"

William continues to wait, eyebrows raised, as if he is assuming she has more to say.

"Well, you know how it is. It's to do with values, with what really matters." Fiona pauses — his silence is clearly unnerving her — and she bends towards him confidentially. "OK, I miss my family. I'd like to see more of little Ollie and Andy. And Charlotte, of course. And you, too, Wills, actually."

To his relief the coffee arrives and Fiona leans back, flushing a little. This gives Will a moment to recover, to marshall his thoughts, and then he looks at Fiona.

"You must forgive me if this comes as a bit of a shock," he says lightly.

Fiona's relief that he taking it calmly is patent. She takes a breath, chuckles. "To me, too," she admits. "It's just . . . well, I think it's worth trying. Rent the cottage, come down for weekends and holidays. My flat doesn't really work for a baby, and I hardly see Andy any more."

"The thing is," he says calmly, picking up his cup, taking a sip, "the cottage is let."

She stares at him. "Let?" She sounds shocked, indignant. "How d'you mean? You didn't tell me."

He pulls his mouth down at the corners: gives a little shrug. "It didn't occur to me that you'd be interested. A friend of Mattie's taken it on a six-month shorthold tenancy. I've no idea how long he plans to stay."

She looks so dismayed that he almost feels sorry for her: almost, but not quite.

"Have you mentioned this plan to Andy?" he asks.

"No, of course not," she answers: she still hasn't recovered from the shock. "You know very well he's at sea. I just get texts from time to time." She shakes her head disbelievingly. "That cottage has been empty for months."

"Mmm," agrees Will, mentally blessing Tim, "but that's how it goes. But I must admit I'm a bit surprised, Fi. I mean, Brockscombe? You always say it's the back of beyond."

"I know, I know. I told you, things have changed. I want to reconnect with my family. Is that so difficult to take on board?"

She looks out of the window, her happiness spoiled, her excitement doused. William watches her.

You walked away from us for pastures new, he thinks. Now you want to stroll back in like nothing has changed.

He wonders how Andy would react to Fiona's plan; and Charlotte and Kat. He was touched when Charlotte asked if they could rent the cottage, delighted that she and Andy wanted to be so close by, but he isn't so sure how Fiona would fit into the small community at Brockscombe. For himself, he knows he would hate it — to have her so close again when he's learned so painfully to live without her — but would he have the right to block such a move?

His relief that at the moment it isn't in question is very great.

"Perhaps you could find a place to rent here or in Ashburton," he suggests.

"In dear old Ashbucket?" It's odd to hear Fiona still calling Ashburton by the affectionate name that the locals use for their town. "Too expensive for a bolt hole. Anyway, it's not the point. I want to be on the spot. I want to see more of Oliver and to be part of his life. Part of the family rather than someone who just drops in occasionally. Surely you can understand that, Wills?"

Of course he can understand it. It's a huge joy and privilege to have his little family nearby, though he makes sure that they have plenty of privacy: he and Kat take nothing for granted.

"And anyway," he says, "Andy might be posted somewhere else. Abroad even. It would be foolish to count on them staying at Brockscombe."

She stares at him, all her earlier jollity dissipated.

"But they'd still have their base at Brockscombe, wouldn't they?"

He shrugs. "Who can say? After all, when Francis dies we shall all have to be moving on. We must just make the most of it while we can."

"Easy for you to say," she says sharply.

He finishes his coffee. "Yes, it is. I'm sorry, Fi. Nothing I can do."

"You can let me know if this new tenant moves on."

"Yes, I can do that. Look, I must get back to the office." He hesitates. "Are you down for long or is this a flying visit?"

"I've booked two nights. I was hoping to come over today and look at the cottage." She pauses. "I suppose your old cousin wouldn't let me rent a few rooms in that great empty house of his?"

William laughs and gets up. "No chance. So will you be out to see us later on?"

She nods. "I'll text Charlotte and see if she's around."

He nods, bends to kiss her and goes out into the bright spring sunshine.

CHAPTER
THREE

Fiona watches him go and then orders more coffee. She's been so sure, so confident, that her plan will work that she doesn't quite know what to do next. It never occurred to her that Cousin Francis would let the cottages to anyone who wasn't family. Andy's cottage was empty for more than a year after the aged retainers moved out, and now the other cottage . . .

Fiona sighs, a short sharp breath of frustration. It's such a good plan that she cannot bear to relinquish it. Just lately, each time she returns to London she carries with her the remembrance of the little world at Brockscombe: the laughter, the closeness — the sense of family that she forfeited five years ago when she put her career first.

Perhaps it had been unreasonable to say that, whilst William could be an accountant anywhere, this was a unique offer that she simply couldn't refuse. After all, he'd been part of his practice for twenty years, joining straight from university, working hard until he was made a partner. Even so . . .

Fiona props her elbows on the table, coffee cup cradled in her hands and stares out into the street. Back then, the lure of London, a top architect's practice —

and Sam, of course — had been irresistible. Sam Deller, the top man, whose cousin had bought one of the Salcombe flats and mentioned Fiona to Sam, had been the biggest draw of all. He was funny, clever, determined, successful. Sam always got what he wanted, and he wanted Fiona. She was unable to resist his charm, his compliments, and — most of all — the fact that he was falling in love with her. How potent it all was: how special, brilliant and desirable he made her feel. Hadn't there been a song about it once: "Falling in Love with Love"?

Fiona sips her coffee reflectively. How ordinary poor old Wills looked beside Sam's glamour; how pedestrian his objectives. On her weekends at home in Ashburton nothing measured up any more: those glorious long walks over the moor that they loved; the fun of a delicious cup of coffee gossiping with Dave and Steve in the Studio Teashop; happy evenings in the wine bar with their friends. These pleasures had faded beside all that London — and Sam — showed her.

When his wife divorced Sam, two years later, Fiona really thought they'd be together, until she realized that there were other women whom Sam made feel special, brilliant, desirable — new women who were much younger than she was. Oddly, it was almost a relief: as if some spell had been broken. Even so, it was only recently that she became aware of something important missing in her life.

Fiona puts down her cup and digs her fingers into her temples, pushing back her hair. She knows the exact moment that she felt this change: it was when

Andy put Oliver into her arms and said, "There you are, Grandmama. Say hello to Oliver."

The weight and the warmth of him, the tiny crumpled face, the feathery twist of dark hair, all these things wrenched her heart. She gazed down at him and wanted to weep at the miracle of life.

"He looks like you," she managed.

"Have a heart, Mum," Andy protested. "Poor little sprog's only two days old. Do us both a favour."

"He's beautiful," she said.

She sat holding him, unwilling to let him go, watching him yawn suddenly, widely, like a kitten; flex the minuscule prawn-like fingers. Then he began to cry. Charlotte whisked him away to be fed and suddenly there was a general hubbub of happy, laughing people that included William and Kat, and Mattie and Charlotte's parents — and, quite suddenly, Fiona saw that she was almost a stranger, an outsider down from London for a few hours to see her grandson. Between one moment and the next everything was different.

Previously, she'd visited only when Andy was on leave. She made very few attempts to develop a relationship with Charlotte, though she was always welcome at the London flat. In Devon, it suited Fiona to stay at the Cott; to suggest that Andy should pop over whilst Charlotte was working, so as to have a pint and then some lunch, or to invite them both for dinner. This way she could retain her independence. So it's not easy, now that she wants to come regularly to see Oliver, to ask Charlotte if she can stay in the small boxroom, which in the early days she rejected, and there's no way she can suddenly ask William and Kat if she can stay with them. Yet with each visit she feels more and more an outsider. She can see that to have a place in Oliver's life she needs to be properly hands-on, totally familiar with every aspect of his life.

It's odd in a way, Fiona thinks now as she finishes her coffee and fishes in her bag for her phone. Odd, because she wasn't specially maternal with Andy — or not that she can remember. Perhaps that was because he was naturally hers, there were no other contenders, she was certain of her place in his life. Oh, there was William, of course — and he was a very good father — but she came first with Andy. Of course, she can't expect to come first with Oliver, or even second, but she can still hope to have a special place in his life.

Fiona pushes away her coffee cup and begins to tap out a text to Charlotte.

Charlotte and Aunt Kat are still sitting peacefully in the sunshine, finishing their coffee. Charlotte stares at the text, her heart sinking, irritation rising, and then pulls herself together. After all, Fiona is her mother-in-law and Oliver's grandmother.

"What?" asks Aunt Kat, watching her curiously. "Not bad news? You look quite grim."

Charlotte shakes her head. "No. Just a bit surprised. Apparently Fiona is down and is asking if she can come to lunch. She doesn't usually arrive unannounced, does she? She always gives us plenty of warning."

"It's odd," agrees Aunt Kat. "Shall you say yes?"

"I don't know." Charlotte feels slightly cross at the prospect of Fiona requiring sustenance at such short notice. "I was going to have a bowl of soup, nothing special."

She wants to say that she likes to be running on all cylinders for her mother-in-law: the house tidy and clean, Oliver dressed in something Fiona's bought him, some food specially prepared. It has always been easier when Andy is around to distract Fiona, to make her laugh and entertain her, though things have changed since Oliver was born. She is completely besotted with him and comes to visit even when Andy is away.

"I expect Fiona drinks soup," says Aunt Kat. "Or you could simply say that you're out but that she can come to tea."

"But I'm not out," objects Charlotte. "Supposing she were just to turn up? She might just drive out, hoping you or William might be here."

"Well then, we'll all be out," says Aunt Kat cheerfully. "You and I and Ollie shall go and have lunch at Riverford or the Staverton Bridge Nursery. We'll buy something delicious to bring back for tea and Fiona shall join us. How about that?"

Charlotte begins to laugh. "You're very naughty, Aunt Kat."

"You mustn't allow yourself to be intimidated by Fiona. Text her and suggest half past three."

"Shall I?"

"Of course. Be quick. It's already a quarter to twelve. She could be here in half an hour and you've got to get Ollie ready."

Charlotte taps out the message, still feeling slightly guilty, whilst Aunt Kat whisks away the coffee things. Inside the cottage Oliver begins to cry and Charlotte jumps up and hurries inside. Wooster raises his head to glance around, sighs heavily, and flops down again to sleep in the sunshine.

When Fiona arrives at Brockscombe, parking in the barn alongside Kat's Smart car, crossing the courtyard to Charlotte's cottage, she's disconcerted to find a little party going on in the big kitchen-living-room, which takes up much of the ground floor.

Oliver is propped on the sofa with Kat, Charlotte is taking cakes from a box, and a slightly built, fair-haired young man is putting plates out on the table. They are talking, laughing at a joke someone has made, at ease and familiar with one another and, all at once, Fiona experiences that same sense of exclusion she has felt before: that she has forfeited her right to be a member of this group. She stares at the young man, wondering if he is the new tenant, surprised by the way that he seems to be fitting in so readily. Already she feels antagonistic toward him; he is in her cottage.

"Hi," she says brightly, and everyone turns to look at her.

"How lovely to see you, Fiona," says Kat, rising to her feet. "This is a nice surprise."

Without Kat's support, Oliver tips gently sideways and begins to cry and Fiona, ignoring Kat, hurries past her and picks him up.

30

"Ollie," she says lovingly. "Don't cry, darling. It's me. It's Granny."

She holds him, joggling him gently, and he stops crying and stares at her in amazement. He twists his head, as if to reassure himself that familiar faces are still near at hand, and Fiona hugs him, willing him to relax.

"Fiona, this is Tim," Charlotte is saying. "He's moved into Number Three," and Fiona, still holding the baby, turns to look at the fair-haired stranger. "This is Andy's mother, Fiona," Charlotte says to Tim.

Fiona nods at Tim, smiling at him, not too friendly. "Hi."

He smiles back at her but his look is slightly unsettling: a searching look, as if he sees past her veneer of social *politesse* to what lies beneath: her sense of exclusion, her need to be part of Oliver's world, her new loneliness. Fiona frowns slightly. This slight, fair boy unnerves her, which is crazy, and she holds Oliver more closely as if he is a shield against her unease.

Tim stands back with his tea and his slice of cake and watches the three women. He was surprised and faintly alarmed on his return to be co-opted to the tea party.

"We need you," Aunt Kat said, appearing beside the car as he switched off the engine and opened the door. "Fiona's turned up unexpectedly and Charlotte's just the least bit edgy. We've bought delicious cakes from Riverford so you'll be well fed."

He climbed out, smiling at her. "Sounds dramatic. Who's Fiona?"

"William's estranged wife and Charlotte's mother-in-law. None of us knew she was here until late morning. She texted to ask if she could come over, so we invited her to tea, and then William texted while we were having lunch to tell us that she was hoping to rent your cottage so that she could come down for weekends and holidays. Charlotte was rather taken aback by the prospect. That's putting it mildly. Please, dear Tim, do not imply that you plan to leave any time soon."

He couldn't help laughing. "But what's so wrong with Fiona?"

"There's nothing actually wrong with Fiona," Aunt Kat said, as they crossed the courtyard. "Actually she can be very good value. She and William separated about five years ago after she took up a first-rate job in London and we were all rather cast aside — well, except for Andy — but now, all of a sudden, we're flavour of the month and we can't quite understand why. Well, it's Oliver, of course."

Tim feels slightly sorry for the unknown Fiona. "I suppose, as his grandmother . . ."

"She loves him," says Aunt Kat. "Of course she does. It's just that it's a tad tactless to be distant and remote for five years and then suddenly expect to be clasped to the bosom of the family because you want back in. Do you see?"

"Yeah. I get that," he answered. "So why am I here? Just to be clear."

"Because your presence will keep things civilized," said Aunt Kat. "Get a grip, darling. Three women, all feeling the least bit threatened. It's bound to get tricky. We need the down-to-earth male influence."

He laughed. "You're forgetting Oliver."

"And remember," she said, as they went into Charlotte's cottage, "that you're staying for ever."

She held his arm for a moment, smiled at him, and pain raked his heart, obliterating the joy he always experienced in her company, lacerating him.

"I wish," he muttered bitterly, following her in.

And here he is, watching the three women, studying their body language, hearing the things that are not spoken. It's as if the foreshadowing of his own end heightens his awareness of other people. It happens all the time now but he says nothing. Instead, he watches. He sees that Charlotte is slightly off balance: that she knows that Fiona is besotted with Oliver, that she understands Fiona's maternal instincts, and is pleased that she loves her grandson. But Charlotte's expression — a polite little smile that doesn't quite reach her wary eyes — shows that there is resentment, too, because Fiona is staking her claim without any consideration for the other members of the family. He guesses that Charlotte feels defensive on behalf of William who has been so kind to her and to Oliver, and whom Andy loves. Yet Tim suspects that Charlotte knows she is holding all the cards here and that it will be very difficult to resist showing her power.

Aunt Kat is slightly detached, fielding Fiona's more tactless comments about the right way to bring up a baby, almost enjoying the drama. At every point, she involves Charlotte as Oliver's mother, emphasizing her capability and devotion.

"It's amazing," Aunt Kat says, "how Charlotte manages it all on her own with Andy away so much and not able to share the load. Keeping up with her work, designing wonderful websites, looking after Oliver, walking Wooster. She even does William's ironing."

Fiona looks at her coolly. "William should do his own ironing."

"I only do it occasionally," says Charlotte, irritably. "Look, do put Oliver down so that you can drink your tea, Fiona. He's fine on the sofa."

"No, we're happy, aren't we, Ollie?" Fiona joggles Oliver in her arms. "We have to make the most of our cuddles, don't we, sweetie?"

She takes a quick sip from her cup and puts it back on the table.

"So are you at the Cott, as usual?" asks Aunt Kat brightly. "We didn't realize that you were down. Did William know?"

"No," says Fiona. She looks faintly uncomfortable. "No, it was a rather sudden decision."

She looks down at Oliver, unwilling to meet either of the two women's eyes, and Tim knows that she's deciding whether or not to tell the truth. He almost sees the moment when she decides to throw caution to the wind: the little intake of breath, the straightening of the shoulders, the defiant lifting of the brows.

"Actually," she says, almost casually, "I wanted to run an idea past William and I wanted to do it face to face. To test his reaction. I met him this morning in Totnes."

"How exciting," says Aunt Kat, almost cosily; all girls together. "Whatever could it be?"

She catches Tim's eye, sends a little wink, and he cannot quite contain his grin.

Fiona looks at Charlotte, chin up. "I was hoping to rent the other cottage as a bolt hole so as to be able to get down to see you all more often. Holidays and Christmas, that sort of thing. What I didn't know was that this young man," she glances at Tim, "had beaten me to it."

Her look is almost hostile and the silence that follows is embarrassing. Even Aunt Kat can't think of an appropriate rejoinder.

"It never occurred to me," Fiona adds, "that old Cousin Francis would let the cottage to an outsider."

"Tim's not an outsider," says Charlotte swiftly, almost angrily. "He's Mattie's friend. They worked together in London."

Tim is touched by her quick defence and he sees that Fiona regrets her tactless choice of word.

"Well, you know what I mean," she says impatiently. "Not one of the family. After all, the cottage has been empty for ages. The tenants are either family or staff. Francis has never had a . . ." She hesitates, seeking for a word: clearly "stranger" will hardly fit the bill.

"No, he never has," Aunt Kat says, understanding her. "And he hasn't now. Tim's a family friend. We feel very lucky that he's come to Brockscombe. After all, I doubt it would ever have occurred to any of us that you'd want to come back, Fiona. You've never been a particularly regular visitor, have you?"

This is carrying the war into the enemy's camp and Tim is impressed, though slightly horrified, at Aunt Kat's temerity, especially remembering what she said about keeping things civilized.

"I must admit," he says smoothly, putting down his plate, moving forward slightly, "that I love it here. I'm just so glad Mattie told me about it. I'm sorry, though, that I've stolen a march on you."

Fiona stares at him, deflected from Aunt Kat's question, and he sees that she wants to regain ground whilst still feeling angry that he is, in a way, her enemy.

"So have you got a job locally?" she asks. "It's a bit remote out here, isn't it? Don't you miss London?"

He wants to laugh — or cry — but he answers truthfully, up to a point.

"I'm having a sabbatical," he says. "I'm preparing for the next stage in my life."

He can see that he's slightly taken her off balance and he recalls Aunt Kat's words: "Remember that you're staying for ever."

"To be honest," he adds, "I simply can't imagine, now, living anywhere else."

He looks at Fiona, knowing that he speaks much more truthfully than she will ever know, willing her to be more conciliatory. She frowns at him, as if he puzzles her, and then turns away.

"Any more cake, anyone?" asks Aunt Kat.

Oliver begins to grizzle and Charlotte takes him from Fiona. "He needs changing," she says. "Would you like some more tea, Tim?"

Fiona relinquishes Oliver reluctantly. "Perhaps I could help with the bath?" she asks hopefully, and Charlotte says, "Yes, of course."

And suddenly the whole dynamic has changed and Tim lets out a sigh of relief: the difficult moment has passed.

CHAPTER
FOUR

As William drives to his office in Ashburton next morning his head is full of Fiona. It is a while now since he had such close contact with her and he is unsettled by it. Since Andy and Charlotte moved to Brockscombe there has been a little more interaction between William and Fiona, but not much. Fiona makes it clear that she comes to see Andy and, more recently, Oliver, and on some visits he hasn't seen her at all.

Now things have changed. Last evening when he got back from the office she was still at Brockscombe, her car parked in his space in the barn so that he had to leave his own in the yard. Kat was listening to some music that sounded like a cross between modern jazz and medieval madrigals, and reading a manuscript. A friend, Michel Brot, a dancer and choreographer who is writing his memoirs, has asked her to check that he is getting his facts right. He sends her each chapter as he finishes it and she is enjoying the process immensely.

"We're in Leningrad," she said, flourishing a page. "In the seventies. *La Fille mal gardée.* Miche makes it sound so exciting. All I remember is how cold and hungry we always were." She looked at William more carefully. "Are you OK?"

"Fiona," he said briefly. "I see she's still here."

"Helping with Ollie's bath, then Charlotte invited her to supper. Just as well you warned us she was here. Charlotte was a bit twitchy about it."

"She completely threw me," he admitted angrily. "I mean, can you imagine having her next door? Here for Christmas and Easter? Turning up at weekends?" Even as he said it he felt guilty. After all, he lives next door to Charlotte and Oliver — and Andy, when he's home — so why shouldn't Fiona? "Don't answer that," he said, sitting down at the table. "Tell me about Leningrad."

Now he knows that the root of his anger is buried deep in resentment. He thought that he was over it but the corroding stain of jealousy is seeping up again; those almost forgotten sensations of hurt that Fiona should leave him so easily after more than twenty happy years. It was quite early on that she told him about Sam. She couldn't help herself: the longing to speak the beloved's name, to confide, overcame any sense of decency or even kindness. She needed to talk, to tell and tell again, whilst he watched and listened, disbelieving and helpless. It was as if she expected him to understand, even approve her new passion, as if it were natural that he should accept this supporting role in her new exciting life. Dear, boring old William relegated to faithful best friend. It was her right to be happy, to be in love: her feelings must take precedence over his and Andy's.

As he crosses the A38 and takes the back lane to Ashburton, William thinks about this. It was ever thus. Perhaps he encouraged it back in those early days when he was in love with her. Fiona was demanding, amusing, driven. Her energy and ambition delighted him. He was so proud of her. That she should be head-hunted by a London practice did not surprise him though the prospect of how it should be managed appalled him. When she saw that he was not prepared to sacrifice his own way of life to this new, untested one, she'd convinced him that weekending would be the answer; that she might be able to do some of the work from home. Neither of them had taken Sam into account. How painful it was when William first suspected: watching her walking around with secrets in her eyes, the fleeting smile on her lips, the surreptitious glances at her phone. Oddly, to begin with, it made her more generous, more loving, towards him. When he challenged her she made a joke about it: there was this guy, one of the directors, who had taken a fancy to her. It was all a bit crazy, a bit mad.

When, wonders William now, did Sam stop being a joke and become a threat? From being slightly hyper, Fiona grew sullen; William's suspicions, his questions, began to irritate her. When she saw that he was not content simply to be prepared to sit and watch her being happy, to listen to her London stories and how Sam pursued her, she became distant. Now it became clear that their life together in Ashburton simply wasn't enough and when finally he confronted her she chose London.

Sometimes he wonders if she saw the whole thing as a game — after all, she didn't want a divorce — and perhaps she always suspected that once the game was played out she might come back.

William shakes his head: it's too far-fetched, too complicated a concept. Nevertheless, he feels threatened — and helpless.

Kat is practising. Each day, using the Rayburn's rail as a barre, she works through her routine: pliés, battements, développés, port de bras. She likes to keep fit, stretched, supple. Miche's autobiography has unsettled her, reminded her of times past, awoken a hunger within her.

"Do you remember *Jazz Calendar*?" Miche has written in a card accompanying the latest chapter. "The first time we partnered each other in 'Friday's Child'?"

Of course she remembers. Kat rises on her toes, turns; right hand on the barre, left outstretched, she begins her pliés "on the other side". When she was just eighteen she'd danced the narcissistic "Monday's Child": androgynous, stylish, her hands flat against her thighs, she'd flaunted before an imaginary mirror. Later, when she joined Miche's dance company, they'd danced the raunchy "Friday's Child" "loving and giving" *pas de deux* — "sex through classicism", as someone said — to Richard Rodney Bennett's jazz score. What fun they'd had back then: what tears and tantrums and joy. When she discovered her own talent as a choreographer — the exciting prework in some small out-of-the-way studio, sculpting on the young dancers, allowing Gyorgy's music to inspire the steps — Miche had encouraged and supported her.

"Come back to us," he says from time to time. "Come home, Irina. There's still work to be done. You've mourned Gyorgy long enough."

In the autumn he will be auditioning dancers for a new musical scheduled for the West End and he wants her to work with him on the choreography. The temptation is very strong. Yet she is fearful; fearful that her talent died with Gyorgy, that she is too old . . .

"Too old?" roars Miche contemptuously, when she says this. "Rubbish, darling. Look at Gillian Lynne."

He always says this — and indeed, Gillian Lynne is her icon.

"I'm thinking about it," she says to Miche. "Honestly. Give me time."

"There isn't any time," he says brutally. "I want you on board for this production, Irina."

Yet it is hard to consider leaving Brockscombe, which has been her first real home since her childhood. Here is security, peace, family. All those years of squalid digs and dreary rented rooms, draughty church halls and stuffy studios, trains and planes and luggage . . .

A knock on the door, a voice calling, "Hello, anybody in?" disturbs her reverie and she flings open the kitchen door to see Cousin Francis standing on the step, leaning on his stick. The mere sight of his tall, angular shape, his brown eyes which are already crinkling into that familiar smile, warms her heart.

"Francis," she says. "Darling Francis. However are you?"

42

He follows her slowly into the kitchen, unfazed by her leggings and oversize sweatshirt and soft ballet shoes: he's seen Kat practising many times.

"I'm fine," he answers. "I decided I needed a little outing so I whizzed down on the stairlift and here I am."

She gives him a little hug, feeling the bony cage of his ribs, aware of his frailty. "Coffee?"

"Oh, yes, please. So what's going on?"

She turns with the coffee pot in one hand. "Going on?"

Francis shrugs. "I just feel that something might be."

"Well." Kat busies herself with making coffee whilst she decides how much to tell him and settles on the truth. "We had an unexpected visit from Fiona. She wants to get a bolt hole close at hand so as to be more involved with Ollie. Actually, she was hoping for the other cottage."

He raises his eyebrows and she bursts out laughing. "Well, you can imagine. A cat among the pigeons, Francis darling. Thank goodness we've got Tim *in situ*. She wasn't best pleased, our Fi. Tim was brilliant."

She puts the coffee pot and mugs on the table and sits down opposite.

"What do you think of Tim?" she adds idly.

His eyes drift away from hers, looking in the distance, as if he is able to see deep into Tim's mind and heart. Francis has a habit of doing this, which always gives Kat an odd sense of being in the presence of someone who has an extra dimension: who can see and hear things unknown to her. It's as if he is consulting a wisdom much greater than his own and she watches him, almost holding her breath.

"I like Tim," Francis says, "but I sense a mystery. I can't decide whether he is running away from something or towards something."

"Maybe," she suggests, "he's just taking time out. You know. Between one thing and the next?"

Francis' eyes drift back again and he smiles at her reassuringly. "Very likely. Has Mattie been down to see him?"

Kat frowns at the question. "No. Why?"

Francis shrugs. "Just wondered. And what about you?"

"Me?" She pours coffee, slightly distracted, wondering if he is able to read her thoughts. "What about me?"

"Are *you* still taking time out?"

Kat heaves a deep breath. "Why do you ask that?"

He indicates the untidy pile at the end of the table: the manuscript with its heading, *A Dancer's Life for Me*: the photos of dancers and stage sets that are splayed out beside it; a CD by a modern jazz composer.

"But Brockscombe is home," she says, as if she is answering his question.

"Is it?"

She stares at him, shocked. "What do you mean?"

"Home is where you live and work and have your being. Refuge is a place where you hide to lick your wounds and recover from pain."

"So you think Brockscombe is my refuge?"

"How long is it now?"

She thinks about it. "Two years, nearly three. I still miss him."

His glance lingers on her practice clothes. "You'll always miss him. So what? You shouldn't let it disable you."

Kat begins to laugh. "Thank you for your sympathy, dear Francis."

"Sympathy." Francis snorts derisively. "So undermining." He leans towards her. "Why would you want sympathy? You've got all this . . ." he hesitates and then taps his head, ". . . this *stuff* going to waste." He nods towards the CD. "Go on. Let's hear it."

She hesitates, then gets up and puts it into the CD player on the shelf. The kitchen is filled with the sound of a Spanish guitar, drums, percussion, and Kat stands still whilst movement and colour and shapes fill her vision. Francis watches her, finishes his coffee.

"I've always wished I could dance," he says wistfully. "Always had two left feet."

She blinks at him as if he is out of focus, and then crosses the floor to bend over him and kiss his thin cheek.

"You are a blessing," she says.

"Does that mean I get more coffee?"

"Yes," she says, "it does."

"And then, dear Kat, you should get back to your practising."

"Yes," she says. "Yes, do you know, I really think I should."

Francis pauses in the sunshine, grateful for its warmth. Slowly, carefully, he makes his way around to the front of the house and stands looking out across the carriage drive, beyond the sunken ha-ha to the woods. Here, out of the shelter of the courtyard, it is much colder: the easterly March wind scours and polishes the clear empty sky to an icy blue. Francis huddles himself more deeply into his coat. He is thinking of Kat's question and what it is about Tim that connects with his, Francis', own experience. There is something he recognizes in the younger man: something held back. Tim, he suspects, is a man with a secret — and Francis knows all about secrets.

As he looks at the airy clouds of spring blossom, listens to the clamour of birdsong, he reminds himself not to be hubristic. It is not in his gift to protect all these people who have gathered by chance here at Brockscombe. Nevertheless, he cares about them — his little surrogate family — and even Tim, who is a stranger to them, has awakened his paternal instincts.

It is odd for such a young man to require a sabbatical, to give up a good job and come to live amongst strangers. It seems that he has no family, though Mattie has known him for a while and is clearly fond of him. No friends visit him. Perhaps it is true that Tim is looking for a new direction in his life but Brockscombe seems an unlikely place to choose: so remote and out of the world.

"Mind your own business," Francis tells himself, but he offers up a prayer for wisdom, lest help should suddenly become necessary, and feeling comforted he goes back to his quarters on the top floor.

CHAPTER
FIVE

In April the cold, sweet, fragile spring is blown away by wild gales that stream in from the south-west. Rotten branches crash down from flailing trees, scattering twigs and dead leaves, blocking the lanes: storm-driven, white-tipped rollers shoulder powerfully along the cliffs, wrenching up boulders, stones, rocks, and dumping them all anyhow along the littoral. Chimneys tumble, slates smash. Delicate blossoms lie crushed and torn, strewn confetti-like in gutters and ditches. Sheep huddle with their gawky, shivering lambs beneath protecting thorn hedges whilst, overhead, gulls are tossed like flakes of paper against the dark, stormy sky.

Tim stands aghast before this display of elemental destruction. Never before has he witnessed such brutal force: never realized with such clarity that puny man is not in control of his universe. Nothing in his quiet city life and hot sunshiny holidays abroad has prepared him for this experience. Oh, he has seen terrible images on television, witnessed the drama and grief at second-hand, but never has he felt the wind's hands tearing at his clothes, battering his face, buffeting him along. He is horrified and exhilarated all at once. As he drives in the lanes at the edge of the moor, peering upwards through the streaming rain at lashing branches and scurrying clouds, he wonders why he is not afraid. But then why should he be afraid? He has nothing to lose.

This knowledge emphasizes his vulnerability, his aloneness. On an impulse he pulls into a trampled muddy gateway and fumbles in his pocket for his iPhone. He scrolls down, presses the key and puts the phone to his ear.

She answers immediately. "Hi."

He relaxes, slumping a little in his seat. "Hi, Mattie. Listen, I'm in a little, narrow lane driving through this massive gale. I've never seen anything like it."

She laughs. "Crazy man. Why would you do that? It can be dangerous. You might get a tree across your car."

"I know." He laughs with her, feels a sudden glorious up-welling of joy. It's always been easy to laugh with Mattie. "When are you coming down?"

A surprised little silence, then: "Oh, well, I'm not sure. I usually wait for an invite from Charlotte."

"You could come here. I mean you could stay with me."

Mattie begins to laugh again. "Well, I could. I mean, why not?"

"Yeah, why not?"

"OK." She sounds amused, intrigued. "So, this weekend then?"

"I know it's short notice. Is that possible?"

"Mmm, just about. I'll drive down after work tomorrow. You'll have to explain to Charlotte, though she'll be relieved not to have the trouble of the camp bed in the sitting-room."

48

"Why should she mind? After all, if I were living somewhere else you'd come and stay with me, wouldn't you?"

"Would I? Yes, I suppose I would. If you asked me."

"Well, then. That's great."

"Tomorrow evening, then. I shall be late, probably not much before ten."

As he drives home the exhilaration remains with him: the degenerative disease that is eating its way into him might disappear; the prognosis might be wrong. Just for today, for this moment, all things are possible.

His optimism buoys him up, carries him through the shopping, the search for bed linen and towels, the dusting and hoovering, so that when she comes driving into the yard, runs skittering across the wet flagstones, he has the door open ready for her and he pulls her inside out of the rain, hugging her, gazing down at her sweet face. He feels strong and confident, full of hope and courage.

Mattie is here with him at Brockscombe: all will be well.

It carries him into the evening, through the supper he has made for her, on to the sofa together before the log-burner, where she gazes at the flames and falls into a doze against his shoulder. She is warm and heavy and he is full of protective love for her, and a longing desperate lust, so that when she wakens, and looks around puzzled for a moment and then smiles at him, he pulls her close, kisses her, and they make love. The relief, the bliss of it — this intimate, passionate act that

49

he'd thought never to perform again — swamps him with such gratitude that he weeps silently, violently, for a moment, crushing her against him so that she can't see him or feel him shaking.

They stumble together up the narrow staircase, perform the necessary acts in the small bathroom, and then fall together into his bed, holding each other closely. The night is full of love.

Saturday is full of family: of meetings with Aunt Kat and William, of Mattie playing with Ollie, a walk in the lane with Wooster, and all of them sharing supper in Charlotte's cottage.

And on Sunday, after lunch, she is gone, with a toot of the horn, a flourish of a hand from the window. Everyone is there to see her off — it's accepted that she has been to Brockscombe to see them all — and Tim's time with her alone has been brief but incredibly special.

He slips quietly away, walking off into the grounds, where hellebores and vincas flourish beside the overgrown paths that wind through the wood. He's still thinking about Mattie, not really noticing his surroundings, so that the cleared area takes him by surprise. He sees small headstones all amongst the overgrown grass and stands still with shock: it is a graveyard. Just for a moment he thinks that these must be the graves of children until he moves closer, bending to read the inscriptions, and sees that these are dogs: Mitzi, Benny, Jimbo . . . each name has an image roughly carved into the stone. There are spaniels, terriers and Labradors here, and on the newest grave —

of a cairn terrier called Brack — is a small posy of primroses.

Tim crouches before the grave in the long wet grass. The carving brings to life the small dog and he can imagine the pricked ears, the bright eyes, the rough warm coat. Long ago he knew just such a little dog: running with him in the sunshine, cuddling with him on the sofa. His name was Ban.

Still crouching before the grave, Tim bends his head, closing his eyes as if to ward off the familiar grief and guilt. It's as if he can feel again the gate-latch, cold and smooth and stiff beneath his small fingers; he can remember how he cried out a greeting to his mother on the opposite pavement, about to cross the road towards him. She was carrying the shopping bag in one hand, waving to him with the other. To his surprise the latch clicked free, the gate swung open — he'd never managed that before — and quick as a flash Ban slipped out, dashing into the road, with Tim behind him.

He can remember his mother's scream as she ran forward, the squeal of brakes, the thump of flesh on metal. He could just see her legs, bent at an odd angle beneath the wheels of the car, shopping rolled everywhere, and then his father came hurrying out, pushing Tim aside, and someone lifted and carried him away.

Afterwards, his father wanted Ban rehomed, he couldn't stand the sight of him. It seemed that he couldn't stand the sight of anyone, family or friends. He took a job abroad and Tim went to live with his grandmother, and with Ban. Ban became the recipient of his tears and guilt, his confusion, his fear. The little dog was his friend, his comfort, his connection with all that he had known and loved for nearly four years.

Tim stands up, wondering to whom Brack belonged: old Cousin Francis, perhaps? But surely it's not Francis who picks wild flowers in this small damp wood to honour Pan or the grave of a little dog?

He wishes now he'd brought Mattie to see Pan, and, as he thinks of her, the courage and hope that have carried him through the weekend drain away from him, leaving him lonely and afraid. That elemental moment, during the storm, breached his defences and allowed his love to betray him into believing that he might have a future with Mattie. He has been so careful to allow nobody to come close to him since Rachel left him. Not that it was a particularly serious relationship. He has no regrets about that. His only real regret is that when he first met Mattie she had a boyfriend and then, when they broke up, he and Rachel had already begun their relationship.

Standing in the dogs' graveyard, gazing around him, Tim tries to convince himself that it was all for the best: that Mattie, like Rachel, having heard the diagnosis, might have left him just as abruptly. At least Mattie doesn't pity him, feel sorry for him. Their lovemaking was genuine, glorious: he felt viable, alive. He hugs the memory of it to him, warming himself in its residual glow.

As he turns he just glimpses a movement in the trees, a tall shadowy figure slipping away out of sight. Tim pauses, peering into the woodland, wondering if it is Rob, but there is no one there. He hurries back, suddenly in need of companionship, of warmth.

The storm has cleared away to the east and the sky is rinsed a shining luminous blue. In the courtyard William is holding Ollie, showing him the daffodils and the cars in the barn, whilst Aunt Kat talks to Francis, who is seated on the bench, and Charlotte comes out of her cottage with a tray of mugs.

"Oh, hi," she calls to Tim. "There you are. Hang on, I'll get another mug."

So here they are: his family. Aunt Kat turning to beckon him into the group, Francis smiling at him, William putting Ollie into his arms and saying, "There now. Here's your uncle Tim."

He holds the warm bundle of baby, hiding the weak tears that are never very far away these days, looking down into the small face that breaks unexpectedly into a gummy smile. He smiles back, touched by Ollie's trustful reaction, and sits next to Francis on the bench. Wooster comes to lean against his knees as if he knows that Tim needs comfort.

"Mattie was in good form," says Francis. "What do you think of her applying for this job at the BBC in Bristol?"

"She's well qualified for it," answers Tim — and then falls silent. Any further remarks seem fraught with implications: of how good it would be to have her closer; of his own future.

He wants to say: "I love her but it's all completely pointless."

He glances sideways at Francis and is taken aback by the compassionate expression on his face: compassion — not pity — as if he is suffering with Tim and wishing he could alleviate the suffering.

Charlotte appears, gives Tim a mug of tea, and takes Ollie from him.

"Andy's Skyping later," she says. "What did you want to tell him, William?"

William strolls over, Aunt Kat joins in, and Tim sips his tea, watching them as the sun sinks and it grows colder, and all the while he can hear the thrush singing in the ash tree below the cottage.

CHAPTER
SIX

In Totnes, in the Thrive Café, Kat sits drinking a macchiato, listening to Miles Davis playing "My Funny Valentine". It is impossible for her to listen to music, any music, without dance sequences forming in her head; she sees dancers moving, making shapes. The café, with its two big windows — one opening into the courtyard garden, the other looking on to Fore Street — the wooden tables, the richly coloured kelims that hang down in front of the cupboard shelves, all are part of the pattern in her head. The jazz, someone busy behind the counter, this man coming in, glancing at Kat and smiling . . .

Kat blinks, the dancers fade, and she smiles back at him. He's rather nice: grey-blond floppy hair, wide curling mouth, a good strong frame. He wears jeans and a loose, navy-blue, high-neck jersey. Immediately she imagines him dancing to the music. She can't prevent herself, it's as natural as breathing to her. He sways and turns and moves, and she can't help her smile widening with pleasure.

He's ordering coffee, unaware of the role into which he has been cast, dropping his jacket and his rucksack on to a chair at the next table, pulling a newspaper from the bag's pocket.

Kat sizes him up: friendly but cautious, unlikely to make the first conversational move lest there should be any misunderstanding.

"They put the jazz on especially for me," she says. "I was first in this morning. Hope you like Miles Davis."

He responds at once. "I certainly do. I used to play the drums in a jazz group when I was a teenager."

"Gosh," she says, delighted with his positive response. "What fun. You didn't keep it up?"

He shakes his head, putting his wallet back in his pocket, sitting down at the table.

"We weren't very good. I don't think Acker Bilk felt threatened."

She's amused at his rueful honesty but before she can speak again a woman comes quickly in. She looks eager, hopeful, and spying the man cries, "Oh, there you are, Jeremy. I wondered if I'd missed you."

Kat watches, interested. Not a wife or a girlfriend, she guesses, but someone who might like to be. This woman, with her carefully dyed silvery-blond hair and smart clothes, is bright with expectation. She stares at Kat with instinctive hostility, and approaches the man's table with a proprietorial air.

"How are you settling in?" she asks, leaning towards him, at once intimate yet diffident.

The man, who has stood up at her approach, answers with a pleasant but slightly non-committal response and Kat knows, she just knows, that he is very slightly irritated by this woman's arrival. She wants to laugh and she feels the old familiar speeding of the heart, the tremor of excitement running through her veins. She never could resist a flirtation.

He is glancing at her, and she makes a little face so as to indicate her understanding, and he half grins in embarrassed acknowledgement of her quick grasp of the situation. He goes to the counter to order coffee for the newcomer, who removes her coat, fusses with a bracelet, smooths her hair. She is plump, confident; someone who organizes things, heads committees, gets things done. When he rejoins her, she sits a little straighter, arranging her face in an expression that is both encouraging and approving.

"Have you thought any more about my little party?" she asks. "I can introduce you to some new people."

Kat watches and listens unashamedly, still aware of the current of his interest. Presently another woman appears, to be greeted enthusiastically by the first. He is flanked now by their admiration and concern. Yet she knows that, despite her lack of make-up, her storm-cloud hair falling untidily from its pins, her leggings and knee-high leather boots, he is much more interested in her than in these smart, pretty ladies.

She sighs with a real contentment, stands up, conscious that he is watching her, and with another smile at him she walks out.

Jerry Fermor watches her go. He wishes Sandra had not arrived just at that moment, that he might have become better acquainted with the tall, striking woman who seemed to know exactly how he felt about Sandra and her friend. It was as if they had connected at a deeper level, by-passing the usual formalities; as if they knew each other very well and were sharing a private joke. He is amused, flattered, and rather disappointed that the encounter is over. He has to concentrate on what Sandra is saying about her party, about the clubs he might like to join and a visit to the cinema at Dartington. They met at a talk in the library given by the writer and historian Bob Mann, and she and her friend — whose name he has forgotten — are very welcoming to the stranger within the gates, yet he slightly prefers the tall, striking woman's less conventional approach.

He's had no special relationships in the four years since Veronica died and, anyway, his two daughters are not very encouraging when other women are around. It didn't occur to them, busy with their careers and their children, that he might be lonely in the roomy old Victorian villa at the edge of the city when he retired from his position as head of the Drama Department at a Plymouth college; that he might no longer be content simply with their visits from upcountry, which get fewer each year as their own lives become busy with work and babies. So they were shocked when he told them he was selling up and buying a modern flat in Totnes. It was almost an act of rebellion; of allowing that dramatic sense within him an opportunity to fulfil itself. Vee always kept him grounded — she was the sensible one — and he was very grateful for her continual cool head and wise counsel, but he was determined to do this: to take the chance to express his personality. It happened

58

so quickly: an offer on the house and the availability of the modern, sleek, bright flat with its views along the river.

"I need a change," he told his daughters. "The house is far too big for me now and I was never much into the gardening. That was your mum's province. I love Totnes: I love the vibe and the café society and the live music in the pubs. I've got great views of the river, I can walk everywhere, even to the station."

When they protested that they wouldn't be able to stay with him he pointed out that he still had a spare bedroom and, anyway, keeping on a big house for the sake of a few weekends a year was unrealistic now that he was retired and alone.

"You can rent a holiday cottage nearby," he said. "I can afford to help you with the expense."

And so here he is: sitting in the Thrive Café with two new friends, planning to go to a party and a film — but still regretting missing the opportunity of getting to know the tall, attractive foreign-looking woman who smiled at him as if she were amused at his predicament; as if he were in some kind of danger. He smiles to himself at the ludicrous idea — but he can't quite put her out of his mind.

CHAPTER
SEVEN

At Brockscombe, in his sitting-room on the first floor, Francis sits in his high wing-backed chair looking out across the garden and the woods to the valleys and the hills beyond. As a child this was his favourite room, his parents' bedroom, and later when he inherited the house he'd made it his study. Liz complained, of course — she wanted it for her own bedroom — but he stayed firm. After all, one spent so little time in a bedroom. It was to Brockscombe and to this room he returned to renew his energy and soothe his spirit.

Back then Brockscombe was full of life: Liz organizing dinner parties and garden parties, the two boys, barely eleven months between them, growing up and filling the place with their friends. Sometimes he thinks he can still hear them as he sits in his chair, dreaming: Liz calling up to him as she goes out into the garden; the boys shouting on the stairs. As he watches from the two tall sash windows facing south and east he sees them playing on the lawn, racing on their bicycles round the carriage drive, running into the woods with the dogs at their heels. Always arguing, always fighting, they were in constant rivalry.

"They don't see enough of you," Liz would say. "They need a strong male influence."

He did his best: told them off, clipped their ears, stopped their pocket money, but they were tough little fellows. Secretly he admired the spirit that drove them onwards: chips off the old block. They looked like Liz. Small, wiry, ginger-haired, they buzzed like gnats around him; shrill, argumentative, exhausting. It was a relief when they went off to school. Even Liz admitted that she enjoyed the peace and quiet, though she missed them, of course. Still, there were exeats, half-terms, holidays. Their friends came to stay; they grew up. Roger went to Cambridge and joined the Foreign Office, Sebastian took a short-term army commission and afterwards went into banking. Now, Roger is in Moscow and Sebastian is in Boston — and Liz is dead.

Francis leans forward in his chair. He can see Rob working at the edge of the trees, clearing out dead wood. Someone is helping him, a tall figure stooping to pick up the rotten branches, loading them into a wheelbarrow. It is Maxie. Francis fetches a deep sigh. His illegitimate son looks nothing like him, though he is tall and rangy: he is like his mother.

Maxie is his first-born and he likes to have him near after all the years of separation, though very few people — not even Maxie himself — know that he is Francis' son. When he was a young MP, back in the fifties, it would have been the end of his career if it were known that he had a mistress. Yet how could he have resisted Nell? And how cruel of fate that he should fall in love with her only weeks after marrying the eminently suitable, practical Liz.

As he sits quietly the distant scene fades and he remembers how he first met Nell at his friends' house in Exeter. She'd recently been employed as nanny to look after their new baby and she appeared in the drawing-room that afternoon just as they were finishing tea. Sixty years on, Francis smiles involuntarily at the memory of his first sight of Nell: her pink cheeks, bright eyes, brown-gold hair. She looked so neat and sweet in her Norland uniform; so delectable and desirable. He was nearly twenty-seven. She was nineteen.

His hosts invited her to join them. Nell was more than just their nanny: their families were old friends. Her father, an army officer, had been killed in the war, her mother managing on a widow's pension in a small flat near the cathedral. Nell was slightly shy but very amusing about the baby, and, when she looked at him, Francis felt all sorts of odd sensations that he'd never experienced with Liz.

It began with a few casual meetings at the house in Princesshay, always chaperoned by the friends and sometimes even the baby. Then he "happened" to run into her on her day off, in one of her favourite cafés that she'd mentioned. They had lunch together. It happened several times: they had lunch or tea, and fell deeper and more dangerously in love. One glorious summer afternoon he took her for a little run in the car and they finished up in the flat he kept in the constituency where he stayed for a few days each week.

Even now his cold, frail limbs recall the warmth of her flesh and the joy of holding her. It became an addiction he simply couldn't fight. He needed her.

Liz rarely came to the flat. She was too busy modernizing Brockscombe, getting to know the families who would help Francis' political career. When he returned home to her his happiness overflowed into his life with her and she was always amused by the enthusiasm with which he took her in his arms, never aware of the guilt and the shame that lay beneath it. He went to confession, tried to end the relationship, but he was too weak: too much in love with Nell.

When Nell told him she was pregnant he was shocked, frightened, but a small part of him rejoiced. His child and Nell's: the prospect filled him with joy. Yet the reality was bleak indeed. His political career was going from strength to strength — and what if Liz should find out? His gut curdled with fear and he seized Nell's hands, not knowing what to say to her, his brain darting about seeking acceptable solutions. Nell saw his fear and said at once that they wouldn't be a burden to him, she and the baby; they would manage somehow. Her mother knew, she told him, and was prepared to help her.

Staring at her as they stood together in the shadowy peaceful flat, Francis was silent with amazement. He thought of the small quiet woman he'd met once or twice and could hardly believe it.

"She doesn't know it's you," Nell added quickly. "I wouldn't tell her, though she knows that the father is a married man. We've talked about it, once we got over the shock, and we both want to keep the baby. She's being amazing. I think it's because she still misses Daddy so much. It's giving her something to live for. There's nothing you can do, Francis. If this gets out, you're finished."

He pulled her into his arms and held her tightly. He wanted everything. "But it's my baby, too."

"I know but, my darling, we have to face the facts. We're moving to live with a cousin of Mummy's near Tavistock. We shall say I'm a widow and we shall manage somehow."

"I want to help though," he cried stubbornly. "I love you. Perhaps I should speak to Liz."

Even as he said it he knew that he wouldn't have the courage.

Nell was shaking her head, still holding on to him. "Let's just wait for a while. Nothing should happen in a rush."

"But I shall still see you and the baby? I can help financially. Please, Nell."

"Of course you shall see the baby," she said gently. "But we must be careful. Please, Francis, you must trust me."

And he had trusted her. She called the baby Maxim. They managed to go forward, meeting when he could manage it. He saw his boy grow from a baby into a toddler and then, when Maxie was two and a half, there was the offer of a post as a junior minister — and Liz announced that she was pregnant.

Francis leans back in his chair and groans as he remembers the feeling of being pulled in so many directions at once; of rushing between London, his constituency and Brockscombe. He barely saw Nell or Maxie for months on end and then, two years later, he had a letter from her telling him that she was getting married.

"You'd like Bill," she wrote. "He's first lieutenant on a frigate running out of Devonport so it's back to the military life for me. He loves Maxie and it will be good to be properly settled. I'll stay in touch, of course . . ."

He knew that he wouldn't like Bill — that he hated Bill — but what could he do? And, to his shame, part of him was filled with relief. He arranged a trust for Maxie and wrote Nell a letter of congratulation. His letter, like hers, might have been from some very dear old friend but there were one or two little code words and phrases, previously agreed on, from which each might take comfort. Then Bill was posted to Singapore, the family were to go with him, and he and Nell agreed that communication should cease. It was more than forty years before he saw Nell and Maxie again.

He can see Maxie now, pushing the wheelbarrow, laughing with Rob, who walks beside him, an arm across his shoulders. Francis catches a glimpse of another figure: hidden from their sight, Tim is walking in the woods. He waved to him once but the boy didn't respond. He stood quite still, staring up at the windows almost in alarm, as if he were seeing a ghost, and then hurried away deeper into the trees.

Francis stands up carefully, balances himself, still staring out of the window. Since his last stroke he confines himself mainly to the top floor of the house.

Here he has his bedroom, bathroom, even a tiny kitchen — and this study, his sanctuary. He moves slowly to his desk and leans forward, resting on his fists, staring down at his papers. He is writing his memoirs, transferring years of notes to the computer. It is agonizingly slow but he is making progress. Francis switches on the computer, lowers himself on to his chair, opens the document and smiles wryly to himself as he reads the heading: "Chapter One. The Macmillan Years: 'You never had it so good.'"

CHAPTER
EIGHT

William walks along South Street, heading for the car park, raising his hand in farewell to fellow members of his singing group who are also on their way home. It has been one of those magical evenings when the group finds a mutual understanding of the music, a common feeling for what the music demands from the singers, and the resultant harmonies resonate and project in a way that usually seems beyond their reach.

It's an exhilarating sensation; addictive. One of the tenors was exultant: "Wow! We really nailed it!" Another buffeted William lightly on the shoulder: "How about that?" And "Quite good," agreed the music director, "but we'll do it again and, this time, tenors, watch your entry on the twenty-fifth bar. You were late!"

Singing energizes William, makes him feel alive. Even seeing someone coming out of the door of the house where he and Fiona and Andy lived for twenty years cannot quench his high spirits. He is able to remember the good times now without bitterness, and this evening, after such jubilation, he can even think about Fiona's proposal to rent Tim's cottage with equanimity.

He guesses that Sam has made it clear that there is no future for her with him and that Fiona is realizing how much substance she has jettisoned for the shadow. Fiona has always been intense, living in the moment, unaware of the emotions of the people around her. She sees each situation only from her own point of view and is incapable of imagining how differently it might affect someone else, yet she could always make him laugh.

Her sense of humour and vitality energized him in the same way his singing has this evening. He felt twice as alive with her; it was as if she coloured his naturally drab grey camouflage into bright colours. Often her strongly held convictions made him uncomfortable — everything was black and white, simple — and after a while he ceased to argue with her, to put a different point of view. Fiona was impatient with the weak or the slow. There were no excuses for failure: to be a runner-up was to be the first of the losers.

William digs into his pocket for his car keys, wondering what she will do next. There will be another plan of campaign, he is sure of that. It half occurs to him that she might want to come back to him and anxiety grips him suddenly. He wonders whether he could withstand such a campaign and whether he would want to. He snorts at the foolishness of the thought: why on earth would she want such a thing? Is it conceivable that she could cast her spell on him again?

He knows that Kat is considering taking up Miche's offer. What if Kat moves to London and Fiona decides that he has plenty of room for her to stay at weekends, at Christmas? He suspects that once Kat is back amongst her old friends and associates she will spend very little time at Brockscombe. It has been a time of healing for her, of rest and renewal, but she has always remained in training as if she knows that one day the call will come and she will return to her work.

William climbs into his car. Deliberately he calms himself, takes a few deep breaths and relives the joy of the singing, the comradeship of the group. He starts the engine, drives out of the car park, and as he goes he begins to sing.

When he arrives home Kat is sitting at the kitchen table, her elbows propped on the table, Miche's chapters spread around her. She glances round as he comes in and he sees that there is a little glow, a brightness that lights her from within. He knows the signs and he experiences the usual twinge of envy at Kat's ability to embark on a new flirtation, to fall in and out of love, leaving very little distress or despair in her wake.

"These spring evenings are so beautiful and so melancholy," she says. "Can you hear the thrush? Heartbreaking, isn't it? In a good way, though."

He dumps his case on a chair and laughs at her. "How can heartbreak ever be a good thing?"

"I think it can," she answers seriously. "Sometimes it's necessary to break, so as to make space and give room to grow. It enlarges the possibility of emotions and reactions."

"Very philosophical," he says. "So who is he?"

She laughs too, beaming at him with affection. "Darling William. I shall miss you if I go to London."

The fear returns and he fetches a glass, then sits down and reaches for the bottle of wine that stands open on the table.

"And will you go?" He is surprised at the realization of how much he will miss her.

She considers his question, shuffling the papers, and he is struck by the gracefulness of her hands even in such a simple gesture.

"I'm not sure," she says at last. "Francis thinks I will. He thinks I should."

William wants to feel irritated by Francis' interference — what does he know? — but he doesn't underestimate his wisdom.

"Miche has unsettled you," he says. "But even if you were to go you'd come back from time to time, wouldn't you?"

"I don't know," answers Kat candidly. "I'd want to. I'd think I would but then again I know how easy it is to get caught up in things." She looks at him rather sadly. "You know how selfish and unreliable I am, darling."

He smiles at her. "None better. But aren't we all? I was thinking, driving home, that if you went then Fiona might want to move in with me."

Kat sends him a shrewd glance. "And?"

"And nothing." He fills his glass and raises it to her. "So I say again. Who is he?"

"A rather nice man that I saw in Thrive this morning. Very sexy."

70

"And what else?"

"His girlfriend called him Jeremy."

He raises his eyebrows. Kat doesn't usually trespass. "Girlfriend?"

She makes a face. "Putative girlfriend. Working at it. All bright and sweet and wriggling about like a puppy." She sips her own wine and sighs. "Such a pity if he falls for it. She's deeply ordinary."

"So what next, then?"

Kat shrugs. "Who can say? I'll probably see him around. Apparently he's just moved to Totnes so our paths are bound to cross sooner or later."

"Meanwhile you enjoyed ruffling the water. Making a few waves."

"Something like that."

She stacks the sheets together, smiling to herself, and he watches her. Perhaps this Jeremy might be the reason she'll need to stay; perhaps things might go on just the way they are now: he and Kat, Charlotte and Ollie, Tim. Silently he raises his glass to this private dream, takes a sip then sets the glass down.

"I'll just pop in on Francis," he tells her, "to see that he's OK and have a chat. Shan't be long and then we'll have supper."

Next door, Charlotte checks on Ollie and goes downstairs to make some supper. One of the dreary things of living alone is that eating becomes a chore. It feels unnatural to sit down in lonely splendour to a properly cooked and served meal; chewing solemnly, resisting the urge to read, or watch the television. How much easier it is to snack. At least now she has Ollie she has someone to share breakfast and lunchtime, but supper is still a solitary affair. Sometimes Tim comes in and they share a curry or a pizza. And she has Wooster — his tail wagging now as she comes into the kitchen — and the comfort of his big, solid presence.

She hears William's car, wishes it was Andy coming home, opening the front door and calling out to her. And she would call back, "Shush. I've just got Ollie off," and he'd give her a hug and they'd talk about how the day had been. Andy is like his father: easy-going, cheerful, competent — and she misses him dreadfully.

"I might get a foreign posting next," he told her. "How d'you fancy Washington?"

She stands at the window looking out at the gardens at the back of the cottages, not knowing how she'd fancy it.

"What would we do with Wooster?" she asked, parrying the question. "We couldn't leave him behind."

And Wooster got to his feet as if he knew what they were talking about and came over, pushing his head against their legs.

"Oh, we'd get him there somehow, wouldn't we, Wooster, old fellow?" Andy said easily, bending to pull his ears. "There would be quarantine, of course . . ."

Charlotte knows that she would miss her family, and it's good here, with William and Aunt Kat next door, and Tim. What she'd really like is for Andy to get a shore job in the dockyard, a ship in refit, so that he could come home each night, except when he was duty officer, and they could just be a little family all together. They've had so little time together since Ollie was born and it would be good to find out what it was like to be a family, to get used to it, before they set out on such an adventure.

These long light evenings unsettle her. She heats soup, cuts some bread, feeling restless, melancholy, so that when her phone buzzes she reaches for it with relief. It's Mattie sending a cheerful message and a photo of her with another girl having supper together. Charlotte sends a reply. She's hoping that Mattie will be offered the job at the BBC in Bristol. It would be good to have her closer — and maybe there might be something developing between Mattie and Tim, though they behave as if they're just good mates — but if Andy is posted to Washington it won't make much difference. She types: *When are you coming down again?*

Mattie replies: *Soon. I'll let you know when I get a date for the interview.*

Feeling more cheerful, Charlotte finishes her supper, settles down at the end of the kitchen table with Wooster at her feet and opens her laptop. As so often during these long evenings, her work is her refuge.

CHAPTER
NINE

At this time of the year, Tim thinks, the countryside looks like a half-finished watercolour. Patches of paint-bright gold, tissue-delicate pink, milky-white green, all washing along ditches, through hedgerows and over bare branches. Through farm gates he catches glimpses of the distant moors rough-sketched against a pale sky; sheep like white stones dotted randomly around an emerald-green field.

Driving with Aunt Kat to Totnes, he is still taken aback by the beauty of it all. He enjoys being driven; it gives him the opportunity to gaze without any anxiety of being distracted or causing an accident.

"It must be wonderful," he says, "to be able to paint."

Aunt Kat, who is negotiating the narrow bridge across the River Dart at Staverton doesn't answer immediately. She waves to the driver waiting to let her through, who responds cheerfully, and then accelerates up the hill, climbing out of the valley.

"I could take a photograph, of course," he carries on, "but it wouldn't be the same. But why not? The photograph would record the scene exactly as it is at this moment so what's the difference?"

He glances at Aunt Kat who, he can see, is thinking about it. She frowns, shakes her head.

"Perhaps the photograph leaves no room for imagination," she suggests at last. "The camera never lies and all that. Though these days that's not quite true, of course. Is there more scope for the imagination in a painting? It's the artist's own view; his unique take on it."

"You mean he can add things or subtract what he doesn't like?"

Kat smiles. "Something like that. It reminds me of a story about F. J. Widgery, the landscape artist, who was painting a moorland scene somewhere on Dartmoor. A hiker paused to look at the work in progress, then he studied the view and looked again at the river in the painting. 'But Mr Widgery,' he said, puzzled, 'there's no water down there.' 'No,' replied the great man, 'but there should be.'"

Tim laughs. "Perhaps that's it. The artist is in control. I'm a control freak."

He falls silent, remembering that he is no longer in charge; that he has been taken over by something beyond his control. He tries to accept each day as a gift but it is hard, on days like these, to know that you might never see another spring. Just now he is glad to be with Aunt Kat. Her warmth and vitality give him courage. She accepts him without questioning or curiosity about his past. He is Mattie's friend.

As they drive into the town, head towards the car park, he thinks about Mattie. He doesn't know what to do. He's fallen in love with her, simply and naturally, as if their earlier friendship in London had always been leading up to this. He loves her but can't tell her, and now it is clear that she is wondering how their friendship might go forward. She isn't nagging — Mattie's not like that — but she feels, understandably, that their relationship has changed since that weekend at Brockscombe.

"Coffee first?" Aunt Kat suggests. "I think it's warm enough to sit outside, don't you?"

She goes inside The Brioche to order and comes back smiling at some exchange she's had with Nat or Jai, looking about. She is watchful, excited. Tim studies her with interest, wondering what's on her mind. He is getting used to the friendliness of the West Country: the way strangers smile, say "Good morning". Few people avoid eye contact, conversations arise out of mere nothings; he is able to watch little children with amusement without fearing that their parents will suspect him of anything worse than being charmed by their antics.

Tim sits in the sun and pretends that he is not under a death sentence. He watches the market traders across the road in the square, the awnings and stalls giving it a medieval air, and sips his coffee. A boy and girl, teenagers, walk past linked closely together: her hand is tucked in the back pocket of his jeans and he cups her face, turning it towards him for a kiss. Tim's heart is pierced with envy at such simplicity. He is distracted by a little commotion at the other table. A man stands there moving the empty coffee cups around, shifting plates. He looks distressed.

"My phone's gone," he says to them. "I must have left it here on the table when I went just now. Did you see who took it?" He glances up and down the street, as if he might see the thief sprinting away. "Did someone sit here after I'd gone?"

"Wait," says Aunt Kat. "Have you checked to ask if it's been handed in?"

He stares at her frowning, as if he can't understand her meaning.

"Handed *in?*"

"Mmm." She nods at him, slightly amused at his incredulity. "It's possible. Why don't you check?"

Still frowning he goes into the café. Tim is fascinated by the little by-play. He glances at Aunt Kat, who raises her eyebrows, gives a little shrug. The man reappears, his face radiant. He is so happy that he actually seizes Aunt Kat's arm and gives it a little squeeze.

"You were right," he cries. "Someone handed it in. It's amazing. My God! I love this place. Thank you."

He dashes away to join his companions and Aunt Kat laughs and then straightens up a little, her eyes fixed on someone beyond Tim's shoulder. He waits until the person Aunt Kat is watching is beside him and then turns his head and glances up at the man, who is smiling at Aunt Kat.

"Hello," she says lightly, almost challengingly. She seems amused.

Tim is aware of the newcomer's caution. He looks down at Tim and murmurs something about the beauty of the morning. He's wearing a knapsack and carrying a newspaper. Aunt Kat makes no suggestion that he should bring another chair and join them, she simply watches him with the same amused expression, and he hesitates, then nods awkwardly and goes into the café.

"Do you know him?" Tim asks, puzzled by the encounter.

"Not yet," answers Aunt Kat serenely, "but I intend to."

Tim bursts out laughing. "You were making him nervous."

"Was I?" She glances through the windows to the interior of the café. "Excellent."

He continues to chuckle as he drinks his coffee in the sun and then, quite suddenly, the terror swoops to engulf him and he wants most terribly to live; to be able to contemplate the years ahead with a reasonable hope of survival: to sit in the sun, drinking coffee and laughing with Aunt Kat.

"'For who plans suicide sitting in the sun?'" he murmurs.

Aunt Kat is watching him curiously. Her previous amusement has died from her face.

"I was just thinking aloud," he says quickly, casually. "A fragment of poetry just came into my mind. Are you a reader, Aunt Kat, or is music more your thing? I often think with poetry, if you see what I mean. Not mine, sadly. Other people's. Does this kind of scene evoke dance, movement? Do you want to create something new out of it?"

And so he distracts her until she is smiling again and he feels that his secret is still safe.

* * *

Whilst Tim goes off to the bookshop and for a look around the market, Kat remains at her table. She's refused his offer of more coffee and sits watching the passers-by, the delivery men, the market traders. A youth on a skateboard jumps and jitters down the middle of the street, weaving around the shoppers, swooping out of the path of a car, and she watches his grace and agility with delight. Patterns form themselves in her head, a sequence of movements — and then Jeremy is standing beside her, smiling down at her with that same half-cautious look in his eyes.

"Hi," she says, filing away the skateboarder for further use and gesturing at Tim's empty chair. "Have you had some coffee?"

"Yes," he says, hesitating with his hand on the chair. "Yes, but . . . would you . . .?"

"Yes, please," she says at once. "Thank you. I'd love another Americano."

He puts his rucksack on the chair and goes back inside to order. Kat waits, surprised at how pleased she is to see him, recognizing that tiny quickening of the pulse.

"Jeremy," she says, when he returns. "That's right, isn't it?"

"Yes." He looks surprised, pausing for a moment before, putting his rucksack on the pavement and sitting down. "But how did you . . .?"

And then she sees him remember; a twinge of embarrassment makes him awkward.

"Actually, I prefer Jerry," he says almost confidentially, as if he is somehow excluding the woman in the café that other day from any kind of intimacy.

Kat beams at him. "Jerry," she repeats. "Hello, Jerry. I am Irina Bulova."

He gazes at her. Her deliberate phrasing is not lost on him and, after a moment, recognition dawns in his eyes.

"You're the dancer. The choreographer," he says, in awe. "I had a feeling I'd seen you before. Goodness! I saw that programme on the television . . . Wow!"

Kat laughs at his expression. Channel 4 had made the programme when Gyorgy died. It was surprisingly successful, giving them both a kind of iconic pop-star status within the world of dance.

"But actually," she says, mimicking him, "I prefer Kat."

"Cat?

"My name is Katerina," she tells him. "My father was a Polish fighter pilot. He was injured when his plane crashed, and my mother was the nurse who looked after him. Irina Bulova is a useful name for a dancer. But to my family and friends I am Kat."

"I feel very privileged to be counted as a friend on such short acquaintance," he says rather formally.

Kat regards him thoughtfully, wondering if he is quite as ready as she imagined for a delightful flirtation. She is used to the quick reactions of artistes, the easy relationships of the theatre, and often takes a short cut through the defence mechanisms and social niceties that are used as protection to mask the real person behind them. Some people find this invasive, threatening, others are relieved to set aside their reserve, to connect at a deeper level. Often Kat finds herself the confidante of long-buried fears, grief, remorse, even on the shortest of acquaintance.

The coffee arrives, which gives them both a moment to regroup.

"Are you settling in?" she asks, and laughs at his expression. "I'm afraid I was earwigging that morning in the café. Do you mind?"

"Not at all. I've got a very nice top-floor flat in one of the new blocks down on the river. Amazing views."

He lifts his cup, sips his coffee, and she can see he's trying to decide if he might invite her to see it; whether it looks presumptuous or might give the wrong impression. Kat wonders if she were unwise to give him her professional name. Sometimes, being famous can cause an imbalance in a relationship.

She tells him about Brockscombe, making him laugh as she describes the set-up, and sees the tell-tale signs as he relaxes: his lifted shoulders dropping, his fisted fingers loosening. Some people hate to be looked directly in the eye but Jerry meets her gaze openly, questioningly, and it is as if they are greeting each other at a very deep level of understanding.

Kat doesn't invite him to Brockscombe or ask about his past; she doesn't delve or probe. She talks about a new production she's seen at the Theatre Royal, a recent biography of a famous actor, a concert at Buckfast Abbey. Jerry talks of his own past productions with his students; his delight when one of them was given a part in a television sit-com. He mentions a film he's hoping to see and she responds with enthusiasm, quoting some of the reviews.

"Perhaps," he says, "we could go together?"

"Great," she says. "I'd love it. I'll give you my phone number."

She notices his breast rise with the silent sigh of relief and delight, and she smiles secretly to herself. Game on.

After Kat has gone, Jerry continues to sit at the table thinking about the encounter. He feels exhilarated, in a kind of delightful shock, so that he doesn't see Sandra until she is very nearly beside him. Instinctively he reaches for his rucksack, prepares to rise so as to make his escape, but her evident delight at meeting him foils his attempt.

"How very nice," she says, and indeed genuine pleasure glows in her round, pretty face.

"Hello," he says.

He can't think why he feels this way: a kind of embarrassed guilt, as if he has been caught out in some unworthy act. She is looking hopefully at the empty chair and he sees the exact moment that she notices the two empty mugs and her slight change of expression from delight to — what, exactly? Suspicion? Irritation? His natural reaction is one born out of pure good manners though he is kicking himself for giving in to it.

"Have you had coffee?" he asks her. "Would you like one?"

Her face brightens at once.

"I'd love one, Jeremy. And you? Look, I'll go and get it this time. My turn. Americano, isn't it? Aha. You see, I notice everything!"

He can see that she's pleased by this tiny familiarity, that she sees it as progress and, as he waits, Jerry thinks again of Kat and how their minds meshed together in an exchange of ideas, experiences, jokes, though he suspects that Kat wouldn't remember what kind of coffee he drinks. The exhilaration possesses him yet again and he has to make a huge effort to concentrate on Sandra once she returns. He feels a tiny unworthy sense of triumph that he has withheld from her the shortening of his own name. It makes the sharing of it with Kat — with Irina Bulova — even more special. They've exchanged telephone numbers and he wonders who will be the first to make contact.

"Don't think I don't understand," Sandra is saying, "that I don't know how hard it is, managing on your own." She sighs sympathetically, chin drawn in, eyes registering care and understanding, and he wants to stand up and walk away from her unasked-for sympathy. "I always say that it doesn't get better, you just learn how to deal with it."

He mutters something, and he can see that she thinks he is simply being brave, and then his phone beeps twice and he reaches into his pocket with a little shrug of apology, glad of the interruption.

Did you really want a third cup of coffee?

He reads the text through again and instinctively glances around, peering into the buzz of people in the market square. He wants to laugh out loud, to punch the air, but he can't. He merely texts back one word: *No!*

Trying to suppress his laughter, he settles back to talk to Sandra.

CHAPTER
TEN

Leaving Bristol after her interview at the BBC in Whiteladies Road and heading for the M5 in her ancient battered VW Polo, Mattie feels happy and full of energy though she by no means imagines that the job is in the bag. She's quite certain that loads of people better qualified than she is will have applied for this post as a researcher. As she reruns the interview in her head she thinks of all the intelligent, impressive answers she might have given: opportunities lost. She remembers one of the job description requirements: "Cheerfulness, emotional resilience and a sense of humour under pressure. Must be a team player." Mattie hopes that she's put these qualities across but still feels that she might not have made the grade. The people were lovely, though, and it was clear that the rig was informal: most of them were in jeans.

After the interview she asked if there was somewhere she could change out of her smart suit ready for the journey west and a sweet girl had shown her the cloakroom and chatted to her. She called the BBC "the Beeb" and told Mattie that she once accompanied Sister Wendy to a shoot and how they sang hymns in the car. By the time they finished talking Mattie wanted the job more than ever.

It's not that she doesn't enjoy working in London but somehow she can't quite get the West Country out of her soul. She dreams about the beaches, the moors, the diversity of the countryside. All her busy, exhausted London friends tell her how much she'd miss the nightclubs and films, theatres and art exhibitions, though few of them ever seem to have the time to go to them. The daily commute, social media, child care take up most of their lives.

She drives across the Suspension Bridge, glancing down into the Avon Gorge, and wonders if even Bristol is too far away from all she loves best. Her childhood, growing up with Charlotte on the western edge of the moor — her father often away at sea, their mother trying to keep their lives balanced despite his long absences — was a happy one. Yomping over the moor with the dogs, picnics on the beach, the yearly trip to the pantomime in Plymouth; it seems idyllic when she looks back. It is odd — and rather enviable — that Charlotte has recreated the wheel with Andy and baby Oliver and Wooster: history repeating itself.

She loves Bristol, though. She was at uni here, and could probably have found a job quite easily, but it seemed necessary to have a go at London; sharing a bedsit with a friend, getting a job in a bookshop and then moving to the publishing house. It's been fun but she can't see where she's going. Ambition seems to have been left out of her character — until now, perhaps. Now she wants this job at the Beeb and to be nearer to her family — and to Tim.

She turns on to the M5, her spirits rising. She so enjoyed that last weekend with Tim, with them all at Brockscombe.

His passion took her by surprise — he's such a quiet, gentle soul — and it was such a relief to respond and allow her love for him to be an open, happy thing. So far their friendship has been such a muddle. He was involved with Rachel when they first met and then she met Josh and started going out with him — and the next thing was that Tim and Rachel had split up and he was leaving his job. Even now Mattie doesn't quite know why Tim has chucked up his job and embarked on this rather odd sabbatical. He certainly wasn't much upset when he and Rachel broke up, though he hadn't been very well at the time. He told everyone that his grandmother had died, leaving him her house in Fulham, where she'd brought him up, and he'd sold it and was planning to take time out to re-evaluate his life.

Mattie was slightly surprised when he reacted so positively to Brockscombe. It just seemed right when he asked her if she knew anywhere he could go but she hadn't expected him to take her up so readily. She knew from the conversations she had with him that he had no family apart from his grandmother but he never volunteered any explanations. Perhaps her death was a kind of catalyst and there are things that he needs now to come to terms with, to understand before he can move on.

She's beginning to accept the fact that she really hopes that she will be included in the moving-on. It's crazy how much she's looking forward to seeing him again, though it was Charlotte who invited her this time.

"Since you'll only be a couple of hours away," she said, "try to get down to see us afterwards."

Mattie phoned Tim. "What about it?" she asked almost jokily. "Shall I come down and see you all?"

"It would be great," he answered, but there was an oddness in his voice. It was warm, even loving, but there wasn't that same excitement as when he phoned her on the day of the storm, and he didn't suggest that she should stay with him.

She wonders if he is embarrassed by the passion he showed that weekend. Perhaps, because of her unguarded response, she played it a bit too cool afterwards. It was such an odd situation at Brockscombe, playing happy families next day after a night of such lovemaking, but in a kind of way it helped. She can go down now and stay with Charlotte and it won't seem unusual or strange, yet she is very wound up about how Tim will be. Her instinct is to give him time; to take things gently.

Mattie gives a little snort. It's true that she can no longer say that she has no ambition. She wants Tim and now she wants the job, if not at the BBC then definitely back in the West Country. It's a start.

Tim finishes his sandwich, pushes his plate aside and glances at his watch. He feels restless, nervous at the prospect of Mattie's arrival. Part of him longs to see her; part of him doesn't know how to handle it. He knows that he should tell her the truth but he can't bear to lose that happy, open friendship she offers him; can't bear the prospect of the shock in her eyes, her sympathy and the special treatment that will follow it. Once they know the truth then nobody at Brockscombe will treat him as an equal. He still hugs to himself that joyful night of love with Mattie. Yet how can he go forward with her without deceiving her? When she phoned and asked if she should come down to Brockscombe after her interview in Bristol, his heart had leaped up with joy. "Yes," he wanted to shout. "Yes, please. Come and stay with me again."

Instead he remained cool, not questioning the arrangement that she should stay with Charlotte. How hard it had been to behave as if she were simply a good friend coming for a visit with her sister.

He pushes back his chair with a violent thrust of frustration and misery. Grabbing his jacket from the hook by the door he lets himself out into the windy bright early May afternoon and takes the path to the woods. Yet even in his misery he pauses to listen to the birdsong; to watch squirrels racing along their twiggy pathways high in the trees; to glory in the tender pink, uncurling leaves of the copper beech. There is a magic in the woods in spring and he cannot help but respond to it.

Today Pan is holding bluebells, their long pale stalks threaded through his small stony fingers, and he wears a garland of periwinkles. Tim stands before him. He wants to do something foolish, like pray or make a wish. Here, in this wild, magical place, he almost believes in miracles: that he might be healed; that Mattie will love him. Standing quite still, allowing his senses to be taken over by the sound of bird-music and the scents of the wet earth, Tim succumbs to the peace that presses in. Briefly his soul connects with something infinite and his heart thrills with unimaginable joy.

At last he turns away, following the mossy overgrown path at the wood's edge, pausing beside the wooden seat that is placed between two trees so as to take advantage of the view across the fields to the high moors. He wonders who put the seat here, who sat gazing out as he does now, sheltered by trees and shrubs. Suddenly he notices that on the broad wooden arm of the seat someone has placed a few objects to make a shape. Leaning to look closer he sees that it is a face: two pine cones for the eyes, an acorn cap for the nose, five small stones for a smiley mouth, a pine-needle switch for the hair.

Tim sits staring at the face. He is awhirl with emotions: amusement, bafflement, even excitement. It's so odd, as if a message has been left specially for him. But by whom? He scans the woodland, peering through the bushes behind the bench. He has this conviction that the child is there somewhere, watching him; watching his reaction to this piece of woodland art.

"Come out," he wants to cry. "Come and talk to me," but he doesn't dare. In this wild, strange place he is afraid of what might happen. Very gently he touches the eye-cones, slightly alters the pine-switch hair. He feels it's absolutely essential that he responds to this message. He gets up and searches around, takes two orange berries from a nearby bush, picks up another cone with a pine needle, and goes back to the seat. Very carefully he presses the orange berries into the eye-cones to brighten them and arranges the pine-needle switch and the cone to make it look as if the face is smoking a pipe.

Tim stares at it, pleased with the result, hoping that the wind doesn't blow it away or that nobody else disturbs it. Another idea is beginning to form in his mind that fills him with a foolish excitement. With one last glance around he turns and walks home.

From the window of his study Francis watches him. He sees Tim stride out into the woods. He looks tense with his hands thrust deep into his pockets, his head lowered. Then he stops as if he is suddenly aware of the life all around him, looking upwards, watching the squirrels. He disappears from sight and Francis wonders which path he will take. Has he discovered Pan? The dogs' graveyard?

It is years now since he was able to walk so far, but in his head Francis can imagine those walks where his ancestors planted rhododendrons and azaleas, camellias and magnolia. The bluebells will be coming into flower now, and the wood anemones and the periwinkles. In spring and early summer he always preferred to walk alone in the early morning, creeping out so that the dogs didn't hear him. Walking silently, pausing in the shadows, he'd see the rabbits playing in the field, spy a blackbird with a beakful of food, poised watchfully on a branch near its nest, observe a pheasant running with its stiff-legged gait before launching itself with a whirring of wings over the fence into the field. It was a time for reflection, for refreshment.

He'd sit on the wooden seat that his father had so thoughtfully placed at the edge of the woods, and watch the rising sun's rays changing the dun-coloured higher slopes of the moors to a celestial pink and gold. It was so familiar, so dear, the slow turning of the year. It held him grounded in its rhythm, teaching him that he was not in control, showing him its mysteries of life and death and resurrection.

When Tim reappears he looks different, almost excited. He walks quickly, with a purpose, and Francis wonders what he has seen to change his earlier mood. He feels a kinship with this boy — he seems like a boy to him — who spends so much time alone; who seems overwhelmed with his discovery of the countryside.

"I've always been a city boy," he said to Francis when they first met. "I've never known anywhere like this. It's so quiet."

"And do you seek quiet?" Francis asked him. "Usually it's the last thing that young people want."

Tim looked at him then; a distant look as if he were thinking things through.

"Yes," he answered at last, very seriously. "I think it's exactly what I need now."

"Then be welcome at Brockscombe," Francis said.

They shook hands, Francis looking down from his great height at this slight young man, and a look had passed between them: of understanding and liking. Francis held Tim's hand briefly in his strong clasp and then let it go.

"Do you like poetry?" he asked, and Tim's face lightened with surprise and pleasure.

"Yes, I do," he said.

Francis smiled and made a sweep with his hand towards the bookcase.

"When you've moved in you must come and see if I've anything you haven't read. I expect you'll find me very old-fashioned, though."

Tim smiled back at him. "I'd like that."

But he hadn't come, not yet. Perhaps, thinks Francis, he needs another invitation; perhaps he is afraid of giving himself away.

He turns away from the window, remembering that Mattie is arriving today to stay with Charlotte. He'll wander down later and see them and hope to catch Tim for a private moment. Somehow it seems important, though he couldn't say why. Meanwhile, he can hear Maxie calling to him, his voice echoing up the stairs, and he goes out on to the landing to welcome him.

CHAPTER
ELEVEN

It is Wooster who is the first to greet Mattie. Stretched on the cobbles outside Charlotte's front door, he raises his head as her car pulls into the courtyard and barks once or twice before getting to his feet and ambling to meet her. He's very fond of Mattie, who buries her fingers in his thick golden ruff and talks lovingly to him before straightening up to wave to Charlotte, who has now appeared carrying Oliver.

"How did it go?" calls Charlotte.

It's odd, she thinks, watching Mattie embracing Wooster, that her very strong affection for her sister should be shot through with a seam of resentment: a kind of impatient irritation mixed with love and loyalty that she never experiences with anyone else.

"You're a bit hard on Mattie, aren't you?" Andy once said to her over some silly thing that Mattie had done — the forgotten birthday of a mutual friend or a double booking for a weekend — and she'd felt defensive at once.

"She gets away with murder," she'd answered. "It's always been the same. Dad used to spoil her rotten."

But afterwards she thought about it, trying to analyse the difference between her reactions to Mattie and to her friends. It was as if it were necessary to keep Mattie's feet on the ground; to stop her showing off, being silly, getting into trouble.

"Keep an eye on Mattie," their mother would say if they were going to a party or to stay with friends. "Don't forget you're the eldest." Or, "Let Mattie have a turn. Remember she's younger than you."

Charlotte resented this mantle of responsibility, this implication that she must always be the sensible one.

Now, as she watches Mattie stand up — laughing at Wooster's greeting and pushing back the long dark hair that corkscrews round her face — a small part of her records anxiously that her sister is looking thinner whilst another part notes, slightly bitterly, that Mattie is able to wear old clothes and still look more eye-catching than anybody else.

"I hope you didn't wear those tatty jeans to the interview." Charlotte cannot help the critical remark even as Mattie flings her arms around both her and Oliver and hugs them tightly.

"Of course I didn't. Though it wouldn't have mattered if I had. Everyone was very casual."

"So how was it?"

Mattie wrinkles her nose, pulls down her mouth. "Don't know. They were lovely but I'm not confident. I expect they'll interview lots of people who are better qualified than I am. Hey! Hasn't Ol grown? Hi, Ol. Give me a hug then."

She takes Oliver in her arms whilst Charlotte, still in this oddly self-observant mood, notices that she doesn't make any comforting observations like, "Of course you'll get it," or, "I bet you were great," as she might have done to a friend. And she wishes Mattie wouldn't call him Ol.

"I expect," she says rather sedately, "that if it's right then you'll get it. Have you lost weight? Did you get some lunch?"

Mattie is dancing with Oliver, twirling around whilst she holds up one of his chubby fists, laughing as she hums "My Favorite Things".

I'm still doing the elder sister thing, thinks Charlotte irritably. Worrying that she doesn't eat properly and she looks tired. But she's quite capable of looking after herself.

She feels a very slight stab of jealousy as she watches Oliver laughing up at her sister. It's always been so easy for Mattie; she could always make people love her. She makes them laugh, makes them feel good about themselves.

"I had a sandwich on the way down," Mattie answers, "but I'd love a cup of tea."

And then Tim suddenly appears from the path to the woods and Charlotte sees how his face changes when he sees Mattie. Briefly she glimpses the joy, the love, before he controls himself and calls out, "Fab-u-*lous*, darling. Definitely a ten."

Mattie waltzes round, laughing. "Tim," she cries. "Isn't this great?"

Charlotte, watching Tim embrace them both, gets a glimpse of Mattie's half-hidden face as she hugs him.

So they are in love, she thinks. So what's going on?

"I'll put the kettle on and make some tea," she calls. "And do stop twirling, Mattie. You'll make Oliver sick. Anyway, it's time for his sleep. I'll take him in."

Mattie passes Oliver to Charlotte but as she goes inside with him she's already begun to feel perversely irritable with herself now: a party-pooper. It's often like this when they are together: that old requirement to protect her little sister still causes friction. The six-year gap was just too much for them to be real playmates but not quite enough to engender any kind of maternal instinct in Charlotte. She'd been an only child long enough to feel that her nose was definitely put out of joint by this new baby to whom, everyone assumed, she would be a second little mother.

Charlotte holds Oliver in her arms, rocking him, gazing down into his small peaceful face. She is weak with love for him. Only now does she understand the fierce maternal instinct: that knowledge that she now has a hostage to fortune and nothing will ever be the same again.

Mattie makes a little face as Oliver is taken from her arms and whisked away. She knows that she sometimes irritates Charlotte but can't always quite see why. There seems to be some unspoken mantra surrounding them that insists that Charlotte is the sensible and serious sister whilst she is irresponsible and emotional: a kind of Elinor and Marianne Dashwood. Just for a moment she wonders whether Tim should be cast in the role of Willoughby and bursts out laughing.

97

"What's the joke?" he asks, unable to keep from smiling at her amusement, but she shakes her head, unwilling to discuss this with him. Her relationship with Charlotte runs too deep for a casual reference.

"Just being silly with Ol," she answers.

"It looks like the interview went well," he suggests. "You seem in good spirits."

"Oh, I don't know." She shrugs and slips her arm in his. "I really want it, Tim, but they didn't give anything away. And, after all, why should I be selected? I bet they get loads of people after it."

He presses her arm against his side with his elbow. "Because you're the best, that's why. Bet you get it."

Mattie feels emotional; grateful for his partisanship and his approval. She knows it's a weakness to need love but she responds to it as a flower does to the sun, expanding and relaxing in its warmth. As they stand, linked together, she wonders suddenly whether she's been foolish in suggesting that Tim should move here to Brockscombe. If there is going to be anything between them it might be much more difficult to conduct a relationship under the eye of her slightly censorious older sister.

Typical, she tells herself, to think of that now when it's much too late.

She's always been the same: impulsive, acting on instinct, rushing in where angels fear to tread. It was always getting her into trouble when she was little: inviting a friend to tea, saying that she was having a party, promising to lend a toy or a book, all without asking permission.

"Just like your father," Mummy would say in an exasperated voice, and Daddy would make a little face behind her back, out of sight, so that Mattie would want to burst out laughing. She didn't because of getting him into trouble, but she loved him for it. Even now she's careful what she says when she goes home to see them and it's only when she and her father are alone together that she tells him about the dramas in her life.

He always says the same thing: "I'm on your side, sweetheart. Don't let the buggers grind you down," and she gives him a hug and feels better, still needing to know that he loves her, that he's on her side.

Now, still holding Tim's arm, she sees how difficult things might be if they should get really serious. Yet at the time it seemed absolutely right to tell him about Brockscombe.

"Charlotte's bringing out some tea." She smiles at him and lets go of his arm. "I know, Tim, let's all go down to the beach afterwards. We could have a fish-and-chip supper at South Milton. Have you been there yet?"

Tim shakes his head. "Don't think so."

"You'll love it," she says confidently.

"We thought we'd all go to South Milton," she says as Charlotte comes out with some mugs on a tray. "Ooh. Lovely fruit tea. Thanks. What d'you think? Ol would love it."

She sees, just briefly on Charlotte's face, an echo of their mother's expression of restrained irritation; sees

99

Charlotte's breast heave with the little sigh of reined-in impatience.

"It would be much too late for Oliver," she answers. "You know he has his bath at half past five."

Just for a minute Mattie wants to make her father's comic face but she doesn't. She feels guilty that she hasn't thought about it, that she isn't being a responsible auntie. Though if Ol was hers she'd probably take him anyway, all snuggled down in his carrying seat, to let him look at the sea and hear the crying of the gulls. Does it matter if he has a late bath? Or misses it altogether? Clearly, from Charlotte's expression, the answer is yes.

"Of course," Mattie says. "I was being silly. Never mind. We'll go another time. Ol's got all his life to go and see the sea and eat fish and chips."

She glances at Tim and sees an odd fleeting expression on his face. He looks immeasurably sad. The next moment he's smiling, lifting his mug as if he's toasting her.

"To the job at the BBC," he says, and all three touch their mugs together and Mattie smiles back at the others.

Tim watches the by-play with interest. As an only child, with very little experience of family life to call on, the relationships between siblings fascinate him: between themselves it seems to be open season all year round. He is fairly confident, however, that were an outsider to criticize either of these sisters to the other they would immediately close ranks: blood is thicker than water.

He's also seen how the presence of a stranger amongst a family group often puts them on their mettle so that they behave with more restraint, though not always.

He drinks his tea, noticing that Charlotte is making an effort to control her irritation and Mattie is being placatory, complimenting Charlotte on the tea, the prettiness of the china — although he can't quite understand why such a simple remark about going to the sea should engender such an undercurrent of feeling. He guesses that it is not simply the suggestion that Oliver should be given a treat at an inopportune time that is the reason. This behaviour is the result of the particular dynamic between them that is continually being played out.

It's where you are in the pecking order, he thinks. Oldest, youngest, in the middle. Or an only child, like me.

Of course he knows it's not quite that simple. Other things play their part, not least the genetic brew — and fate.

All these inputs subconsciously shape us, he thinks, so that our reactions become almost as automatic as dear old Wooster's there, who at the mention of a particular word or the opening of a box begins to salivate at the prospect of a biscuit.

Tim leans to pat Wooster, who responds gratefully, flattening his ears and thumping his tail on the ground, and munches the biscuit that Tim slips to him. He licks his chops, looks hopefully to see if there might be another one, and settles down again with his heavy head resting on Tim's feet.

CHAPTER
TWELVE

The talk has finished, the speaker clapped, and the audience is beginning to leave. Jerry has already seen Sandra sitting several rows ahead of him, noticed how she kept glancing anxiously around until she spotted him, and now he is hoping to get out of the library before she catches him. She's with her friend so maybe she has plans anyway, and won't be suggesting that he joins them for tea.

He sets off at a fairly quick pace but he hears her voice calling him and reluctantly he slows down and turns round, arranging a half-pleased, half-surprised smile.

"Sandra. Hi."

"Jeremy." She stands beaming at him and, as usual, her indefatigable goodwill defeats his intention to be polite but firm and keep walking. "Glad you made it. We were hoping you might be ready for a cup of tea. Good talk, wasn't it?"

"Very good. The thing is, though," he makes the pretence of glancing at his watch, "I'm meeting someone at half past."

"Oh." Her change of expression is almost ludicrous: disappointed, a very slight reproving pulling-in of the chin. "Oh, I see. I assumed that perhaps . . ."

She allows her words to falter to a stop but Jerry hardens his heart against her disappointment. He raises his hand to the friend who has now caught Sandra up, smiles at them both and turns away.

"Just a moment, Jeremy." She doesn't give in. "I wanted to invite you to Sunday lunch. Just a few of us have a rota going and it's my turn this week. I'd love you to meet some of them. There's a retired lecturer from Exeter University. I'm sure you'd have a lot in common with him, and his wife was a head teacher."

The smile — hopeful, kind — is back and he is unable to refuse. Anyway, he can't think of an excuse and it would look rude to just say "No, thanks," when she means so well.

"That's very kind," he says. "Thank you."

"Wonderful." She is beaming again. "Come early and I'll show you those books we were talking about."

"OK. Great," he says. "See you on Sunday then."

He hurries away, down Fore Street, and across The Plains. His flat is in one of the buildings that once were warehouses, and he goes into the entrance hall, takes the stairs at a run, and lets himself in. His first action almost always is to go into the sitting-room and look down at Vire Island and along the river. Today, though, he hardly sees it; he's thinking about Kat. He takes his phone from his pocket, stares down at it for a moment, and then begins to tap out a message.

I suppose you're not around for a cup of tea?

He sends it, paces a bit, wondering if he's crazy; it's years since he felt so hyped up. Almost at once his phone rings and he flips open the lid.

I could be. Where are you?

In my flat. Where shall we meet?

What's wrong with your flat?

Jerry gives a snort of amusement: what indeed? He sends the address, tells her there's a parking space — and then panics. He dashes around tidying up, putting things away, checking that the visitors' lavatory has a towel. Then he stands in the middle of the sitting-room, staring round him and trying to see it through her eyes. It's a modern flat and very little of the big furniture that looked so right in the Victorian villa would have been appropriate. He shared the good pieces amongst his children, kept one or two smaller favourite items, but decided to make a whole new start. He's chosen light-coloured wood, Impressionistic-patterned blinds, plain upholstery. The paintings are watercolours or charcoal sketches. For the first time since he was a student, he's had the freedom to choose exactly what pleases him most. No cushions or shawls, none of the china ornaments that Veronica loved so much. Sometimes he feels guilty — as if he has rejected their life together — but he needs to stay minimalistic.

Sandra has already been to the flat, bringing some home-cooked treats — her hints had become quite impossible to ignore — and she looked around this big, light room and then smiled at him. It was a roguish, very nearly patronizing smile.

104

"I can see that this is a man's place," she said. "It's definitely missing a woman's touch. Not what I'd call homely."

He busied himself with making coffee, not commenting, but next time they met for lunch in the town she brought a little parcel for him. It was a cushion: a small silky cream affair with a puppy embroidered on it. He was surprised at how cross this made him but he accepted it as graciously as possible and went along with her arch comments. When he got home he threw the cushion on the bed in the little spare room. He'd simply have to remember to get it out if he invited her again; meanwhile he was annoyed that she was attempting to impose her taste on him. After a bit he calmed down and felt guilty. It was simply a kind gesture, a generous act.

A ring at the bell and Kat is here. She comes in and at once his nervousness vanishes. She brings with her no delicious treat for tea, no cushions, only a bunch of primroses wrapped loosely in a tissue. She hands them to him, follows him into the sitting-room and looks around her.

"How lovely to be high up," she says. "Lots of light."

She makes an odd movement, almost as if she is translating the light and the shapes of his room into dance. When she looks at him he feels a strange mix of feelings: excitement and an odd kind of fellowship.

"Feel free to dance," he tells her lightly.

"I shall," she answers.

"I'll put these in water and make some tea." He hesitates. The primroses are wet with rain, and he bends his head to breathe in the faint scent.

"I wondered after I picked them if you'd have a small enough vase," she said. "They were just there, in the hedge, and I couldn't resist."

He raises his head. "But I thought you weren't allowed to pick wild flowers these days."

She stares at him in amazement. "Aren't you? Why on earth not?"

He feels rather pedestrian, shrugs. "Just some sort of protection for the countryside. They're beautiful. What sort of tea?"

Veronica always drank fruit tea; Sandra likes Earl Grey.

"Builder's?" she says. "Darjeeling? Whatever you're having."

He goes into the long narrow kitchen, puts the primroses on the surface by the sink, and fills the kettle, wondering where he put the teapot, realizing that he has no cake. He opens a cupboard, brings out a packet of biscuits and looks at them anxiously. He's opened them, forgotten to put them into the tin, and now he wonders if they've gone soft.

Kat leans in the doorway watching him, amused. "I like your flat."

She doesn't offer to help, look for a vase or ask how he manages on his own. She and Sandra, he thinks, might be from different planets.

"I've got some fruit tea bags somewhere. And Earl Grey. I drink pretty ordinary stuff, I'm afraid."

106

"Pretty ordinary suits me," she says. "I don't like smelly tea."

"Nor me," he says, relieved. "Actually, I'd rather have coffee, myself."

"Me, too. Coffee then? Or why don't we have a glass of wine?"

She nods at the bottle standing by the coffee machine. He glances instinctively at his watch, nearly five o'clock, and sees her smile as if she is mocking his conventionality.

"Yes, why don't we?" he says recklessly.

He picks up the bottle and holds it towards her so that she can see the label.

"Merlot? Or there's some white in the fridge."

"Merlot sounds perfect. Only a small one, though, please. I've got to drive home."

Briefly he wonders what she'd say if he asked her to stay but knows he hasn't got the courage. He feels completely out of his depth — and he's loving every minute of it.

CHAPTER
THIRTEEN

As she drives home Kat is feeling slightly guilty. She likes Jerry — it's so easy to connect with him — yet she is wondering whether he has the right temperament for a flirtation. Their talk is effortless; he loves the theatre. It's so good to make him laugh, to gasp and stretch his eyes, to fall in with new ideas and concepts.

Yet she suspects that, deep down, Jerry is a conventional soul. He's stepped out of his comfort zone by buying a modern flat and is experimenting with a re-emerging personality that has been overlaid with marriage and fatherhood. He's beginning to build a new life with new friends and he's ready to embrace something exciting and different.

What she can't decide is whether this is a vulnerable time for him when he should be protected from himself. Perhaps, after all, the woman in the café would be better for him.

Whizzing along the main road on her way home, Kat can't helping laughing to herself. Jerry had several glasses of wine and grew more loquacious, inviting her to the cinema later this week at Dartington.

"Love to," she said at once. "How about tomorrow?" — and could see that he was slightly taken aback and incredibly pleased, rather as if he were a teenager and this were his first date.

Unlike Gyorgy or Miche, Jerry has a gentleness about him that is terribly attractive. She is used to driven, selfish artists who are ready to sacrifice anybody to their creations. There is nothing ruthless about Jerry. She's well aware that his admiration is feeding her ego, that she likes the early indication of devotion in his eyes. He is flattered by the attention of Irina Bulova, which, in turn, is feeding his ego.

He asked her about Gyorgy, about the music he'd composed for her, and she tried to describe the magic between them that informed his music and her choreography.

"You must miss him, all of it, dreadfully," he said, not mawkishly but with an intensity of understanding.

In that moment she was swamped with the bitter pain of missing and longing but she caught herself up and stretched out a hand to him. He hesitated, just for a second as if surprised, and then took her hand between both of his warm ones.

"Yes I do. Terribly."

He chafed her hand and then let it go, as if he didn't quite know what to do with it.

"It's the same for you, though, isn't it?" she asked, remembering his conversation with Sandra in the Thrive Café. There are photographs of his wife and his family on the shelf and he instinctively glanced towards them.

"Yes. Yes, of course."

They were silent, as if the ghosts of their former loves and lives were hovering near them. She could feel his unease and wondered how to restore the earlier light-heartedness.

"So this film, then," she said, picking up her glass. "Shall we meet in the Roundhouse?"

"Yes," he agrees. "Or in the White Hart?"

"That would be good," she says at once. "We can have a drink in the bar and then wander over to the Barn. Lovely."

Yet she was aware of a subtle shift in the atmosphere, as though that invocation of their past lives had altered the dynamic. It was time to go. She finished her drink and got to her feet.

He stood up quickly, not certain if he should try to persuade her to stay, not knowing quite how they should part. She could sense him wondering if they should shake hands, kiss briefly, or just smile. His anxiety touched her heart. Forty-odd years of happy marriage hadn't equipped him with the knowledge of how to conduct an affair.

"Thanks for the drink." She brushed his cheek very quickly and lightly with her lips. "Saved my life. See you tomorrow. Six thirty-ish."

She hadn't looked back at him, still standing at the open door, but hurried away down the stairs.

Now, Kat turns off into the lane that passes the Staverton Bridge Nursery, crosses the river, and slows down as the level crossing gates swing closed. A steam-engine clatters past and she sits watching it, thinking about Jerry.

"Cruelty to dumb animals, darling," she says to herself.

This was a saying Gyorgy always used when she'd flirted with young men who were dazzled by her fame. As Kat waits for the gates to be opened she wonders what Jerry is doing; what he is thinking.

"It's just a visit to the cinema," she mutters defensively, as though Gyorgy is listening. "How can that possibly be a problem?"

Jerry is standing staring at the photograph of Veronica, who gazes back at him, holding one grandchild in her arms and another by the hand. The photograph is nearly fifteen years old and Vee is wearing her motherly smile. It manages to be happy, commanding and confident all at once.

He studies it. Is there reproach in that steady gaze? He thinks of Vee, back then, when on those odd social occasions he'd drunk more than usual or paid slightly too much attention to a pretty woman. Glancing around — flushed with a sense of wellbeing, with pleased surprise at his ready wit — he'd meet that steady gaze across a dining-table, across a room full of revellers, and he'd know exactly what Vee was thinking. "You're making a prat of yourself, Jerry." That glance was the equivalent of a douche of cold water and generally restored him to his senses very quickly.

And, he reminds himself now, he was always very glad of Vee's restraining influence. She was quite right. He *was* too susceptible to flattery, too delighted when

111

he made an attractive woman laugh. She'd prevented him from making a fool of himself.

He can imagine what Vee would be saying to him now, and a part of him knows that she would be right, but this time he doesn't want to hear it.

"It's just a visit to the cinema," he mutters, turning away, picking up Kat's empty glass. "How can that possibly be a problem?"

CHAPTER
FOURTEEN

Tim takes the toy car out of the paper bag and looks at it, shiny and new in its plastic pack. After a moment he tears at the wrapping and removes the car, running it across the palm of his hand, thinking that it looks less of a present and more . . . more what? Something left in the same way that the pine-cone face was left on the arm of the bench: a sign of friendship.

He sits down at the kitchen table, still rolling the car to and fro, and wondering why he didn't take Mattie to see Pan or the dogs' graveyard or tell her about the face on the bench. He fully intended to but at the last moment it felt all wrong. It's too important to treat it as some light-hearted entertainment though he doesn't really know why he feels so strongly. He was unable to think of how to introduce it without either making it all sound rather twee and silly or investing it with too much significance, thus arousing everybody's interest. He simply couldn't bear the idea of Mattie, Charlotte with Ollie, perhaps even William and Kat all tramping into the woods to see these things that are so special to him.

Now, Mattie has gone back to London, her brief stay over, and he's missing her. His muscles ache today and he feels tired but he's set his heart on a walk into the woods. He swallows his medication and pulls on a coat. The early May weather has turned chill and damp. The fresh new leaves are fuzzy with shining raindrops and mist drifts like smoke in the river valley.

He walks slowly, his hands thrust into his pockets, the toy car clutched in one fist. Part of him is relieved that there was very little opportunity to have time alone with Mattie. It is still possible to maintain the fiction that he is a fit, able man and to enjoy her natural response to him.

Sometimes he rehearses what he might say to her: "I have this degenerative disease, which attacks the muscles. Soon I might not be able to walk and eventually it will affect my respiratory passages. Then I'll die. But nobody can quite say when because, apparently, it's a very rare form of it. It could be months or maybe longer, but I don't really have a future."

He can imagine her reaction, the slow change of her expression to horror and terrible pity, and instinctively he shakes his head at the prospect of it.

As usual the peace of the woodlands — the banks of flowering azaleas, the scent of bluebells, the flittering of the birds in the canopy — calms his fear and alleviates his misery.

Pan is still holding the bluebells, though they are drooping now, and he's still wearing the necklace of periwinkles. Tim pauses as usual for his moment of homage and then moves on. He feels a mix of hope and anxiety as he eagerly approaches the wooden seat. The face is there on the broad arm and at first it seems as if there is no change here either. Then he sees that the switch of pine he left for a pipe has been removed and the stones of the mouth have been rearranged so that it turns down to form a sad face.

Tim studies it. He wants to laugh, delighted that the child is joining in the game. Very carefully he brings out the little car, places it on the wooden arm beside the face, and then stands back to look about him. There is no sound, no movement.

He sits down on the damp seat and stares out across the fields. Today the moors are shrouded in mist but now there is a radiance in the damp air: a brightness that touches the trembling raindrops with light and gleams on wet green leaves. A phrase slips into his mind: "There lives the dearest freshness deep down things . . ."

"I expect you're too young for Gerard Manley Hopkins," Francis said yesterday on one of his visits to the courtyard, "but I brought this for you to look at anyway. You never can tell with poetry."

He took the rather battered book, touched by the old man's thoughtfulness, and watched Mattie hugging him and how Francis looked down at her with his penetrating gaze. Mattie's response interested Tim. She looked back at Francis gratefully, smiling as if she welcomed his scrutiny, as if his presence brought her some kind of relief. They clearly seemed to understand each other and this exchange comforted both of them. She began to tell him about her interview, guiding him to the bench where they sat side by side, whilst Tim

115

leafed through the book of poetry. He noticed that some phrases were heavily underscored, and there were remarks pencilled in the margins, and it was rather moving to read these and gain an insight into the old man's private thoughts.

He glanced up to find Francis' eyes on him, though his head was still inclined towards Mattie, and Tim gave an almost imperceptible nod and raised the book as if thanking him.

"There lives the dearest freshness deep down things . . ." That phrase struck a chord, and now, out in the wood, it comes vividly to life. Life is surging up all around him from deep down in the warm earth, fresh and sweet. His plan, to finish his life before he becomes helpless, seems so much more difficult to contemplate out here in these woods. Here, miracles can happen. Hope springs up, twining and climbing around his heart, like the honeysuckle in the thorny hedge.

Tim gets up, casts one last glance at the toy car and sets off towards the dogs' graveyard. He knows that his longing to see the child is simply a desperate flight back to the past: his past. He longs to see the small happy boy that he'd been before he stood at the garden gate with Ban; before his mother died. Somehow, then, there might be some sense of forgiveness. He longs for a sign that he is not alone.

As he approaches he sees a heap of something pink on Brack's grave, as though a scarf has been dropped on it. He hurries forward and then stops abruptly. Someone has gathered the camellia's fallen flower heads and arranged them into the shape of a heart. Tim

116

stares down at it, his own heart hurrying and fluttering in his side. He feels weak and, without thought or intention, he subsides to his knees. Coming just at this moment, and crazy though it is, he feels that is a sign that he and Ban are at last forgiven. He can't stop the tears that stream down his cheeks and he scrubs his arm impatiently across his face knowing that he is behaving like an idiot. Yet he continues to stare at the camellia heart, at the stone etching of the little dog, and he cannot stop weeping.

Presently, weak and exhausted, he stumbles to his feet and begins to make his way back home.

Unpacking Oliver from the car, Charlotte sees Tim emerge from the woodland path, wave his hand and disappear into his cottage. She waves back unperturbed by his hurried retreat. She's learned that living in such close proximity teaches people to respect the others' privacy. Anyway, she's quite pleased to be able to take Oliver in and get him down for his rest. A lunchtime session in Plymouth with some of her friends — all naval wives with small children — has been a rather uproarious affair and Oliver is fractious. Charlotte's looking forward to having a few minutes' peace and quiet.

She misses Mattie after she's gone: it's always been the same. Even when there have been arguments and irritations she is sad to see her sister go. As she carries Oliver inside, Charlotte still can't quite imagine setting off to Washington for two years and leaving all her family whilst Oliver is still so young. She feels that it's rather a lot to ask of her. She said as much to Francis when he came down from his lair to see them all during Mattie's visit.

He sat silently, listening to her working through her thoughts: how she'd prefer to have time to live here with Andy learning how to be a proper family; that she needs time to adjust. Wooster came to lean against his knees and Francis gently pulled his ears as he listened.

"I suppose you'd still be learning how to be a proper family in Washington," he said thoughtfully when she finished. "It might draw you even more closely together and make you strong and independent as a little unit. It's an amazing opportunity for you all. After all, you'd be in a very safe environment. How many young people would leap at such a chance! Quite a promotion for Andy, I imagine. And what an experience for Ollie."

Charlotte was slightly put out by this positive take on the prospect before her. She had expected more consideration.

"Oliver will be far too young to be affected by it," she answered rather snappily.

Francis pursed his lips thoughtfully, still pulling the ears of Wooster, who was panting, grinning fatuously with delight.

"Is one ever too young to benefit from life experience, I wonder. Surely everything has an impact on him one way or another, even if he can't actually remember the details later on."

Now, Charlotte lowers Oliver into his cot and looks down at him. He's very drowsy but content. She's pleased that he was so good with the other children,

118

amazed and amused by them in turn, and very good-tempered until the journey home. Yet she still cannot imagine her little family far from home in a foreign country.

It occurs to her that she is frightened. She realizes that during this separation Andy is becoming a stranger to her; she's forgetting what it's like to have him around, talking to him, being in bed with him. She's known him for less than three years and for a great deal of that time he's been at sea. He hardly knows their child. How will it be when they are together in a place where she knows no one: no parents an hour away across the moor, no Mattie dashing down to see her, no William and Aunt Kat next door? Even Tim is becoming more familiar to her than Andy.

Charlotte folds her arms across her midriff as though she is holding herself together. Her mother is sympathetic, but her own years as a naval wife have toughened her, and her father is more concerned with Andy's promotion than Charlotte's anxieties as to whether she will cope, about which it is clear he has very few fears. He gives her a hug, tells her she'll be fine and that they'll come out to visit them. She finds it difficult to explain her true feelings and demand sympathy. *She* is generally the one who is tough and strong, exhorting her sister or her friends to pull themselves together during bad times, insisting that they must refuse to allow weakness to triumph.

Staring down at Oliver, her arms still wrapped about herself for comfort, Charlotte realizes that this is the first time in her adult life that she has felt truly weak and frightened. Up until now she has had very few challenges and she begins to see that her lack of sympathy with other people's problems is due to her inability to connect. Her assumption that they should be able to cope is a result of her own lack of experience and empathy.

Becoming a mother was the first step to this new self-awareness; separation from Andy was the second. Dimly she sees that her default mode is a critical one; she is impatient with muddle, indecision and neediness.

Oliver is sleeping peacefully, unaware of her turmoil, and she covers him gently with his blanket and goes out, closing the door quietly behind her.

CHAPTER
FIFTEEN

It's almost lunchtime by the time Fiona arrives at the Cott. She loves this long, white-painted fourteenth-century building, with its heavy golden thatch and low beams. It's so cosy in the winter with its log fires burning at each end of the bar, and in the summer it's fun to climb up to the big decked terrace and sit under the wooden pergolas with a cold drink. The pub is already quite busy but Anton comes out from behind the bar to take her case and show her to her room, and by the time she comes down again he has her favourite cocktail waiting and a table reserved.

She likes this attention, it makes her feel special, and she sighs with pleasure as, having ordered her lunch, she sits back to enjoy her drink and look around. It's quite a shock to see Kat sitting a few tables away with a man that Fiona doesn't recognize. There's no reason at all why Kat shouldn't be having lunch in the Cott with a friend but something in the way they are together prevents Fiona from making herself known. She shifts back in her chair, slightly out of sight, so that she can watch them without being seen.

He looks nice, thinks Fiona, though rather conventional for Kat's taste. Her men usually have a certain "*Sturm und Drang*" about them, which this fellow, with his greyish-fair floppy hair and pleasant smile, seems to be lacking. Nevertheless they are clearly enjoying themselves. He is telling Kat a story and she is listening intently, watching him with enjoyment, responding with enthusiasm. Fiona can see him expanding in the warmth of her attention.

They eat and talk with ease, as if they are old friends, but some subtext tells Fiona that this isn't necessarily true. There is between them a rather charming shyness. Kat touches his wrist lightly but doesn't look at him: he stretches out his legs and when they encounter hers he draws back abruptly. It reminds Fiona of the early days with Sam — oh, the thrill and anticipation of those first meetings! — and she feels envious of Kat and her unknown companion.

They're not lovers yet, thinks Fiona, but they're well on the way.

Her salmon arrives, and she begins to eat, but her attention remains fixed on Kat and the man with her. Now Kat is talking. She makes one of her incredibly elegant and graceful arm movements and nearly knocks his glass of wine over. He grabs at it, managing to save it, and they both explode with laughter. Their plates are cleared away but they barely notice.

Fiona is riveted, but now there is a distraction. Two newcomers walk in, look around, and go to the bar. They are both women in their sixties, rather alike with their neatly coiffured hair, careful make-up and smart clothes. One begins a conversation with Anton, who is clearly telling her that there is no table free at the moment but the other woman, who has wandered further into the bar to look at the specials board, stops suddenly. Her attention is fixed on Kat and her companion and her unguarded expression — a blend of shock and indignation — makes Fiona want to burst out laughing. She wonders if this woman is his wife and, if she is, how Kat will react.

Fiona watches the woman watching Kat, sees her sizing up the situation and deciding how to act. Glancing back at her companion, who is still in conversation with Anton, the woman makes her way forward until she is standing at Kat's table.

Fiona strains to hear the conversation, laughs out loud at the man's face, which shows a mix of surprise, horror, and an attempt at polite pleasure. Kat is quite hidden from sight. It is clear that the woman is not his wife but she intends to seize the opportunity to muscle in. She waves her arm to indicate the fullness of the bar and the availability at their table for two more. She has the element of surprise and Fiona sees the man glance helplessly at Kat, not knowing how to refuse her request to join them. Fiona glimpses Kat's face and begins to laugh again. She pushes aside her empty plate, picks up her bag and gets to her feet.

"Kat," she cries, as she approaches their table. "Great to see you. Sorry I'm so late but I'm still in time to join you for coffee, aren't I?"

The woman turns quickly, Kat is briefly taken aback but almost immediately regains her poise.

"Darling Fi," she says, unable quite to hide her relief. "I'd almost given you up. Do come and sit down."

Fiona smiles at the woman, a bright and dismissive smile calculated to freeze her out, and sits down on the settle beside Kat. The woman hesitates but her friend — who has not noticed the by-play — has quickly bagged the table vacated by Fiona and is now calling insistently to her. Frustrated, she turns away, looking back to say, "I'll see you at the exhibition in Birdwood House on Tuesday then, Jeremy."

"So," says Fiona, dropping her bag on the settle and beaming at him. "I hope I'm not interrupting anything. Do introduce me, Kat."

Kat murmurs, "Great timing," and then more loudly, "This is Jerry Fermor. Jerry, this is my cousin William's wife, Fiona Taylor."

Jerry looks ill at ease, almost shocked by Fiona's unexpected arrival and Kat's reaction. It's clear that he feels uncomfortable with this little pantomime and glances anxiously after the woman as if fearing that they have been rude. He shakes Fiona's hand and she hurries into the breach.

"I've only just got down from London," she says. "The traffic is terrible. I bet you forgot I was coming, Kat, didn't you?"

"Well, I did, darling," Kat admits. "Though Charlotte reminded me this morning. But it's lovely that you're in time to meet Jerry. He hasn't been to Brockscombe yet so he hasn't met the family. You're the first."

"Be afraid, be very afraid," Fiona warns him jokily. "Craziest set-up ever."

He smiles at her and she can see he's beginning to be a little more at ease although the atmosphere he and Kat created has been shattered. They order coffee, and Fiona tells them about the project she's working on, and presently Jerry gets up and goes to pay the bill at the bar. They both watch him pause to speak to the woman and her companion.

"Who is she?" Fiona asks.

"Sandra. A rather dreary little friend," Kat answers. "She clearly thinks I'm poaching, though he's a free agent. Thanks for that, by the way, Fiona. I've clearly underestimated your thespian skills. Were you there all the time?"

"Some of it. You looked so cosy I wasn't going to interrupt but then I decided I might be the lesser of two evils. He's rather nice but I'm not sure he's up to your weight, Kat."

"Neither am I, but I'm going to give him the opportunity to try."

They both laugh and Fiona feels a new and surprising rush of affection for Kat. Something sticks in her mind and she frowns, trying to remember it. Ah, yes. "This is my cousin William's wife, Fiona Taylor." That's what Kat said when she introduced her to Jerry. And, although it's technically true, it's not how she is usually perceived any more. It's as if Kat has given her something to which she can return: something on which she can rebuild her relationship with her family. William's wife. She's grateful to Kat who, with reason, has been very much on William's side since the

125

separation. It feels good to be back in accord rather than cast in the role of the outsider.

"Were you going on somewhere?" she murmurs to Kat as Jerry puts his wallet in his pocket and heads back. Sandra leans out to detain him, to have another little chat.

"I think it might be wise," says Kat, watching them. "We hadn't made any plans beyond lunch."

"Well, you could take him to Brockscombe. Or you could use my room if you think he's up to it."

They're both laughing when Jerry gets back to them and Kat stands up.

"Thank you for my nice lunch," she says. "Would you like to come back to Brockscombe? Fiona will be coming to see her family and we can all have tea together. What d'you think?"

Fiona can see that Jerry is still slightly off balance, that he is not used to these tricks, and she smiles at him.

"Do come and meet my grandson," she says. "He's quite perfect and I don't get much chance to show him off."

It's such a charming request that Jerry is unable to refuse and they all go out together into the car park.

"We'll put Jerry in the middle," Fiona says, "and then he can't get lost."

She watches Kat and Jerry get into their cars and then she unlocks her own and climbs in feeling happy. She's still amused and exhilarated by the scene, and looking forward now to seeing Ollie and Charlotte —

126

and, later on, William. Fiona reverses out of the space and follows Jerry's car down the lane.

Kat glances in her driving mirror once she's past the roundabout to check that Jerry is still behind her. She's rather surprised — and amused — at Fiona's partisanship. The whole scene reminds Kat of just how much fun Fiona could be, and of happy days before she went off to London. Despite her support and love for William, Kat feels a new sense of empathy with Fiona. After all, it would have been hard to resist such a huge career opportunity and it's possible that, whilst still finding her way in all the excitement and challenge of her new responsibilities, Fiona was probably caught off balance with Sam. Kat guesses that he was a very attractive and experienced man and difficult for Fiona to resist. The working relationship has a very powerful dynamic, as she knows only too well.

She glances again in her mirror, glimpses Jerry's serious expression, and makes a little face. It was clear that he wasn't amused by the way Fiona got rid of Sandra. He was embarrassed, even shocked, and she wonders how he will react once they are alone together again.

It was being such a good lunch, too; a follow-up arranged after the film just to keep things moving along. He talked about how he missed his work and his students, of a trip to London to see a new play, of the possibility of joining a local amateur acting group. She was just working towards the suggestion that they might make the London trip together — she wanted to see

Miche — when Sandra had come barging in, ruining everything.

What is now clear to Kat is that she's slightly misjudged Jerry. She quite expected him to be at one with her over Sandra's appearance: that he would find it as irritating as she did and be amused by Fiona's rescue tactics. Instead it has made him uncomfortable. He's such a good man; kind, rather hesitant, very amusing. He's so different from Gyorgy, Miche and the others that she's fascinated by him. She hadn't wanted to play the family card yet — if at all — but neither had she wanted to leave him at a loose end with Sandra. Fiona's suggestion was the only immediate option. The important thing is not to rush things.

Kat indicates right, in plenty of time for Jerry to pick up on it, and brakes, waiting for a gap in the traffic. He follows her down the lane towards the bridge and she pauses to make sure it's clear before she leads the way over the level crossing and on to Brockscombe.

As Jerry follows her car he's experiencing a whole mix of emotions. He can't remember when he felt such confusion. He'd forgotten what it was like to have such fun without any sense of responsibility. With Kat he can shed his long-familiar role as husband, father, grandfather, and the persona that goes with them, and simply be himself. There are no expectations, no judgements, apart from his own need to keep up with her; to make her laugh, to entertain her. He can hardly believe that she — so famous, so talented — should enjoy his company.

128

The lunch was a great success — until Sandra showed up. He'd been so wrapped up in Kat that he hadn't considered that he might know any of the other diners. Suddenly there was Sandra, with that now-familiar expression that combines eagerness and disapproval; surprised that she should find him and Kat there together but indicating that, given the bar was full, it would be a good idea if she and her friend could share their table.

He was cross, disappointed, that their tête-à-tête should be so disrupted but good manners insisted that they should be polite about it. Kat's readiness to side-step the usual courtesies and to enjoy Fiona's orchestrated arrival rather shocked him and, irritated though he was by Sandra's intrusion, he felt the need to make up for it by apologizing and then — she was quick to seize her advantage — agreeing to have lunch with her after going to the exhibition. This, in its turn, irritates him even more. He feels manipulated.

"The trouble is," Vee used to say, "that you're too nice. You let people walk all over you."

It exasperated her to see him attempting to accommodate awkward people, to placate, to restore harmony. However, even he cannot see a mechanism by which he can create any kind of relationship between Kat and Sandra. And he doesn't want to: they belong in separate parts of his life. Sandra has introduced him to new friends, societies, clubs. Kat is entirely different: she is from another world and he is utterly bewitched by her.

And now here he is driving out to meet her family, about whom she hasn't spoken so he doesn't know quite what to expect. Suddenly this new spirit of adventure she has awoken in him surfaces again, sweeping away irritation and anxiety. His spirits rising, feeling the now-familiar and exciting sensation of being out of his depth, Jerry turns into the courtyard and parks besides Kat's car.

CHAPTER
SIXTEEN

By the time William arrives home the courtyard is quiet. Tim and Kat's cars are missing though Fiona's is tucked in beside the barn. At least she's not in his space this time, he thinks. He is feeling just the least bit grumpy. Singing has been cancelled — two married members on holiday, tenor and soprano, and their musical director unwell — and he'll miss the company as well as the physical bonus. A couple of hours singing revitalizes him: it's a great workout for the lungs, the intercostal muscles and the diaphragm, and he always feels more alive, more energetic, for several days after his Friday evening singing.

As he climbs out of his car, wondering whether to pop in on Francis, Fiona appears from Charlotte's doorway. She looks in good shape, sexy in her jeans and a loose shirt, smiling at him. Just occasionally he can pretend that they've never been apart and then all their familiar ways and shared past click back into place between them. Perhaps it's because he stopped off at the pub for a pint, he warns himself cynically, but he receives her kiss with something of the old pleasure and his grumpiness recedes.

"You're looking good," he says. "Been putting Ollie to bed?"

"I have. I got soaked during bath-time and Charlotte lent me one of Andy's shirts."

She links her arm into his, pulls him close, and he is pierced with lust borne out of familiarity and a sudden need for physical release. Gently he disentangles himself under the pretence of trying to find his door-key whilst he attempts to get a grip on his emotions. She seems intent on following him inside so he drops his briefcase down on the bottom stair and goes through to the kitchen.

"Drink?" he offers. "Did you have a good trip down?"

"Yes to both," she answers, perching on a chair at the table, crossing her legs. "Lots of traffic, though. I had a very nice lunch at the pub, and guess who was there. Kat and her new man."

He can see that she's hoping to surprise him but he simply pours her a glass of wine and pushes it across the table.

"Ah," he says, non-committally. "So she introduced you?"

Fiona looks disappointed. "You knew about him, then?"

"Mmm." He sits opposite, smiling at her expression. "I knew but I haven't met him. So what's he like?"

She's smiling again, ready to share, to gossip. Just like the old days.

"Not in her league but rather a sweetie. Nice-looking. Sexy in a boy-next-door sort of way. The really

132

funny thing is that there's another woman competing for him who actually came in while he and Kat were playing footsie under the table."

His eyebrows shoot up in surprise and she gives a little crow of delight. She's always liked to shock him.

"So what happened?" It's rather nice to go along with this; to let her entertain him. "And where were you all this time?"

"Hiding at a table in the corner. I saw them, you see, and decided to be tactful and steer clear. Then this woman and her friend strolled in. If you could have seen her face, Wills, when she saw Kat and Jerry. God, it was priceless."

"Jerry? That's his name?"

"Kat calls him Jerry. The frumpy friend calls him Jeremy."

He smiles and frowns and shakes his head. "Why?"

Fiona shrugs, swallows some wine. "Shortening a name is a sign of affection, I suppose. I like it, don't you? That why I call you Wills whilst most people call you William. And you call me Fi."

He refuses to pick up on this. "So then what happened?"

"Frumpy friend tried to barge in. The bar was full and she was going to pressure them into letting her share their table. I got a glimpse of Kat's face looking like thunder so I decided to make my entrance. I went over and apologized for being late, sat down next to Kat and saw off frumpy friend with my death stare. You know."

She looks at him intently and then very slowly crosses her eyes, and he bursts out laughing. He can't help himself. This has always been one of her tricks. At parties, across a dinner table surrounded by friends, it was her way of privately expressing amused dislike of something, encouraging him to share the joke.

Fiona laughs with him, clearly delighted at the success she's having at this retelling of the story.

"So what happened then?"

"Well, Kat thought my arrival was screamingly funny but Jerry was just a tad discombobulated. I think he felt a bit sorry for frumpy friend. He went over to her when he was paying the bill and seemed to be apologizing. Kat wasn't best pleased but couldn't decide quite what to do next. I offered my room but we decided he might not be up for it."

"Honestly, Fi. You didn't?"

He hasn't laughed so much for ages: must be the wine on top of the pint of real ale. She's laughing too, thoroughly enjoying herself.

"I did. But then I suggested that we should all come out here together. For some reason that seemed to hit the spot. So we came out in convoy, had tea with Charlotte and Ol, and then Kat decided to take Jerry off somewhere."

"Where?"

Fiona shrugs. "How should I know? Back to his place? Everything was very jolly when they left but it's not easy to keep up the momentum, darling, when you're in separate cars."

He's still chuckling, feeling relaxed, in tune with her.

134

"So are you staying for supper? I could cook."

"Oh, darling Wills, I'd have loved it but Charlotte offered and I said yes."

He's surprised at how disappointed he feels, but perhaps it's all for the best. He feels vulnerable and fears that Fi might take advantage to make another bid to pursue her plan for a bolt hole. At times like these he can remember exactly why he fell in love with her, and married her, and he knows he mustn't allow himself this moment of weakness.

"If Kat doesn't come back why don't you come and join us?" she's asking. "Charlotte won't mind. You know she loves it when everyone's together."

"I might," he says. He really doesn't want to be alone, to cook a lonely supper. He wants feminine company. "Perhaps you could go and check, just in case?"

"Sure."

She gets up, still looking sexy, infinitely desirable, and heart-rendingly familiar. She hesitates, looking at him, and he's terrified that she might approach him, touch him, and that then he would simply seize hold of her and kiss her.

"Great." He turns a little away from her, pretends to be interested in some letters that are lying on the table. "Don't come back specially. Just send a text and I'll come on round if it's OK."

Still she hesitates and he summons all his willpower to keep turned away from her. Then she goes out, he hears the door close and gives a huge sigh of relief . . . and regret.

★ ★ ★

Tim stands at the landing window listening to the thrush. This is the time of day when he feels most vulnerable, most alone. Very often he and Charlotte share supper. She can't leave Oliver, of course, so sometimes he takes a prepared meal round so as to do his share. They are quite at ease together, though now and again she attempts what he calls "the three-degree interrogation" about his future and he has to stonewall her. He understands that this is her way of showing an interest in him, even caring about him, but he can't afford to lower his guard.

Meanwhile he thinks about the child in the woods and what the next step might be. It's become a game that takes his mind away from his private suffering. The toy car was gone when he went back two days later and the stone mouth of the face was rearranged into a smile. He smiled, too, to see it, and sat for a while on the seat hoping someone might appear. As he waited patiently he could hear the cuckoo down in the valley and its ancient, haunting call filled his heart with delight and an odd melancholy. He thinks of his mother and how her life was cut short by such terrible chance and his own action. If only he hadn't tried to open the catch on the gate; if only it had remained stubbornly closed as it always had before. It is as if the child who decorates Pan and leaves his toys embodies the happy child Tim was before his life was changed for ever.

Now, he gives a little jump as someone raps on the door and then opens it a crack and shouts: "Are you in there, Tim? It's William."

136

"Yes," he calls with relief, hoping for rescue from his loneliness, and hurries down the last flight of steep stairs.

"We're having a little get-together at Charlotte's. Bit of a picnic. Like to come?"

William looks in a very good humour, rather as if he's been invited to a party, and Tim's spirits rise.

"I'd love it," he says. "Shall I bring something?"

"What have you got?" William follows him into the kitchen. "I'm supplying the wine and some cold roast beef."

"I've got some Sharpham brie," Tim begins to search in the fridge, "some olives, roast tomatoes," he piles the cartons out on to the working surface, "and a packet of sliced ham."

"Bring it all along," says William cheerfully. "Got a bag?"

They go out together and into Charlotte's cottage, where she and Fiona are assembling food on the kitchen table, watched by Wooster.

"Rather like a tapas without the glamorous bits," Fiona says when she sees them. "I feel really awful that I'm not supplying anything."

"You can share with me on the wine," William tells her and she gives him a surprised and gratified look, which he pretends not to see.

Tim notices, though, that there is a very different atmosphere this evening from Fiona's previous visit. Fiona is much more relaxed, helping Charlotte whilst deferring to her as to where things are kept and whether she should wash the salad leaves, joking with

William and clinking a glass with him when he passes her a drink.

It's as if, thinks Tim, she has reverted to someone she once was, taking back to herself a familiar role. Gone is the spikiness of a woman trying to lay claim to territory that is owned by those she has hurt and betrayed. Something has happened to energize her and give her courage.

He remembers Kat insisting that he should come to the tea party to help to keep it civilized. "Three women, all feeling the least bit threatened. It's bound to get tricky. We need the down-to-earth male influence," she said. Surely it can't be simply William's presence here tonight that has changed the dynamic: William, whom Fiona has hurt the most? Or can it be Kat's absence?

He sees that Charlotte is quite relaxed — though Oliver is not present to cause any possessiveness — and talks to Fiona about small domestic things as they finish laying the table.

Tim receives his glass from William and raises it to him. "Here's to the unexpected."

William looks sharply at him and then smiles, such a sweet smile.

"I'll drink to that," he says — and Fiona catches the exchange, and smiles too, and raises her glass to them both.

CHAPTER
SEVENTEEN

When Charlotte wakes the next morning she feels restless. It was such a good party, everyone in harmony, and Fiona had been so easy and such fun, so different from on her previous visit. Charlotte wonders if she's slightly misjudged her. It's rather unsettling, when you've made up your mind about someone, to find them presenting a different side.

She talks to Oliver as she gets him dressed and feeds him his breakfast, and he smiles at her and blows bubbles and bangs his fists on his tray. Wooster is stretched out on the floor and Oliver leans out of his chair to look at him and make unintelligible noises.

"That's Wooster," Charlotte tells him. "He's a good dog, isn't he? And you're a good boy. What shall we do this morning?"

Last night William decided he would do a return match and he invited everyone to a barbecue supper in the courtyard this evening. Charlotte offered to help but he refused, saying that even he could manage a barbecue. He suggested, however, that she might get some bedding plants for the tubs and stone troughs now that the daffodils are over. There's some potting

139

compost in the barn, he told her. It would be nice to have the courtyard livened up for the barbecue.

"We'll go to Staverton Bridge Nursery," Charlotte says to Oliver. "We'll buy some plants and have coffee in the café. Or out on the balcony if it's warm enough."

She wipes his face, takes him out of his chair and swings him round. Oliver chuckles and Wooster sits up to watch.

"You can come, too," she tells Wooster, "as long as you're on a lead and behave yourself."

She wonders whether to invite Tim but decides against it: she fears that she's becoming rather reliant on his company. If she sees him as she goes out she'll suggest it, otherwise it might look a bit unfriendly, but she won't make a point of it.

By the time she's changed Oliver, made him up a drink and got herself ready, there's no sign of Tim, and William's car has gone from the barn.

"I expect he's gone shopping," she says to Oliver as she straps him into his seat. "Gone to buy our supper. Off we go."

She reverses out of the barn, turns out of the gate and sets off down the lane, talking to Oliver as she drives, singing to him; giving him a commentary of their journey.

"Look," she says. "See the sheep, Oliver? 'Baa, baa, black sheep, have you any wool?' Look at the magpie on the gate."

She doesn't know how much he takes in but it seems important to connect him with his surroundings. They have to wait, pulled in tight to the hedge, for a tractor coming up the hill towards them and Oliver gazes at this huge monster in silence as it rattles past them.

There is no train at the level crossing today, no steam-engines to show him, and Charlotte drives on over the bridge, slowing down so that he can see the river flowing away and curving out of sight beneath the overhanging trees.

At the nursery she parks the car, loads Oliver into his buggy, and lets Wooster out. He's already wearing his lead, so she can simply grab it as he jumps down, and he walks beside her, very well-behaved, knowing he'll get a biscuit when it's coffee time.

Charlotte wanders into one of the big greenhouses, looking at the bright palette of flower-colour washing along the big trestle tables. In here the air is moist and warm, full of the vegetative scents of new plants and damp earth. As she pauses, trying to decide what will flourish best in the old stone troughs and the painted tubs, she hears an odd cheeping noise. Looking about, she sees that on a nearby table there are some wooden bird-houses for sale and, even as she watches, a bluetit with a beakful of insects darts into one of them. Going closer, she sees a notice: "These are not for sale until the babies have flown." Now she can hear the baby birds cheeping and the parent appears again at the edge of the hole, pausing for a moment before flying away.

Charlotte laughs. "Look, Oliver," she says. "There are baby birds living in there."

Oliver has seen the parent bird. He watches it intently and appears to be listening, and she knows that he can hear the babies in their nest. Suddenly she feels a great sense of excitement at the prospect of all the things there are for him to discover that she will be able to share with him. She walks around the aisles, looking at the profusion of bedding plants, mentally making her choice. Presently, she carries the small pots to the counter and makes a neat collection of them, then she pushes Oliver out into the sunshine, round the back of the café on to the decking high above the river, and parks the buggy by one of the tables. She secures Wooster's lead under the foot of the chair, tells him to sit and goes inside to order coffee.

By the time she returns, carrying her cup of cappuccino, Oliver is asleep and Wooster is stretched beside him, nose on paws. Charlotte sits down and breathes a sigh of contentment. She relaxes as she gazes across the woven willow fencing, down into the steep valley and through the trees beside the river. Through the new flush of green leaves she can just make out the old station house and one or two steam-engines on the track.

She sips her coffee and thinks about Aunt Kat and Jerry and Fiona, and how surprised she was when the three of them appeared after lunch. She's still not quite certain of Jerry's status. It was Fiona who seemed to be in control, giving her a hug and saying: "Look who I found having lunch in the Cott. This is Jerry. This is my daughter-in-law, Charlotte, Jerry. She's a brave naval wife and Andy is very lucky to have her. Oh, and we mustn't forget Ollie."

And Jerry came forward to be introduced to Oliver, and then Wooster came bounding out, and somehow

142

she never did quite grasp his relationship to either Aunt Kat or Fiona. Jerry, however, has a brother who was in the navy and he was able to talk intelligently to her about what it was like to be married to someone who went away a great deal; how lonely it could be and how difficult to make and keep some sort of bond between the absent father and his children. He was sympathetic and amusing, and very sweet with Oliver, whilst Wooster sat beside him with his head on his knee, panting his approval.

It was clear that both Aunt Kat and Fiona were entertained by this, though neither of them said very much, and Charlotte was aware of an unusual empathy between them. By the time she took Oliver in to change his nappy and then came back to offer more tea, Jerry and Aunt Kat had disappeared and Fiona was sitting with Wooster, looking rather pleased with herself.

"They apologized for dashing off," she said, "and Jerry said it was great to meet you and Oliver, and he hopes to see you again. They have some kind of date with someone or something like that. I do hope you didn't mind me bringing him over without warning? It was just one of those spontaneous things. He's a bit lonely since his wife died."

Charlotte said of course she didn't mind, that she liked him, and did Fiona want to do the bath-and-tea routine with Oliver and stay to supper? And then, somehow, that had turned into a lovely evening with William and Tim coming round as well and, though she couldn't put her finger on it, there was a really good atmosphere. Aunt Kat didn't appear and her car wasn't there when Fiona left to go back to the Cott.

"I think they mentioned a film at Dartington or something," Fiona said casually. "I'm sure she'll be back any time."

It occurs to Charlotte that Aunt Kat's car wasn't there this morning and she wonders, with a tiny internal shock, if Aunt Kat spent the night with Jerry. Surely not: apart from them both being old, he was so . . . well, respectable, and not at all the kind of man one associates with having a bit of a fling. He and Aunt Kat hadn't seemed particularly involved with each other, either . . .

The shriek of the steam-engine rouses Charlotte from her reverie and she glances at her watch. It's time to pay for her plants and load them into the car. Then she'll take Wooster for a walk on the path down to the river and go home and have a good planting session.

Tim watches Charlotte planting up the troughs and tubs; watching how, with quick, deft fingers, she beds the plants into the dark, chocolatey-cake-crumb brown earth. She has a knack with colour and shape and he tells her so. She looks pleased and stands up to look at her work, dusting her hands on an old apron that William has given her to wear.

"I still think it's a bit ambitious," she says, "to be having a barbecue. It's only May, after all. We'll probably all freeze. William says we'll just have to wrap up."

144

They both look across the courtyard at William, who is assembling the barbecue, which lives in the angle of the walls. He is clearly enjoying himself and Tim smiles to see him busy and happy.

"It'll be OK," he tells Charlotte. "At least it's dry. It's a pity Mattie can't be here."

He speaks without thinking and Charlotte glances sideways at him.

"Yes. Yes, it is. She'd enjoy it."

"Wasn't it a pity she didn't get the job?" He heard from her only a few days ago and she was very disappointed.

Charlotte nods her head sympathetically. "She's really gutted but she says she isn't giving up. It's made her determined to move back. She's coming down to see the parents for the Bank Holiday weekend so I've said I'll go over with Oliver. It's Mum's birthday."

Mattie hasn't said anything to him about the weekend and Tim feels oddly disappointed about that, but, after all, there's no reason why she should. There's a little silence and then Aunt Kat appears looking rather pleased with herself and as if she's enjoying a private joke. Tim studies her curiously, thinking of what Charlotte told him about the way she and Fiona had brought Jerry back after lunch at the pub. William glances round.

"Is he coming?" he calls.

Aunt Kat nods. "Yes, he is and he says thanks for inviting him. About six, like you said. Seems a bit early."

William looks pleased. "I've invited Francis, that's why. He might come just for a drink. He keeps early hours these days."

"Quite a party," says Aunt Kat, still with that secret look of self-satisfaction. "Those tubs look wonderful, Charlotte. You are clever."

Charlotte looks almost embarrassed by so much praise, mutters something about going to wash, and goes inside pulling off the apron.

Tim looks at Aunt Kat, eyebrows raised.

"So who is it that's joining the party?" he asks.

"Jerry Fermor," she answers. "My new best friend. Just moved to Totnes from Plymouth so I'm helping to get him bedded in — if you see what I mean?"

She looks at him so mischievously that he bursts out laughing.

"I've never heard it called that before," he says.

"A good old West Country expression for making somebody feel at home, darling," she says.

"What's the joke?" asks William, appearing beside them. "Come and help me with the big table, Tim. It's in the barn. If it really is too cold we'll have to retreat to the kitchen but I hope it won't be."

Still laughing, Tim follows William. He's looking forward to the barbecue, and to meeting Jerry, but he still wishes that Mattie could be here.

146

CHAPTER
EIGHTEEN

By the time Jerry arrives in the courtyard the party has begun. He feels apprehensive, still in shock after his night with Kat and wondering how she will greet him. Her text inviting him to the barbecue arrived whilst he was making himself a rather late lunch and, though he was already longing to see her again, part of him was inclined to refuse the invitation. He tried to imagine strolling in, greeting Kat casually and pretending nothing much has happened, and his nerve failed him. Would she have told Fiona, for instance? Perhaps they all know.

He remembered how she'd taken him into her embrace; her long arms and legs enfolding him, drawing him in. Just for a moment, he'd been nervous, embarrassed, but then quite suddenly the whole act of love with her seemed so easy, so natural. They'd fallen asleep, still entwined together, and when he wakened he was almost afraid to move. But then she, too, woke a few moments later and there was no awkwardness. She simply rolled away from him and said sleepily, "I need a pee, Jerry, and I've forgotten where the loo is," and he got up and put the light on for her in the bathroom across the passage, leaving the bedroom unlit lest she

147

should feel embarrassed by her nakedness. He wondered what the form was; whether he should get back into bed, or whether she would want to leave, so he dragged on his dressing gown and sat on the edge of the bed feeling rather foolish.

Even then she'd handled it all so easily. "I'm absolutely starving," she said, as she came out, bundling her hair up with both hands, smiling at him. "Are you?"

And he suddenly realized that he was. "Bacon?" he suggested. "Croissants from yesterday. Not fresh."

"Perfect, darling," she said contentedly. She'd picked up his discarded shirt, wrapped herself in it and they'd gone into the kitchen and fried bacon and dunked the croissants in their coffee, and afterwards they went back to bed and made love again.

By the time he wakened the second time the sun was pouring in and she was dressing. He struggled up on to his elbow but she merely bent over him, kissed him and said, "That was just lovely, darling Jerry. See you very soon," and slipped away, leaving him in a complete whirl and wondering what happened next in these situations.

What he certainly hadn't expected was to be plunged into a family gathering quite so precipitously. He stood staring at the text, not knowing how to respond. This whole experience was way outside his comfort zone, and he wondered if perhaps he should quit now before it became too complicated, but even as he began to form an excuse another text pinged in: *Cold feet? You need extra socks xx*

Her instinctive awareness of his feelings both touched and amused him. That was when he knew he was already in too far: he was way out of his depth but he was hooked.

And so here he is, driving into the courtyard and parking his car behind Fiona's Fiat, and here is Kat, detaching herself from a group of people and coming to meet him. He gets out, still feeling nervous, and she leans to kiss him lightly on both cheeks and murmurs: "You made it! Congratulations. You win a cookie."

He laughs. "I prefer bacon and croissants," he replies.

Kat hooks her hand lightly into the crook of his arm. "Later, perhaps. First you must suffer William's 'burnt-offerings'. Come and meet him."

As he goes with her to meet them all, he's feeling exhilarated again: deep in, way over his head, and loving every minute of it.

Francis, sitting between Tim and Charlotte, observes Jerry's approach. He sees Kat's greeting, the little private joke that relaxes Jerry and makes him laugh, so that he moves now with more ease and confidence. Kat is always elegant, always graceful. Her long skirt flares out around her ankles as she walks and as she turns her head to smile at Jerry her eyes are almost on the same level as his. His Anglo-Saxon fairness and chunky frame are a perfect foil for the dark hair and eyes of her Middle-European ancestors.

Francis watches them with pleasure. There is a symmetry, a physical ease between them, which makes him believe that they are lovers and he silently applauds Jerry's bravery for coming amongst them all. On either side of him Tim and Charlotte sit, alert and interested. Wooster struggles up from his recumbent position, near William and the barbecue, and goes to greet Jerry, who bends to stroke him, to renew their acquaintance. Tim stands up when Kat brings Jerry to be introduced but Francis exercises an old man's privilege and remains seated. Jerry takes his hand in a firm grip: another good mark. Francis still believes that a strong handshake denotes a strong personality. As Tim hurries away to fetch a glass of wine, Jerry sits down and leans forward to smile at Charlotte.

"Where's Oliver?" he asks. "Don't tell me he's not coming to the party?"

She smiles at his little joke. "Fiona's bathing him and getting him ready for bed. I left them to it. I thought it might be nice for her to have a break from me breathing down her neck and telling her how to do it."

Francis smiles appreciatively at this self-honest observation.

"After all, it's not as if she's never bathed and put a baby to bed before," he observes gently.

"Mmm," agrees Charlotte briefly, rather reluctantly.

"But not *your* baby?" suggests Jerry sympathetically. "It's rather different, isn't it? That's what my girls used to say when their babies were very small."

She glances at him, surprised by his partisanship, and makes a little face and shrugs.

"Silly, though, isn't it?"

"But understandable."

Tim brings him a drink and Jerry stands up to take it, smiles at them, and wanders off towards William and Kat.

Charlotte stirs restlessly. "I think I'll just go and check that they're OK and she's remembered to give him his bottle."

She goes into her cottage and Tim sits down again. Francis raises his eyebrows.

"Not drinking?"

Tim shakes his head. "I don't much these days, what with one thing and another."

Francis is silent; he sips his gin and tonic thoughtfully.

"I like the Gerard Manley Hopkins," Tim says suddenly. "It's very . . . relevant."

One or two things fall into place and a terrible suspicion creeps into Francis' mind.

"I wish you'd come and see me," he says. "Will you? I'd like it so much."

"Yes. Thank you." It sounds as if Tim has suddenly made up his mind, put aside any reservations he's had about revealing himself to Francis. "I'd like to."

"Good." Francis searches for a change of subject. "Isn't it a pity that Mattie and Andy aren't here to make up the family?"

"Yes, it is. Of course, I've never met Andy."

"I'm sure you'll get on very well when you do."

It sounds rather like an order and he sees Tim give a little smile. He glances at Francis almost challengingly.

"If I'm still here," he says lightly.

And Francis knows now that his guess is right and he feels his gut lurch with fear and horror.

"You will be," he says. He drops his hand briefly on Tim's fist, clenched between them on the bench. "Come and see me."

Then Fiona appears, flushed and exuberant from bathing Oliver, and drops down beside Francis.

"I'd forgotten how exhausting babies are," she says. "Be an angel, Tim, and get me a drink. Wine, please. Red. Bless you," and as Tim gets up she smiles at Francis and settles herself comfortably. "I haven't see you for years and years," she says. "You're looking great."

He laughs, quite ready to enjoy her flattery, and to let bygones be bygones if that's what William wants.

"You're looking pretty good yourself," he answers. "For a granny."

They both laugh and when Tim returns with her glass she raises it to Francis.

"I'll drink to that," she says.

"Glad you could come," William says to Jerry. "I'm sorry I missed you yesterday afternoon. It sounds as if you had a good time."

"I certainly did. We met Fiona in the pub and she invited me here to meet her grandson. It was very sweet of her."

William nods. "She's very proud of Oliver. Well, we all are, of course, but she doesn't see him quite so much as we do."

152

As he turns the pieces of steak and checks out the sausages he wonders just how much Kat might have told Jerry about his and Fiona's situation. Fiona is being so amenable, such good value, that — rather foolishly — he hopes that Kat hasn't explained everything to Jerry. It's crazy but he's enjoying the old familiarity, which has unexpectedly resurrected itself, and — just for this weekend at least — it's great to joke and laugh as if the last five years never happened.

William takes another pull at his ale. He's drinking a bit too much this weekend but he feels more relaxed than he's been for ages. It's good to have everyone here together, no squabbling and back-biting, enjoying themselves and being happy. And he likes Jerry. Kat sent him a text the night before: *Staying over. C u a m*, with a smiley emoticon, and he was feeling so relaxed and jolly after the supper party that he simply replied: *Enjoy.* When she arrived home he could see that she was in good spirits and so he suggested that Jerry should be invited to this impromptu barbecue.

William hesitates to mention anything of a personal nature but he approves of anyone who might keep Kat here at Brockscombe.

"It's just a shame," he says to Jerry, who has taken to himself the responsibility of buttering some rolls piled next to the barbecue, "that Andy can't be here. He loves this kind of thrash. I'd like you to meet him."

"You must miss him," says Jerry sympathetically. "Charlotte's doing a great job with Oliver, isn't she? She must miss him, too. She's lucky to have you so near at hand with Andy away for so long and a new baby to look after."

William beams at him. Yes, he definitely likes this Jerry Whatshisname. He slips Wooster a small gobbet of steak.

"Have another drink," he says, but Jerry shakes his head.

"I wish I could but I'm driving," he says, "so I'm taking it slowly."

"Why don't you stay the night?" offers William, feeling full of hospitality. "We've got a perfectly good spare bedroom."

Just for a moment he sees in his mind's eye the spare bed loaded with Kat's belongings but he shrugs it away.

"That's very kind," Jerry is saying, "but I couldn't possibly impose on you at such short notice. Anyway, I haven't any things with me."

William is about to protest that he could lend anything required but the image of the spare room recurs more forcefully and he decides to accept the situation gracefully.

"Next time," he promises Jerry. "Next time you must stay with us."

Jerry agrees, and so the goodwill between them increases.

"Look at them," says Fiona, sitting with Kat on the bench. "Sweet, isn't it? All that male bonding over the sausages."

"What is it with men and barbecues?" wonders Kat.

154

"Atavistic, sweetie. The hunter-gatherer thing. All that chasing prey and building campfires and cooking bits of raw meat on the ends of their spears and being matey."

"And what about the women?"

"Ah, well, we'd be back at the cave gathering berries and nuts and stuff, and looking after the babies and growing nourishing things."

Kat shakes her head. "Not me, darling. Not a nurturer, me."

Fiona laughs, sips her wine. "Did you never think of marriage, Kat? Not even with Gyorgy? You loved that man."

"Mmm, but not in a having and holding and forsaking all others kind of way, and I certainly didn't want to have his babies. It was to do with what he was, how he thought, and the music he composed that simply translated itself into movement." She shakes her head. "I can't explain it. Did you feel like that with William? All possessive and maternal?"

Fiona studies him affectionately. "I suppose I did in a way. William never tried to smother me. He always gave me space. But I did want a baby. I adored Andy. Still do."

"And now Ollie."

"Yes. And now Ollie." Fiona shifts sideways and turns to look at Kat. "We missed you at supper last night."

"Did you?" Kat is grinning. "Sweet of you."

"Mm-hm. Charlotte was worried that you weren't back when the party broke up. I made up some fiction about you going to a film. What did she say when you showed up this morning?"

"Nobody saw me. And before you ask, it's none of your business."

They begin to laugh just as Tim and Charlotte come out carrying bowls of salad and William calls that supper is ready.

"The baked meats await us. Oh joy. Scorched on the outside, raw in the middle, packed with E. coli," murmurs Fiona. "Can't wait."

"Wooster is at hand," replies Kat. "Make sure he's near our end of the table."

"And bring the bottle," says Fiona.

"Aren't you driving?"

"Jerry can drop me off on his way home. And I invite you all to lunch at the Cott tomorrow and then I can come back with you and fetch my car afterwards. Don't be a party-pooper, Kat. I've never had such a good weekend at Brockscombe and I don't want it to stop yet."

The thrush is still singing in the ash tree when Francis slips away just as they all gather around the barbecue to collect their plates, with Wooster in close attendance. He pauses with his hand on the gate to watch as Kat puts an arm around Jerry's waist and gives him a brief hug, and he notes Jerry's quick response. William is choosing a special piece of steak for Fiona and she is clearly teasing him about his cooking skills, which makes him protest and pretend to look hurt so that she leans forward and gives him a quick conciliatory kiss.

156

Tim is helping Charlotte to salad, talking to her and making a gesture to reassure her that Oliver will sleep through the noise.

It seems, in this moment, that they are all his beloved children, his family. Francis gives one last look and then passes through the gate into the shadows.

PART TWO

CHAPTER
NINETEEN

She can hear the lark somewhere high above her but though she shades her eyes she cannot see him against the blue dazzle of the skies. Just here, sheltered by an outcrop of granite and tall banks of golden-flowering gorse, it is hot. Mattie smooths out her thick plaid rug, kneels down and opens her small wicker hamper. She loves picnics. When she and Charlotte were very small a picnic was their favourite treat: helping their mother to pack up the car with rugs, the hamper, the toys of the moment and whichever dog was presently in their lives. The moor was their back garden. They knew where the first bluebells would bloom, played on the shingly little riverside beaches that the tourists never found. They loved the cloudy shapes of the hawthorn blossom and the bell heather washing in a purple tide around the side of a tor.

Even now, Mattie never travels without her rug and her hamper containing a Thermos flask, sachets of fruit tea, some biscuits and the makings of a sandwich. Driving down from London she's had just this place in mind, imagining it: up behind Ashburton at the edge of the moor, tucked out of the wind with its view across the valley to the high stony tors, watching the cloud shadows drifting across the hills, with the scent of the gorse all around her.

She sits cross-legged, holding her mug of tea, leaning back against the warm rough rock. How peaceful it is: no sound except for the lark's song and the distant rushing of the riverwater deep in the steep-sided coombe below. Just for this moment nothing seems to matter very much. Anxieties, disappointments, weariness, all fall away from her as she breathes deeply and turns her face to the sun.

It's still early. She left London at six o'clock and it's now just after ten. There's plenty of time to decide how the day should be spent before she arrives for her mother's birthday celebrations in Tavistock. Mattie has a few hours in hand and she wonders where she might spend them, and with whom. Nobody is expecting her quite this early and she's kept her options open.

Before she can make up her mind she hears the rhythmical pounding of paws on the hard ground, the rustle of dry bracken, and the dog appears. It hesitates, tail wagging, and Mattie gives a little cry of recognition. She sets down her mug and scrambles up, and Wooster greets her ecstatically, swiping her cheek with his tongue, panting with excitement.

Mattie begins to laugh — her cover is fully blown — and she goes out to meet Charlotte, and comes face to face with Tim.

"Oh, my God!" she cries, and he stares at her in amazement, and with relief.

162

"He got ahead of me," he says. "He just suddenly galloped off and I couldn't keep up. I wondered who he'd met. But what are you doing here?"

She sees that his shock is passing and he cannot contain his delight at seeing her.

"Tim," she says, stretching out her arm to him, still holding Wooster with her other hand, "come and see my little cave. What on earth are you doing with Wooster?" She stops suddenly. "Is Charlotte here?"

"No, no. I've started to take Wooster for walks. It gives her a break and I'm rather enjoying it. Like a kind of 'rent-a-dog'."

Mattie laughs. "But how amazing that you should be here."

"Charlotte brought me here a couple of times. It's one of her favourite walks, she says, and now it's mine. And Wooster's, of course."

"We came here as children for picnics." Mattie hesitates, wondering how to explain. "I got away really early and just decided to come here before I made a plan."

"And was I going to be part of that plan?"

She looks at him, sees his hopeful, tender expression, and looks away again. "You might have been. See how well I'm organized? Don't you think it might have been fun to live in a cave? Come and have a tea or some hot chocolate. I always have a spare mug for a visitor."

"Do you?" He sits beside her on the rug and Wooster flops at his feet. "Isn't that rather a dangerous practice in the wilds like this? I'll have a hot choc, as you've got one."

"Coming up." She tears the sachet and empties the powder into the mug. "It's not quite like the real thing, but hey! Who cares on a day like this?"

She hands it to him and sees that odd now-familiar look on his face: wistfulness, bitterness, determination. She wishes that he would tell her his secret: why he's taking this sabbatical and how he really feels about her. She passes him a biscuit and breaks off a piece for Wooster.

"Do you think he needs a drink?"

They both look at Wooster who stretches out, nose on paws, gazing over the moor.

"I know he had a good go-down at the leat," says Tim doubtfully. "I think he's OK for a minute. I've got some water and his bowl in the car."

Mattie grins at him. "You'll be getting your own dog next. What breed would you go for?"

"Cairn," answers Tim. "I had one when I was a child."

He breaks off abruptly and looks away to the high moors as if he wishes he hadn't told her. She watches him thoughtfully, drinks her tea.

"Tim," she says — and he turns to look at her and she sees tears in his eyes — "can you hear the lark?"

He listens to the liquid, bubbling song and she sees him smile.

"This place is magical," he says. He looks at her. "I have you to thank for this, Matts. Bringing me to this place. To Brockscombe. To Devon."

She reaches a hand to him, and he seizes and kisses it, and she puts her empty cup down and kneels close to him. Reaching blindly behind him, he puts his own mug, half-full, out of harm's way, and kneels up to hold her closely.

"I love you," she says, almost conversationally. "I might just as well say it. You don't have to say anything back. It's OK, but I just need you to know it."

He holds her so tightly she can barely breathe and presses his face into her throat. "I do love you," he cries, his voice muffled, almost as if he is in some kind of anguish. "I do, but it's just . . . it's not that simple . . ."

She turns her face, seeking for his lips, and they subside gently down on to the sun-warmed rug whilst Wooster sleeps, still and solid as a stone lion, guarding their privacy.

She's never experienced quite such urgent lovemaking, almost as if he feels he might die before he can finish, and afterwards he presses her close to him, breathing quickly. Instinctively she feels that it's best to be prosaic and she moves her head just a little so that her lips are against his ear.

"I don't know about you," she murmurs, "but after that I think more tea is in order."

He gives her one last quick hug and releases himself. She rolls away, tidying herself and talking to Wooster, who has raised his head and is watching them. Tim stands up, zips up his jeans.

"I'll take him down to the car and give him a drink," he says. "It's not very far away."

"Don't be long," she says, picking up the mugs, emptying his cold chocolate out on to the grass. "Then we'll make a plan as to where to have lunch."

He smiles at her, gives her a quick kiss. "Thanks," he says. He hesitates, as if not knowing what to say to her, and she gives him a little push and kneels down again beside the hamper. She feels languorous, deeply peaceful and very happy.

He walks quickly — Wooster racing ahead — trying to breathe deeply so as to stop the wildly erratic beating of his heart. Her declaration of love is almost more than he can bear and he simply does not know what to do or to say. He knows that he will have to tell her the truth but the thought of losing that innocence between them is unbearable. Mechanically he unlocks the car, takes Wooster's bowl from the boot and fills it with water from an old plastic bottle. Wooster laps gratefully, tail slowly wagging against Tim's legs.

Tim can see Mattie's car at the other end of the car park. There are quite a few cars parked and he marvels that nobody came past and saw them. He wonders if he is quite mad, out of his mind, making love in the middle of the morning out on Dartmoor. What did someone say about knowing that they were to be hanged wonderfully concentrated the mind? Perhaps it's the same principle.

Even as he tightens the top back on to the bottle he sees Mattie walking off the moorland track, carrying her hamper with the rug under her arm, and his heart lurches with fear. Having quickly encouraged Wooster into the back of the car, he hurries over to her. She smiles at him reassuringly.

166

"It's OK," she calls. "Change of plan. It occurred to me that lukewarm drinks were a bit of an anticlimax, especially with such a good hotel not very far away. I thought we might drive in tandem to the Two Bridges Hotel and then we can chill and have lunch there, too. Is that OK?"

With a rush of relief he knows that it's absolutely right. It would be difficult sitting together on the rug making conversation after such an emotional moment. He knows that he should tell her the truth but the moment has passed and a change of scenery is the right decision.

"Sounds great," he says. "I haven't been there yet."

"Good," she says, packing the rug and the hamper into the back of her car. "Wooster loves it there and you know you can trust his good taste. Follow me."

She gives a little flourish with her hand and climbs into the car and he hurries back, gets into his own car and follows her out of the car park and on to the moorland road.

She drives slowly and he knows that she is savouring the sweep and grandeur of the landscape. He wonders how it looks in the snow. Perhaps he might see it: perhaps he might take the chance and postpone his plan to take his own life before this terrible disease takes it for him. His fear that he might wait too long, that he will become helpless and dependent on strangers, curdles his gut and a sudden muscle spasm in his right leg reminds him of his mortality.

He realizes that Mattie is signalling, turning left, and he follows her. She drives past the big, granite-stone building into the car park, and he parks beside her car and climbs out. Wooster jumps out eagerly, then hesitates as a flock of geese sweep past, honking and hissing, swaggering down to the river.

"Wow," Tim says. "Do they live here?"

"They certainly do. Wooster knows he has to mind his p's and q's with that lot. It looks tempting down by the river, doesn't it, but I'm not sure it's quite warm enough yet. Let's go and look inside."

Despite the sun the breeze is still chill and he's grateful to go inside and to see two fires burning in great inglenook fireplaces at each end of the bar. Sofas are set at right angles round big, low tables and he grins at Mattie with delight.

"This is just perfect," he says. "Look at Wooster."

Wooster has already claimed his place by the fire at the end of one of the sofas and Mattie laughs.

"Fair enough. Let's have some coffee and then we'll look at the menu for later on."

As they sit together, a large cafetiére now on the table in front of them, Mattie suddenly turns to Tim.

"Oh, gosh! I wasn't thinking. Is Charlotte waiting for you to bring Wooster back? She doesn't know I'm down yet. We're all forgathering for tea with my parents."

"No, no. You're OK. I'm dog-sitting for the weekend. Charlotte thought that with everybody there, plus your parents' dogs, it would be a bit of a crowd so I offered to have Wooster. There's no rush."

Mattie subsides back, leaning against him, relaxing in the warmth of the fire.

"Good," she says. "Isn't it nice to be free?"

They sit in a companionable silence for a while and then he leans forward to refill their coffee cups.

"I'm really sorry, Matts," he says, "that you didn't get the BBC job."

She makes a face, and he slips an arm about her and gives her a little consolatory hug.

"I was gutted," she admits, "but actually I think something even better has come up."

She sits back, holding her cup, and he half turns towards her expectantly, eyebrows raised.

"It's another research post but it's at Exeter University in the History Department."

She glances at him quickly to check his reaction and he is unable to hide the delight at the prospect of having her so near.

"And would you like that?"

"Well, I got my degree in History at Exeter and it would be nearer home. My old tutor might put in a good word for me."

He smiles at her, touches a strand of curly hair that falls across her shoulder.

"You really miss this place, don't you? And I can see why."

"Well, I do. It's crazy, but driving down today I could hardly wait to get up on to the moor and breathe that fantastic air and just . . . well, you know, gaze out at all that space." She looks at him. "You feel like that about it now, don't you?"

He nods. "It's everything. The beaches, the moors, the harbours and the little fishing villages. It's been like

169

a miracle to find a place where I feel I've come home. A bit late in the day — "

He stops abruptly and she jumps in quickly.

"Oh, but why? It's never too late, Tim. You're still young. You've got your whole life to explore it. I'm so glad you love it as much as I do."

Now is the time to tell her, to explain that though he loves her, adores her, it would be unfair to burden her with the problems ahead. But even as he tries to frame the words another couple come in and sit down on the sofa opposite, and once again the opportunity is gone.

CHAPTER
TWENTY

Later, when he drives back into the courtyard, Tim is struck by the air of silence. There are no cars in the barn, all the doors and windows of the cottages are closed. No sign of Oliver's buggy, or a book lying on the bench, or mugs on the table. It looks deserted, and so it is.

Charlotte and Oliver have set out for Tavistock, Kat has driven off to Bristol with Jerry to see a performance by a modern dance company at the Hippodrome, William is singing in a choral concert at Exeter Cathedral and then staying with friends.

"It's just you and me tonight, mate," Tim mutters to Wooster as he unlocks his front door.

Wooster sniffs around the courtyard as if seeking his little family, but he is quite content to follow Tim inside. His basket is tucked in a corner of the kitchen, just as it is in Charlotte's, and he clambers into it and settles down. Tim opens the back door and wanders into the small paved garden. William's garden is the biggest: two gardens made into one when the two cottages were knocked together. He has made raised beds at the end of the patch in which to grow vegetables, and the borders are full of flowers and shrubs. There is a bird table and feeders, which William has left fully charged: he loves to see the birds feeding.

Tim watches them across the fence. Slowly he is beginning to recognize some of them and William is encouraging him. There is a very small greenhouse in one corner and some chairs and a table under a little pergola. It is ordered and tidy, rather like William himself, and Tim glances rather guiltily at his own little patch.

Charlotte has helped him fill the three wooden tubs with bedding plants but there is very little else. He isn't very imaginative when it comes to gardens. He said as much to Aunt Kat.

"Me neither, darling," she said. "Gardeners like to be in control, you see. They like to bring order out of chaos. Give me chaos every time."

Remembering, he laughs — and then he sighs. How difficult it will be to leave these people. His day with Mattie is like a glow in his heart: it was utterly magical. Yet he knows he must be truthful with her and still he does not quite know how to frame the words.

Instinctively he glances past the cottages and up at the big house. Immediately after the barbecue, nearly three weeks ago, Francis had a fall. There is the suspicion that it was another stroke and he's been in hospital but now he is home again, and soon, so William says, will be ready for visitors.

Tim thinks about the old man, wonders if he gets lonely up there, although he knows his little team of helpers are regularly in and out. But he wonders how

172

much Francis must miss his wife, and his sons, who rarely visit — so William says — and whom he is now too ill to visit. When William gets back, Tim thinks, he will ask if he can go up to see him. The old man's perspicacity has made him cautious; anxious that he'll blurt out the truth to that compassionate gaze. Now, suddenly, he'd like to talk to him.

He hears the familiar ping of a text arriving and takes out his phone. It's from Mattie.

Perfect day. Are you both back at B? All good here xx

He thinks about all the things he would like to say in reply, but he decides to keep it simple.

Thank you for making it perfect. W and I are safe home xx

He goes back inside, glad of Wooster's company. He thinks of Mattie saying, "I love you . . . You're still young . . . You've got your whole life to explore it . . ." and he sits down at the kitchen table, buries his face in his hands. He feels vulnerable, frightened at the prospect of dying, of non-being . . .

Wooster heaves himself out of his basket and comes to sit beside him, leaning against his legs. His bulk and warmth are so comforting, so reassuring, that Tim bends down to hug him and draw courage from him. There is none of the familiar sounds: William arriving home from the office, Aunt Kat calling to Charlotte as she takes the washing off the line, Oliver crying. It's not just the silence, however, it's the sense of emptiness; of desertion.

As he gratefully strokes Wooster's heavy head, Tim thinks again of Francis alone in the house and wonders how he copes with such isolation.

Tomorrow, he tells himself, tomorrow I'll go to see him.

Francis glimpses Tim from his window but before he can catch his attention the boy has gone inside. He moves slowly, pushing the Zimmer frame before him, avoiding the pile of books Maxie has left on the floor. He hates the Zimmer frame but he isn't taking any chances, old fool that he is. The fall was his own fault, sheer clumsiness, and now he's even more of a nuisance to those who care for him. He must be more careful. There is still much to do for those whom he loves — and he includes Tim, now, in that small group.

He's not sure what he can do for Tim. It's hubristic to think that he might be able to help him, yet he can't quite get him out of his mind. Ever since he spoke of Gerard Manley Hopkins' poetry at the barbecue Francis has been anxious that Tim has far more on his mind than a sabbatical.

Afterwards he wondered if he'd been imagining things but an instinctive fear keeps him drawn towards the boy. Then he had that stupid fall and was put out of action. It would be terrible if an opportunity was lost through his own stupidity.

Francis moves slowly across the room, sits down at his desk and opens his drawer. At his lowest ebb someone was vouchsafed to him; a stranger offered him comfort. He sits in silence, listening to the thrush

174

singing in the ash tree, remembering. Nell wrote to him, telling him that she was expecting Bill's child, and he knew then that he'd lost her, that there would never be a future for them together. He told himself there never had been: that he had forfeited his right to be with her and Maxie when he'd sacrificed them to his career and to his marriage. He stood at his study window staring out, full of guilt and the sense of loss. Liz and the boys were visiting friends and, on a sudden impulse, he drove to Buckfast Abbey to go to a midweek Mass. Afterwards he went into the restaurant for coffee. It was nearly lunchtime, and very busy, but there was a space at a table where one man was sitting alone reading something printed on a sheet of paper. Carrying his tray, Francis gestured hopefully towards the empty seat and the stranger smiled and nodded.

It was only as he sat down opposite the old fellow that Francis saw he was wearing a clerical collar. Well, that wasn't very surprising here at the Abbey. He was thin, angular, with a thatch of white hair, dark brown eyes and a singularly sweet smile. It was odd but he seemed familiar, although Francis couldn't remember seeing him at any of the services.

"Thank you, Father," Francis murmured.

The priest looked at him intently, an unexpected expression of compassion and understanding, as if he knew everything about him.

Francis said: "I think I've met you before but I don't know where. My name is Francis Courtney."

The priest smiled his warm, inclusive smile and gave a little shrug. "Maybe you have but it doesn't really matter, does it?"

Francis sipped his coffee, pondering that odd reply. Suddenly he longed to pour out his problems to this man, to seek some kind of absolution. He glanced at him again and was struck by the knowledge that the priest already knew his troubles, his wickedness, his failures, and had already forgiven him. He wanted to tell him about Nell, and how he'd been unfaithful to Liz; about Maxie and the cowardly need for silence.

The other man folded the paper, pushed his cup aside and stood up. Francis felt a sense of loss; he wanted to ask him to stay with him. The priest paused beside him and for a brief moment he gripped Francis' shoulder. "My name is Theo," he said. As he walked away Francis sat quite still, feeling even now the imprint of his fingers and the pressure of that strong grasp. It was a few moments before he noticed that the priest had left the piece of paper on the table. He picked it up and glanced quickly round but the man had disappeared.

Francis sat, undecided what he should do, and then unfolded the paper and read the words typed on it.

Who can free himself from his meanness and
    limitations,
if you do not lift him to yourself, my God, in
    purity of love?
How will a person

brought to birth and nurtured in a world of
   small horizons,
rise up to you, Lord,
if *you* do not raise him by your hand that made
   him?
You will not take from me, my God,
what you once gave me
in your only son, Jesus Christ,
in whom you gave me all I desire;
so I shall rejoice:
you will not delay, if I do not fail to hope.

Francis read the prayer twice and gradually a great
sense of peace descended upon his heart. The priest
was nowhere to be seen. Francis made his way outside,
still looking for him, still clutching the paper, and then
drove home to Brockscombe.

Now, Francis takes an envelope from his drawer,
draws out the much-creased and folded paper and
rereads the words printed on it. The prayer has
sustained him and encouraged him all these years. He
remembers Father Theo's smile and the grip of his
hand. He feels inadequate to help Tim, being so
damaged himself, but he knows he must make the
gesture.

CHAPTER
TWENTY-ONE

When Tim wakens he is still determined to follow his plan. Just after breakfast, however, there is a knock at the door. Wooster barks and Tim goes to see who is there. A middle-aged woman with a kind, tired face smiles at him.

"I don't think we've met before," she says, "but my name's Stella. I look after Francis. He's feeling better and he's asked me to invite you up for a cup of coffee if you're free."

Just for a moment Tim is caught off balance. It's as if Francis has read his mind. Wooster comes out and greets Stella as if she is an old friend.

"Hello, old fellow," she says to him. "You can stay with me in the kitchen."

"Right," says Tim. "That's good. Really good. So what do I do? Just walk in?"

"Give me chance to get finished upstairs, say half past ten?"

"Great," says Tim. "Thanks."

He goes back inside feeling surprised and pleased, looking forward to seeing Francis, though a small part of him fears it. Will he be able to continue to dissemble, to maintain his fiction with Francis? Perhaps they will simply discuss poetry? Tim begins to look through his collection, wondering how widely read Francis is: how modern. He becomes absorbed and then, glancing at his watch, realizes that he'll be late if he doesn't take Wooster for his walk straight away.

Half an hour later Stella is waiting for him as he opens the gate and crosses the yard to the farmhouse. She leads him along a passage, past the kitchen and into the hall.

"Up you go," she says to Tim, putting a restraining hand on Wooster's collar. "Door's down on the right. He'll be looking for you."

She puts a hand in her apron pocket and produces a biscuit with which she lures Wooster back towards the kitchen and Tim hears the door shut. He hesitates for a moment, looking upwards, and then runs up the stairs. He stops at the top, looking each way along the spacious landing and then he sees the shadow in the doorway and hurries forward.

"Tim," says Francis, balancing on a Zimmer frame, holding out his hand. "This is kind of you. Stella's brought the tray up so we shall be left in peace for a while."

He shuffles back to allow Tim to go past and he enters the big, sunny room with an exclamation of pleasure. With its book-lined walls and the big desk, this is just the kind of room he's always wanted for himself.

"What a splendid eyrie, sir," he says. "And what a view."

"It's mainly for the view that I commandeered it," Francis admitted. "My wife would have liked it for our bedroom but I considered it a waste. Better things to do in a bedroom, I told her, than stand looking out of windows."

Tim gives a crack of laughter and looks at the old man with amused surprise. "I have to agree with that."

"Of course you do and I wish you'd call me 'Francis'. Pour the coffee, will you? My hands shake too much these days. I like mine black."

There is a comfortable armchair on each side of the little rosewood table and Francis lowers himself into one of them while Tim deals with the coffee pot. He's surprised how much at ease he feels.

"So you've settled in?" the old man continues. "You're happy here?"

"I love it here," Tim answers. "It feels like home."

"That's a great compliment." Francis accepts the pretty bone-china cup and saucer that Tim pushes towards him. "I was born here. I've lived here all my life. My children were born here."

"I envy you," Tim says, looking around him. "It must be wonderful to have a place of your very own in the world. To be stable and rooted. You are very lucky."

The old man watches him over the rim of his cup and Tim looks back at him. There is something here, some kind of recognition between them, that he can't quite define.

"I have been lucky," Francis admits. "Much luckier than I deserve. But I've been very selfish, too."

Tim hardly knows how to answer.

180

"I'm sorry," he says inadequately. "We're all selfish, though, aren't we?"

"Probably. It's that sense of guilt we struggle with that can be so destructive, don't you find?"

Tim frowns. It's almost as if Francis knows about his own secret, but how can he? The old man is watching him and Tim feels an overwhelming desire to tell him the truth but still he resists.

"I can't imagine," he says rather lamely, trying for a lighter note, "that you've ever been capable of real treachery."

"Ah, but I have," says Francis sadly. "I betrayed my wife. I was unfaithful to her with a much younger woman who bore my illegitimate child. I have never acknowledged him as my son and I made his mother swear that she would never tell another soul that I was his father. I was afraid for my career, you see. And for my pride, of course, though I pretended that it was for my wife's sake, and for my legitimate sons. And even now, I can't quite admit it, though Nell and Liz are dead and it no longer matters. I can't face the thought of what my sons would think of me."

Tim stares at him, shocked. "God," he says, "that's hard. For all of you."

Francis nods. A little pause. "I see you walking in the woods. Have you found Pan?"

Tim is relieved at the change of subject. "I have," he says. "And there's someone who garlands him with flowers. Are there children locally who go there and into the dogs' graveyard?"

"So you've found the graveyard, too. It's a long while since I've been there. I can't walk so far these days."

"So it isn't you who puts flowers on Brack's grave?"

Francis gives a great sigh; he smiles reminiscently. "Ah, dear old Brack. Short for Bracken. What a fellow he was. A cairn. Cheerful, cheeky. You know the breed?"

Tim sets down his coffee cup carefully in its saucer. "I had a cairn like Brack when I was a child. I called him Ban."

His breath comes quickly. The day with Mattie has breached his defences and suddenly he feels weak and tired. Francis is watching him with that same compassion and he has a great longing to tell it all at last.

"What happened to Ban?"

"I opened the garden gate, though I'd been warned not to. I didn't mean to. It had always been too stiff before. But that morning the catch clicked open and gate swung enough for Ban to get out. My mother was just across the road coming back from shopping. Ban ran out to meet her and I followed him. My mother ran forward to stop me dashing into the road and was hit by a car. I killed her."

Francis is silent for a moment. "It was an accident. A terrible accident."

"Yes." Tim stares at his cup. "I know that really but somehow it doesn't help. My father couldn't bear it and simply left. Disappeared."

"What happened to you?"

"I went to live with my grandmother. My mother's mother. She looked after us. Me and Ban."

182

"How old were you?"

"Four. Nearly five."

"How terrible," Francis says. "How very terrible."

"So many people ask, you see. When you're little, I mean. 'Where's your mummy?' and you have to explain that she died in an accident. Even when you're older and you make friends people want to know, don't they? About your family. You can never get away from it. Anyway, why should I? It was my fault she died but I've never told anyone the whole truth before."

He feels empty and exhausted. He's kept this secret for so long that now — suddenly dragged into the light — it almost seems unimportant. He rubs his forehead with his fingers, drinks some coffee.

"I'm so sorry, Tim," Francis says. "Please forgive me. I had a feeling that there was something weighing on your mind and I wondered if it might help to talk. I had no business to interfere. I was completely out of order."

Tim shakes his head. "You weren't interfering. You were trying to help me. I've never told anyone before. It's too . . . well, just impossible, really. Is that why you told me about your secret? To encourage me?"

"Something like that. We're all damaged, aren't we? We all have weaknesses, fears, secrets we keep hidden. Sometimes it's good to unburden ourselves. Forgive me, Tim."

Tim is silent. He wants to tell Francis the rest of it but he can't do it. He already feels too emotional — and, anyway, it's not fair on the poor old man who looks so frail and vulnerable.

"It's wonderful being here," Tim says at last. "It's been the best thing in my life. There's nothing to forgive, Francis. And I'm glad I told you. And thank you for telling me. For trusting me." He hesitates. "So who is it that puts flowers on Brack's grave and brings posies to Pan?"

He smiles, trying to bring a lighter touch, but this time it is Francis who hesitates, shakes his head.

"There's a footpath across the field to the hamlet," he says. "Anyone might come that way."

Tim watches him; he feels that Francis is withholding something. His expression is inward, remote and immensely sad.

"Is there anything I can do for you?" Tim asks. "I know you have people to help you but is there anywhere I could take you in the car? Just for an outing, perhaps?"

Francis looks up at him. "Yes," he says quickly. "Yes, there is. Only you'd have to be able to deal with my wheelchair."

"I expect I could manage that," Tim says. "What do you have in mind?"

"I'd like to go to Mass," Francis says unexpectedly.

"To Mass?"

"Yes. At Buckfast Abbey. I prefer to go to one of the weekday services when it's quieter, and I haven't been for a long while. Do you think you could manage it?"

"I'm sure I can. I imagine that Bank Holiday Monday will probably be pretty busy at the Abbey so shall we say Tuesday?"

"You know the Abbey? You're not by any chance a Catholic?"

Tim shakes his head. "No, though I've visited the Abbey a couple of times. But Gran made sure we went to church on Sundays so I'm not a raw beginner."

They both laugh, tension eases. They drink their coffee and make a plan for Tuesday.

CHAPTER
TWENTY-TWO

The return to the courtyard begins with William's arrival from Exeter. He's in very high spirits, energized as always by the singing and meeting with his friends. Added to that is the text from Fiona suggesting that she might come down the following weekend. Ever since the barbecue there has been a little flurry of texts between them and he's enjoying the contact.

He wonders if it would be foolish to attempt to re-create the party spirit with another barbecue. It's a good way to be all-inclusive. He knows that Charlotte won't come to his cottage in the evening, leaving Oliver unattended, which means any other kind of party has to be in her cottage, which is a bit tough on her. The barbecue was such a success that he's tempted to repeat it. Perhaps even Cousin Francis will be able to attend if he's feeling better.

He decides that he'll pass the idea in front of Kat before he makes a decision, and wonders how she got on with Jerry in Bristol.

"Staying the night together?" he repeated, looking at her with admiration. "What a quick worker you are."

"Seems rather crazy to travel back late at night." She gave a little shrug and then grinned at him. "Don't worry, darling. Separate rooms."

He laughed. "I'm impressed. Jerry is a really nice bloke but I would have said that he's just a tad conventional."

"Oh, he is," she said at once. "But I'm working on it. He needs liberating."

"From what?" William asked suspiciously. "Or should I be asking 'from whom'?"

"From a frumpy friend," she answered with a burst of laughter. "That's Fiona's phrase, by the way, so don't blame me."

"I'm intrigued," he said. "Lucky old Jerry, is all I can say, to have two women vying for his attentions."

Kat became serious. "He's very sweet," she said reflectively. "Very genuine. He doesn't like to hurt people."

"Sounds like me," William said, only half joking, expecting a compliment.

But Kat was silent for a moment. "You're much more single-minded," she said at last. "Look at the way you stood up to Fiona when she wanted you to give up all you'd worked for to go to London. Jerry would have gone."

He was almost shocked by her reply. "Do you think I should have gone?" he asked, after a moment.

"No," she answered at once. "No, I don't. Everything you'd worked for was here. This was your life. But I can see her side of it, too. It's hard to be offered such a chance and have to turn it down."

"It was such a pity that we couldn't make weekending work," he said sadly.

Kat smiled at him almost pityingly. "It wasn't just that, though, was it? It was Sam. He threw her totally off balance. He was outside her experience and, on top of the new job, she lost her head."

"You sound as if you feel sorry for her," he said.

"I do a bit," Kat replied. "It's odd but during that barbecue weekend I slightly saw it all in a different light. To begin with I was just so angry on your behalf, so partisan, that I hadn't really stopped to think how it must have been for her. I'm not excusing her, I'm just saying that I feel a bit more tolerant."

Now, as he switches off the engine and gets out of the car, William remembers how he felt pleased rather than upset by Kat's admission. In his new mood, this sense of happiness with Fiona, he wants everyone else to feel the same way: to be more friendly towards her.

He sees that Kat is not yet back and he isn't expecting Charlotte, who is staying the weekend with her parents in Tavistock. Tim is here, however, and at this moment his door opens and Wooster hurries out, giving a welcoming bark or two, followed by Tim.

"Welcome home," he says. "Though it seems a bit odd, me welcoming you back."

"Why?" asks William. "It's your home, too."

"We missed everyone, didn't we, Wooster?" says Tim. "So, was it good?"

"It was very good. We joined with several choirs to sing Fauré's *Requiem*. I think it went well. How have you been?"

188

"Fine," says Tim. "I had coffee with Francis yesterday. He seems much better. I'm taking him to the Abbey on Tuesday."

"Are you?" William is surprised; pleased. "That's very kind. He likes to go to Mass but it's difficult for him now he no longer drives. Stella takes him sometimes but the wheelchair causes a bit of a problem in her car and he hates to be a nuisance. And how has this fellow been?"

He stoops to embrace Wooster, who licks his face obligingly.

Tim laughs. "I've loved having him. He was good company. I'm just going to give him his supper and then take him for a walk. Want to come?"

"I'd like that," William says. He's still on a high and suddenly he feels it would be a bit anticlimactic to be alone. "Tell you what, let's take him down by the river and then go to the pub for a pint."

"OK," says Tim. "I'll feed him and then I'll give you a shout. We'll take my car. It's got his rug and stuff in the back."

William swings his bag out of the car; as he strides across the courtyard he begins to sing.

When Kat arrives home she finds William and Tim sharing a pizza in the kitchen. Wooster is fast asleep by the garden door. In truth she is pleased to see them. The visit to Bristol has been such fun that she was very slightly put out to find that, on their return, Jerry was engaged to go to a supper party.

He was quick to point out that this had been in his diary long before the arrangement to go to Bristol and it hadn't occurred to him that it would in any way interfere with the plan.

To be fair, Kat has to admit to herself, it didn't: they were back in plenty of time. Nevertheless she feels just the least bit miffed that he didn't seize an opportunity to extend her stay with him; that he took her at her word that they'd have lunch in Bristol, catch the train home, and that would be that. She'd left her car at his flat and her options open and so she was surprised when, having made them both tea, he told her — looking rather sheepish — that he was going out later. She wondered if it would be with Sandra but she kept her cool, smiled as if it were perfectly natural, finished her tea and drove home.

"Thank God," she told herself, "that I didn't take my overnight case in. I'd have looked an absolute fool."

Jerry was a good companion: amusing, interesting and attentive. They enjoyed the train journey but she could see, on their arrival at the hotel, that he was slightly ill at ease checking in at the desk, despite their having booked separate rooms. Having arrived, Jerry seemed unable to take control of the situation and it was left to Kat to orchestrate the evening: a walk around the waterfront, a light early supper before arriving at the theatre, arranging for sandwiches and a bottle of wine to be left in her room for later, after the performance.

He thoroughly enjoyed the ballet. She knew a few people in the company and afterwards she took Jerry backstage to introduce him. She could see he was impressed by her reception, delighted to be with her, and they walked back to the hotel arm in arm and talking happily. When she invited him into her room for a drink she was aware of his slight hesitation, quickly hidden, of his glance along the corridor. She wondered, amused, whom he thought might be watching: did he think perhaps one of his family might be staying here? She saw his delight at the little supper laid out, followed almost immediately by a tightening of the lips, which indicated an irritation that he hadn't thought of it himself.

Immediately Kat began on an amusing anecdote involving one of the dancers he'd just met, poured him a glass of wine, and smoothed their way through this slightly awkward moment. Making love was easier: she simply took her clothes off and held out her arms to him. The lovemaking was good, but the single bed was uncomfortable, and before too long he slid out, got dressed, and vanished away to his own room.

She lay for a while, her arms folded behind her head, missing him. She was used to men who were careless of the conventions, indifferent to what other people might think about them, and Jerry's diffidence was rather touching. It was clear that he loved being with her but that her fame was causing an imbalance in the relationship.

In the morning she went down to breakfast to find him already sitting at a table with a newspaper.

"I didn't want to disturb you," he said, standing up to pull out her chair.

"I had rather the same idea," she said.

He seemed a little more at ease, as though the most demanding part of the weekend had been accomplished, though she saw that he still glanced at each newcomer to the breakfast-room.

"Expecting somebody?" she asked lightly at last.

He flushed. "No, no, of course not."

But she wondered if he was slightly on the qui vive lest one of his friends might also be spending the weekend in Bristol and he was anxious about how he would deal with the situation.

Now, as she gets out of the car and goes into the cottage, she can't help wondering if Jerry is regaling Sandra with the more glamorous moments of the weekend and it's a relief to see Tim and William sitting at the table eating pizza, drinking ale and evidently enjoying themselves. They pull out a chair for her, cut her a slice of pizza, and ask her about the visit.

Kat describes the performance, tells a few stories about the dancers, but of Jerry she says nothing at all.

CHAPTER
TWENTY-THREE

Charlotte and Oliver are the last to return to Brockscombe. She is surprised at how pleased she is to be back on her own patch. It's good to go to Tavistock and see everyone, it makes a change to have help with Oliver and a bit of a rest, but she doesn't like him to get out of his routine and it's difficult to lay down the law, what with Mum spoiling him and Dad making jokes about her having more rules and regs than the navy.

Mattie was looking radiant, talking about the prospect of a job at Exeter Uni and getting the dogs overexcited. Later, she said that on her way down she'd had lunch with Tim at the Two Bridges Hotel and, just for a moment, Charlotte was a bit hurt that they hadn't invited her and Oliver along, given that she had to pass the hotel on her way to Tavistock.

"It was on the spur of the moment," Mattie said quickly, seeing her expression. "I sent him a text and he just happened to be up on the moor walking Wooster."

And, after all, thinks Charlotte, they're perfectly entitled to want some time together: she wouldn't want to play gooseberry. Even so, Mattie is still evasive about the relationship and it's difficult to find out just how serious it is.

Charlotte is pretty certain, though, that Mattie planned to see Tim on her way back. On Sunday evening Dad said, "Oh, by the way, Mattie, is it OK if I hitch a lift with you to London tomorrow? I'm going up for a reunion thrash. I can get the train back but it would be nice to have some company on the way."

Just for a second Charlotte saw a flash of chagrin on Mattie's face before she said, "Yes, of course. Lovely. I shall want to get away after breakfast to try to beat the traffic, if that's OK." And then a bit later she noticed her sister texting. It might have been a coincidence but some sixth sense told Charlotte that's how it was: she'd arranged to meet Tim and was having to cancel. Though why she felt she had to is a bit of a mystery. It's not as if he hasn't met the parents. He was introduced when they came over to Brockscombe and he's seen them a few times now when they've visited. The three of them could have had coffee somewhere.

Anyway, it's none of her business. Charlotte begins to unload Oliver from the car and glances around to see if Wooster is about. She wonders if he's missed them.

"You wouldn't want to take Wooster to Washington," Dad said. "Crazy idea. We'll have him here until you get back," and then Mattie said, "If I get the Exeter job, I'll have him," which was almost as crazy as taking him to Washington.

Everyone was very excited about Andy's posting, assuring her how great it would be. It's odd that they never seem to notice that the more they tell her how much she'll enjoy something, the more she digs her heels in and feels stubborn about it. After all, how do

194

they know what she feels or how it will be for her? It irritates her, people assuming they can influence her by sheer willpower. It's the same way they still call Oliver "Ollie" or "Ol". They know she doesn't really like it but they still do it as if by continual usage they'll change her mind.

Charlotte dumps her case by the car and carries Oliver indoors. It's good to be home.

Tim hears the car, goes to the window, and Wooster gets up, tail wagging expectantly. Tim hesitates. He wonders exactly what Mattie has said about their meeting and he feels just the least bit equivocal about seeing Charlotte.

"We'll tell her," Mattie said in the car park at the Two Bridges Hotel. "Of course we must. We'll tell her about having lunch here but I'd rather like to keep the rest to ourselves. Do you mind?" She looked at him anxiously. "Only because . . . well, it's kind of private, isn't it? Special."

He nodded and put his arms round her and held her closely. "Very special," he said.

"What about meeting up on my way back on Monday?" she asked hopefully.

He nodded. "But not there," he said. He spoke without thinking and saw a shadow cross her face. "Not because it wasn't special," he said quickly. "But simply because it was. Next time it might be raining or there might be someone walking or anything . . . "

He didn't know quite how to explain what he meant: that something spontaneous, an unplanned meeting, is

195

so much more likely to have that particular kind of magic than an organized event that has expectation automatically built in to it. But she nodded, understanding at once.

"What about here?" she asked. "Or do you feel the same way?"

He smiled at her. "Not quite. The fires will probably still be lit on Monday and there will probably be a sofa free. It's not quite the same as your cave."

"We could meet here," she said, "and then drive on a bit if the weather's fine. I know a nice little beach down by the river. I'll have the hamper primed."

He laughed. "You do that. Let's throw it in the lap of the gods."

She stretched up and kissed him. "Let's do that then. I'll text when I leave. I'll tell Charlotte we had lunch here, and the parents if they ask. I'd better go."

He and Wooster watched her drive away, hand waving from the window. It hurt him to think that she might be wondering why he wouldn't tell her the obstacle to their love: she must realize that he wasn't involved with anybody else. Perhaps on Monday . . . But then he had her text saying that her father was cadging a lift to London. He wondered if he should suggest they all meet but he lost his nerve.

Now, he goes out to see Charlotte, Wooster running eagerly ahead.

"Hi," he calls through her open door. "Welcome home."

Wooster barges in and Charlotte comes to meet him. She looks happy, glad to be back, and he smiles at her

196

and waves to Oliver, who is sitting in his chair at the table.

"Did you miss us?" she asks.

"We certainly did. We had lots of walks and we met up with Mattie at the Two Bridges Hotel. It was really lucky. She texted to say that she was making good time and just driving up on to the moor and Wooster and I weren't that far away. I've never been there before. It's really good."

He listens to himself lying with such ease and feels a bit guilty but Charlotte has obviously heard it from Mattie anyway so she doesn't look suspicious.

"It's a pity she couldn't come in to see you on her way home," she says. "Only Dad's going with her and he'll want to get on."

He nearly says, "I know," and realizes how easy it is to get trapped. Instead he says: "Did Ollie enjoy himself?"

"Mum always spoils him," she says, "but that's what grannies do, isn't it?"

"Mine did," he says lightly. "But I don't think it did any lasting damage. Well, I suppose you'll be wanting Wooster back. I can keep borrowing him, though, I hope?"

She immediately assumes the expression that Mattie calls "Charlotte's organizing face": a little frown and a pursing of the lips.

"I still think you should have a dog of your own, Tim," she says. "I mean, why not? You're so good with Wooster and it would be great company for you. Of course you can borrow him but why not have one of your own? Or is it because you don't know what you might want to do next? You're not thinking of leaving just yet, I hope?"

All the alarm bells are ringing now and he feels trapped. Usually everyone goes along with the sabbatical idea, his having the inheritance, which means he can take time out, and he's relaxed into a sense of safety.

"I've got no plans to leave for a while yet," he says, smiling at her, "but a dog's quite a responsibility, isn't it? Well, look how you're worrying about taking Wooster to Washington."

It's rather neat, he thinks, to turn it back on her and distract her from his own problems. She gives a little snort.

"Mum and Dad have offered to have him," she says. "They think it would be madness to take him to Washington. Even Mattie offered, which is utter lunacy."

"Did she?" he asks, surprised. "How would she manage him in London?"

"There's this job at Exeter University. Did she tell you? If she gets that then she thinks she could cope with him somehow."

"Oh, yes. She did mention it."

Charlotte shakes her head. "How would he be when she's at work? The trouble with Mattie is that she doesn't think things through. Just wanting to do something is enough and all the problems will instantly dissolve. It's what Dad calls her 'can do' approach to life."

Tim laughs. "Well, I suppose it's good to be positive."

Charlotte looks bleak. "It's OK for her. Even when things go wrong she always has people flocking to help her out."

He watches her, suddenly feeling sorry for her. It can't be easy, with Andy away, to carry on her life; waiting, wishing she could share things with him, taking all the responsibility for Oliver. Tim doesn't know how to offer comfort and even whether she wants it. Knowing Charlotte, he suspects she might see it as a weakness.

"I was just thinking about doing a sandwich for lunch," he says. "Come and join me."

She hesitates, frowning, as if tempted, and then shakes her head. "I ought to get on and I've got to sort something out for Oliver."

He waits, sad that she can never quite let go, but wondering if she's afraid to relinquish her hold just in case she might be swept away, out of control. Perhaps her rigid discipline is the only way she can cope with this odd life of hers.

"OK," he says gently. "Good to have you back. I'll get Wooster's things, shall I?"

"Yes, he'll need his basket." She pauses as though she's still having a little struggle with herself. "Look, why not bring your sandwich round and have it with us? I haven't got much in, I'm afraid. I've got to do a supermarket run later. But it would be good to have some company."

"Great," he says. "Sure you don't want to share my sandwich? There's plenty."

She laughs and suddenly she looks younger, happy again. "Go on then," she says. "Why not? Thanks, Tim."

He hurries back to his own cottage to assemble a little picnic lunch and suddenly he thinks of Mattie with her hamper, the rug spread on the moorland turf, her "cave" of granite and gorse. He remembers her saying, "Can you hear the lark?" and how hot the sun was. At those moments it's almost as if he can control this wretched disease and will it away: defeat it. How odd that, out of the blue that morning in London nearly six months ago, he should have casually asked Mattie the question: where should he go? He'd put his life in the hands of the gods and they brought him to Brockscombe.

Tim packs the picnic into a plastic box, balances it in Wooster's basket with the remains of his food and goes to find Charlotte.

CHAPTER
TWENTY-FOUR

Mattie is rather late getting away — her father has a telephone call that has to be dealt with — and she feels regret as they cross the moor that her plan to meet Tim has been ruined. The weather is hot and sunny — unusually for the late May Bank Holiday — and she would have liked to show him her little shingly beach by the moorland stream, all hung about with alder and willow. They would have sat on the rug on the short, sheep-cropped turf, looking for a dipper, whilst Wooster enjoyed a paddle.

This time she drives out of Tavistock on the Lydford road, the quickest route to the M5, but she wishes she was heading for Princetown and the Two Bridges Hotel, pulling in off the road over the little bridge, and seeing Tim waiting for her at one of the tables in the sunshine. It's such a missed opportunity that she feels quite resentful towards her father, who sits beside her, unaware of her emotions, and droning on about which of his oppos are coming to the reunion.

She thinks about Tim saying, "I do love you. I do but it's just . . . it's not that simple," and she wonders why it's not simple. What is holding him back? Perhaps it's because he hasn't got a job — but he had one and gave it up. She's certain that there's nobody else. She knows that Charlotte would tell her if he had visitors or was away at nights or at the weekends. So what can it be? Of course, he might simply be one of those guys who find it impossible to commit, and yet he couldn't hide his delight at the prospect of her moving to Exeter.

It's odd to be in love like this, with someone she rarely sees and who remains so elusive, though, of course, she's known Tim for more than a year. She was grateful that Charlotte was tactful and made no remarks about him in front of Mum and Dad when she told them they'd had lunch together. Mum raised her eyebrow and said, "Oh, that was nice, darling," with a tiny question mark on the end of it as if she'd like to know more; Dad had just given her a little wink. Neither she nor Charlotte had ever told them much about Tim apart from the fact that he'd had an inheritance from his grandmother and was taking a career break to decide what he really wanted to do. They'd all got on quite well, Charlotte told her, when the parents visited Brockscombe. They knew Mattie had worked with him, of course, and so they probably assumed that if there had been any kind of relationship between them it would have shown by now.

Perhaps, she thinks, it will be easier if I get the job in Exeter. He'll be able to come and see me and we won't be quite so much under everyone's eye. I'm glad he's at Brockscombe, though.

It's odd that she isn't able to tell even her closest friends about her feelings for Tim. They know he's gone to Brockscombe, and that she sees him from time to time, but that's all. She plays down the mystery of his sudden departure and now they hardly think of him. It's because instinctively she knows there's something he's not ready to tell her yet that she keeps their love a secret. After all, it would have been easy enough to tell Mum and Dad that she'd made a date to have coffee with Tim on the way back, but something prevented her. He made no suggestion that the three of them could have coffee together, and she would have been uncomfortable if he had, even though she doesn't know quite why. Whatever it is that is preventing him from allowing their love to be a simple open thing keeps her silent too.

Yet he seems such a genuine man — kind, friendly, funny — and a generous, passionate lover. She is so much in tune with him and she longs to be with him now in her little secret cave; the rug spread out, the hamper open, his arms round her as they listen to the lark.

"It's such a glorious day," her father says, "that we really ought to be up on the moor having a picnic rather than rushing back to London."

"Yes," she says, rather bitterly, "we should, shouldn't we?"

"Still, we'd better crack on," he says cheerfully, unaware of her irritation. "We're already running a bit late. Put your foot down, darling. We'll have a bite of lunch at Sedgemoor."

Jerry drives slowly through narrow lanes, where shiny yellow buttercups and bright pink campion fill the ditches with vivid colour, and powdery heads of tall creamy cow parsley brush at his open window. As he idles along he hears the evocative call of the cuckoo in the valley and he stops to listen to those two magical notes, feeling the sun on his face and his arm, unwilling to drive on. He knows why he is so reluctant, why he is driving so slowly: it is because this meeting with his family is going to be a difficult one. His daughters and their husbands, with their assorted children, have clubbed together to take a holiday cottage for half-term week. It's at Thurlestone, practically on the beach, which is not far for him to drive and it will be great to see them all again, yet he feels nervous. It is the first time ever that he has met with his family when he has something to hide.

He knows, he just knows, he will not be able to talk about Kat. Mentally, every possible conversational opening regarding their relationship defeats him. He can imagine his daughters raising their eyebrows, their wary expressions, their almost tangible loyalty to Vee, as he begins to try to discuss Kat with them.

It would be much easier to talk about Sandra, whom he has met in a conventional way — not in a casual pick-up in a café — through a local history club. She has introduced him to her friends and now there is a gentle flow of meetings, concerts, clubs that his children would find perfectly acceptable. The domestic, maternal Sandra is not such a threat to their mother's memory as is the life force that is Kat.

Indeed, Sandra has even offered to give the whole family lunch.

"How wonderful for you to see them all," she said, her round pretty face beaming at the prospect of this pleasure in store for him. "Such a shame that it'll be such a squash in your little flat. Listen. Why don't I do a lunch? I've got plenty of room, a big garden, and lots of toys and books that my grandchildren love. You can host it and pay for it but just use my place to entertain them. Much nicer than an hotel."

It's such a kind offer that he is deeply touched and agrees to think about it. It was certainly different from Kat's reaction.

"Good grief, darling," she said, looking horrified. "All nine of them at once? But, of course, you're used to it, aren't you? Well, let me know when the coast's clear."

Remembering, Jerry laughs; he can't help it. Slowly, though, the smile fades and he wonders how the future will embrace them all. The sensible thing is, he tells himself, to introduce the idea of Kat slowly so that they hear about her obliquely, as it were, until they get used to her name being mentioned.

He tries to imagine them all together, Kat playing with the grandchildren, and fails utterly. In a different situation he's quite sure they would be delighted to meet her, be impressed with her work and her international reputation, but as their father's lover — not a chance. He remembers Kat and Fiona laughing in the pub, routing Sandra and enjoying every minute of it. His daughters would be slightly shocked, even disapproving. One works in IT and the other is a teacher, and neither of them has the wacky, bohemian outlook on life that Kat — or even Fiona — has.

Yet the very fact of not mentioning her almost feels as though he is lying to them, or deceiving them in some way. He feels a little chill of fear that Sandra might drop him in it by mentioning the trip to Bristol. Although she was perfectly polite about it — "Oh, is that who she is? I think I might have heard of her but the ballet isn't exactly my forte" — it was clear that she was irritated by this jaunt. Going more or less straight on to her supper party last evening — which he hadn't liked to refuse after the business at the Cott — he found it impossible to lie about the weekend, where he'd been and so on. If she has a fault, he thinks, Sandra does rather go for the third degree in questioning to satisfy her curiosity.

Of course, he made it sound a much more casual affair, majoring on Kat's friends in the company, almost implying that she was staying with them, but he's beginning to find living a double life rather tricky. Yet it's so life-enhancing, being with Kat: she makes him feel twice as alive. He can't give her up.

He decides to play it by ear. At some point he'll run the idea of lunch at Sandra's past the girls and see how they react. If they find it attractive then he'll have to take his chance about how discreet she is. If they decide they'd rather he took them to a play-park or another place of entertainment then he'll tell Sandra tactfully that they've made other arrangements.

Jerry pulls up at the junction, turns out on to the main road, and heads towards Thurlestone.

206

CHAPTER
TWENTY-FIVE

The midweek Mass at Buckfast Abbey becomes a habit. Tim drives Francis, manages his wheelchair, and sits through the service gazing at the amazing stained-glass window in the chapel. The liturgy is familiar and though he does not receive Communion he is given a blessing. He doesn't know why the touch of the priest's hands on his head and the murmured words are a solace, but they are and he looks forward to them.

Afterwards he wheels Francis out of the Abbey, across to the café, and they have an early lunch together. It's the hottest June on record and they sit outside on the balcony, looking over the gardens and the lavender beds, enjoying this sharing. And indeed, thinks Tim, it is good to share with Francis. Other little jaunts occur. They drive across the moor to the Two Bridges Hotel and sit by the river in the sun; Francis enjoys a pint of Jail Ale and laughs at the strutting and hissing of the geese. He calls them "the Mafia". Tim takes him to a concert at the Abbey, where William's choir is singing with other choirs, and drives him to Torcross beach where they sit in the sun and eat ice cream.

Tim is constantly surprised at his affection for this elderly man who is old enough to be his grandfather. There is an agelessness about Francis. He doesn't talk endlessly about his past nor does he have a fund of anecdotes culled from his political life. Instead he engages with Tim as if he were his contemporary: they discuss poetry, music, ideas. It's as if that one revelatory discussion, where each told a crucial secret about themselves, has brought them closer than if they'd known each other for years.

One day, after Mass, Tim admits to Francis that he's been trying his hand at poetry: "It's rubbish, of course," he says defensively, "but it's very therapeutic."

Francis doesn't immediately ask to read it or protest that he's sure it's very good.

"Writing's a gift I've always envied," he says reflectively, "or indeed any of the creative arts. Music or painting. Where on earth do you begin?"

"I didn't start until I moved here," Tim tells him. "When I'm walking on the cliffs or on the moors I find that I'm trying to find phrases that might describe them. It's impossible really. I started by making lists of words that related to something I felt." He stops and bursts out laughing. "Does that really sound as pretentious as I think it does?"

Francis laughs, too. "It's no more pretentious than me trying to write my memoirs. At least it's not all about you. After all, why should anyone be interested in the political maunderings of an old buffer nobody's heard about?"

"I suppose it depends whether you know any scurrilous stories about those in power at the time?" suggests Tim. "Or would that be libel?"

Francis shrugs. "I think that it's more to do with trying to make sense of my life. To see some sort of pattern. There was never any serious thought of publication."

He looks around the café, as he often does, almost as if he's hoping to see someone he recognizes and, when Tim raises his eyebrows, Francis smiles at him.

"I met an old priest here quite by chance once, years ago. I was at a very low ebb and he put me back on course. He pointed me towards the writings of St John of the Cross, which have come to mean a very great deal to me. It's foolish but I always hope I might see him again, sitting at a table reading a sheet of paper with the 'Prayer of a Soul in Love' printed on it. He left the paper on the table when he went and I still have it."

"Did he leave it on purpose?"

The old man shrugs. "Who can say? I like to think so. I think that's what prayer is all about. That we're taken care of in those dark moments. I was in a very bad place and I came here looking for help. Father Theo was my miracle."

Tim smiles at him. Francis' faith touches him; he envies him the simplicity and strength of his belief.

"Shall we go and smell the lavender?" he asks.

Francis nods and Tim gets up and wheels him outside into the sunshine.

William's barbecues are also becoming a regular event — on Fridays now, to kick off the weekend. It's fun, once a week, for everyone to gather outside in these warm evenings and have a little party. Each person contributes and he enjoys getting everything organized: he chooses the meat, Tim provides the wine, Charlotte brings a pudding.

"I feel rather *de trop*," says Kat.

"You can supply coffee," grins William. "You know. 'From each according to their abilities; to each according to their needs' or whatever."

"I didn't know you were a Marxist, darling," she says.

It's a good way to catch up and, though it's accepted that friends are welcome, it tends to remain a family affair. Francis usually manages to come down from his lair to join them and, one Friday evening, Mattie was there, celebrating getting the job at Exeter. That was a very special, celebratory barbecue and William drank too much and sang.

It was even better when Fiona was staying. She thoroughly entered into the spirit of the party and William rather basked in her approval whilst telling himself not to be a bloody fool. She and Kat seemed to be getting along very well these days, though he noticed that Kat never invited Jerry along again.

"He's very welcome," he said to her. "It doesn't have to be just family."

"I know," she said. "But it doesn't quite work. I don't know why. And it's fun when it's just us, isn't it?"

"Well, it is," he agreed. "It's very relaxed. Though it was lovely when Mattie came, wasn't it? Maybe she'll manage a few more when she's moved down."

"She can stay overnight with Charlotte," Kat said. "Or with Tim."

He looked at her. "Anything going on there, do you think?"

She frowned, looking puzzled. "I think so but I'm not quite sure how — or what? Perhaps this is how the young have love affairs in this modern age. Or perhaps they're just good friends."

"Perhaps," he said, but he was still puzzled.

Meanwhile his relationship with Fiona is easy again. She says no more about getting a bolt hole and William is beginning to wish that he hadn't been quite so negative about it. He wonders whether it's time to offer her the spare bedroom occasionally but needs to sound Kat out first. It's such a volte-face that he's embarrassed to mention it, though a little plan is forming in his mind. Andy is getting a week's leave early in July and William wonders whether this would be the moment to broach the subject. It's not that he wants to muscle in on Charlotte and Andy — they need privacy — but perhaps Fiona could stay over for just one night to see her son. He could organize a barbecue for that last Saturday night.

William feels rather excited at the prospect of them all being together but he knows that he needs to think about it very carefully. He'll mention it to Kat and then talk to Charlotte before he even gives so much as a hint of it to Fiona.

CHAPTER
TWENTY-SIX

Market day. The stall-holders and the market traders are busy setting out their wares, awnings and canvases flap and flutter in the warm breeze; a pretty girl pushes a wooden barrow laden with vases and jugs full of bunches of fresh flowers to her pitch beside a pillar at the market's edge. Across the street a busker is playing the Spanish guitar. As Kat wanders between the stalls, stopping to look, to chat, she listens to the Latin American music and wants to dance. The shoppers, locals and holiday-makers fill the square with bustle and noise, and she breathes in the scents of old books, Indian cotton, flowers and cheese.

Glancing idly across the high street she sees them: Jerry and Sandra standing together. He looks down at her as she talks, pretty in her summer clothes, bursting suddenly into laughter and clutching at his arm as if she might fall over with mirth. He doesn't make any effort to remove her hand and Kat watches them, trying to analyse her reactions: jealousy, irritation, amusement? Oddly, she feels a sense of anxiety. She's met plenty of Sandras: passive-aggressives, wearing their victims down by a relentless tide of good humour, determination, a quiet sense of grievance and the assurance that they know best. Jerry is no match for her.

Kat wonders if she should stake her claim: cross the road and take his other arm, kiss him. She can see a way forward with Jerry, a sharing of their lives together even if she goes to London. He was at ease with her friends at Bristol: his drama training stood him in good stead with these people of the stage. She can imagine him visiting London, spending time with her, having fun; and she will want to come back to see her family and be with him here. It could work, she is certain of it. He brings a kind of stability, calmness, which she values.

Even as she wonders what to do there is a little stir at the edge of the pavement. A pair of holiday-makers put down their shopping bags, walk into the road and, in perfect time with the guitarist, perform an Argentinian tango. Briefly Kat sees Sandra clutch Jerry even tighter, her mouth rounded into a rather shocked, surprised "O" as if she slightly disapproves, and then all Kat's attention is taken by the dance. In their shorts and sandals it should be incongruous, but it is not. They move beautifully together and with the music; there is dignity, even passion and drama. Nobody takes much notice; a car drives carefully around them, shoppers pass to and fro. When the music finishes the couple simply step back on to the pavement, pick up their bags and disappear into the crowds.

Kat steps forward and begins to clap, others follow suit, even the guitarist is smiling. Now Jerry has seen her. He looks uneasy, as if he has been caught out, but he is clapping too, now, so that Sandra's hand has been dislodged. Kat laughs and waves to him, signalling her delight in the performance, and his anxious expression widens into a smile. Her heart gives a little tick and a jump: how dear he is to her. She crosses the street, still smiling.

"Wasn't that wonderful?" she cries, including Sandra in her delight. "I could hardly believe it. Only in Totnes. Nobody turned a hair, did they?"

Sandra is looking at her warily: chin drawn in, eyes narrowed.

"Rather dangerous," she says reprovingly, "dancing in the road. Not a very good example to the children."

Kat stares at her with surprised amusement, wondering if she can be serious. "I don't think it was too anarchic, was it?"

Sandra looks to Jerry for support. "You're a teacher," she says brightly. "What do you think?"

Kat meets his eyes. She wants to burst out laughing but she sees that he is discomfited, pulled two ways at once, and she feels sad, irritated, and sorry for him all at the same time. She touches him lightly on the arm and turns away.

"See you later, Jerry," she calls over her shoulder. "And remember, no dancing in the street!"

Jerry watches her go. He wants to run after her, to explain to her and make her understand how he feels: how impossible it is for him to hold a balance between her and Sandra. But something prevents him, some deep-down, ingrained desire to be conciliatory,

214

reinforced by forty years of marriage, that makes it impossible for him to act outside of his conventional, well-mannered upbringing.

"What an extraordinary thing to say." Sandra stares after Kat with an expression of disbelief on her face. "What a very odd woman she is. And are you," she adds almost carelessly, "seeing her later?"

"Yes," he answers wretchedly, cursing himself for not having the courage to tell her to mind her own business. "Actually . . . yes, yes I am. And so what are your plans now?"

He can see that she's wrestling with indecision: to question him further about Kat or seize the opportunity to make the most of her chance with him.

"Well, I think it's coffee time, don't you?"

She smiles at him and she looks so arch, so hopeful, that he hasn't the heart to refuse the implied offer — especially as he's longing for refreshment.

"I think it might be," he says. "Shall we sit outside in the sunshine?"

"Oh, I don't think so," she answers at once. "It gets so hot and I'm no good in the glare of the sun. It's because I'm so fair-skinned. Not like your Russian friend," she adds.

He begins to say that Kat isn't Russian but decides against it. It will simply lead them deeper into the morass. They pass along the busy pavement, now jostled together, now separated, and he thinks of Kat and the way she looked at him, eyes brimming with mirth, inviting him to share the joke. And once again he wants to turn round and run after her, to see her face and to hold her tall, dancer's body close against him.

"This is nice, Jeremy," says Sandra, leading him into shadowy coolness and settling at a table. "So much better out of the sun. Now, what shall we have?"

CHAPTER
TWENTY-SEVEN

Fiona sits at the kitchen table watching William unloading the dishwasher. As he puts things away, talking about what's been happening since she was last down from London, she thinks how extraordinary it is that she should be here. After the separation, when William moved to Brockscombe, they met only at family events where, for Andy's sake, they were always amicable. So successful were they on these occasions that some of Andy's friends didn't know anything had changed. It was only once Andy and Charlotte moved in next door and Oliver was born that she visited Brockscombe.

It seems odd, and yet familiar, to be sitting here in this domestic setting and talking to William about family things. She can see that he is enjoying it, which is also slightly surprising remembering his reaction when she'd asked about the cottage as a bolt hole. There has been a sea change since that first barbecue after she'd met Kat and Jerry at the Cott.

As she looks around the kitchen Fiona notices familiar objects: some hand-painted china on the dresser, the brass-bound clock on the wall, a watercolour painting. Even during the sharing out of their belongings they hadn't quarrelled. The new flat in London required modern pieces and a minimalistic approach, not cottage-style furniture, so in the end she took very little apart from her books and personal items.

"What happened to the kitchen table and chairs?" she asks suddenly.

William straightens up and glances round. "They all went in the sale. Francis lets these cottages partly furnished and actually some of the furniture is very old and much better than anything we had. This oak table is nicer than our rather tatty pine, don't you think?"

She has to admit that it is but she feels a little pang at the thought of his parting so easily with things they'd chosen so happily together when they were starting out. He's looking at her as if he can guess her thoughts.

"Well, you didn't want it, did you?" he asks. "We agreed that anything surplus would go into the house clearance sale and we'd share the proceeds."

This is perfectly true: she walked away from it all uncaringly — why should he be expected to cherish the things she rejected?

"No, no, I know. It was just seeing a few familiar bits and pieces. Takes me back."

She smiles at him, wanting to establish a rapport, a sentimental link to their past, but he remains wary.

"Francis let me store some things in the house," he says. "I'm not sure you'd want any of it. Mostly it's Andy's stuff. Books and toys. You know the kind of thing. I thought they'd be nice to pass on if he had kids of his own."

"And now he has," she says lightly. "It was good of you to think of that, Wills. I suppose, knowing you as I do, that I just assumed you'd do all the right things."

She means it, too. He's a good man and his instincts will always lead him to do what's best for the people he loves.

"Unlike me," she adds, grinning at him, "who only ever thinks of Number One. It's all about me, me, me."

"That's not true," he says, laughing too. "At least, not all the time. Although now you're here you might like to look at a few of the things I saved. If anything happens to Francis and I have to lift and shift then I shall need to make a few quick decisions."

The laughter fades from her face and she frowns. "How do you mean? Would you have to leave Brockscombe?"

"Oh, yes. The boys would certainly sell it. Neither of them has any feeling for the place and it's too big to keep as a kind of family holiday cottage. They'll sell."

"But where would you go, Wills?" She's really upset at the thought of his having to find a new home. "You love it here."

He makes a little face, shrugs. "It was always on the cards. I do love it here, especially with Charlotte and Oliver next door, and Kat. It's been a lifesaver for me but I always knew the score."

She feels herself colouring, flushing with the shame of her own selfishness.

"I suppose I wasn't thinking straight," she says. "I never did quite know what the relationship is between Cousin Francis and you but I assumed that you'd probably have certain rights and privileges, if you see what I mean."

"It would be crazy to give anyone rights over one cottage in such a big complex. It would certainly affect the value of the place. No, no, I knew it wouldn't be for ever. Anyway, let's not worry about that now. It's not your problem."

And this is true, she tells herself. She has no right to query it or make suggestions. At the same time it throws a new kind of slant on the future and she decides that she needs to think about this very carefully.

William watches her disappear to see Oliver and Charlotte and wonders why he didn't mention Andy's leave. He's discussed his idea that Fiona should be offered his spare room for a night or two with both Charlotte and Kat with positive results.

"Well, she'll definitely want to see him," Charlotte agreed, "though, if you don't mind I'd rather it was the last weekend than the first. The first is always a bit strange, getting used to each other again, and I'd want some privacy with Andy and Oliver. But the last weekend is emotional, knowing he's going and all of that, so having people around can be quite good."

William understood that. "If you're certain," he said. "You and Andy and Oliver are the important ones here."

"I'll leave you to arrange it with her," Charlotte said, "but stay firm about the second weekend."

He promised he would and later he mentioned it to Kat.

"Much nicer for Fiona to be here than at the pub," Kat said at once. "It's always difficult to know when you can turn up when you're not on the spot and it's nice to have your own space to disappear into when you feel like it. Of course she'll want to see Andy — we all do — but Charlotte and Ollie come first. It'll be bad enough for them to have us around at all, I should think. We need to be very tactful. I can see Charlotte's point about it being the last weekend for Fiona. I'm sure she'll understand that."

"You seemed to be getting on better with her last time she was here," he ventured.

"I know." Kat looked puzzled, thinking it out. "I think we very slightly demonized her after she left. We cast her in the role of the wicked witch, didn't we? I'm not making excuses for her or anything but I think the more we did it the more she reacted to it, so that it became a self-fulfilling prophecy. That last time, when I met her at the pub when I was with Jerry, I saw her as the old Fiona, the one we used to know and love, and everything slipped back into focus."

William wasn't sure how to respond. He still felt bitter and hurt when he thought about Sam, and how Fiona had behaved, but what Kat said was true: his anger had eroded any love and kindness between them until only dislike was left. It had been so hard at those family events to present a jolly, smiling exterior, to pretend that he and Fiona were still good friends, but it was necessary for Andy's sake.

Then, this last time, it was as if something that had been painfully out of joint suddenly slipped back into place. He was able to be friendly to her and, in turn, she was able to respond so that a small miracle occurred. It was so good, so important to him, that he was unable to broach the subject of his invitation to her to stay during Andy's leave whilst she sat here in the kitchen. He was afraid that she might question him: "Why now? What's changed?" And how would he answer?

He knows it's foolish but he didn't want to risk this new *entente cordiale*, but now he regrets his pathetic timidity. As soon as he is alone with her again, he tells himself, he will ask her if she would like to stay for a night or two during the special occasion of Andy's leave — and beyond that he refuses to think.

"Did William tell you his plan?" Charlotte is asking Fiona as they watch Oliver lying on his rug, kicking his legs.

She sees by Fiona's blank expression that she's jumped the gun, but, after all, it doesn't really matter which of them invites Fiona and she's been so much nicer just lately; less prickly and sarcastic.

"Andy's got a week's leave next month and we were wondering if you'd like to come down for the last weekend of it," she says. "William thought you might like to stay with him and Aunt Kat so as to get in a bit more quality time rather than dashing between here and the pub."

Fiona's face first shows surprise, and then such delight that Charlotte almost feels embarrassed.

"Just a night or two," she mumbles, "but not the first weekend, if you don't mind."

Fiona shakes her head quickly. "No, of course not. I quite see that you want to be on your own, the three of you. I'd love to, of course I would."

"William was going to ask you. It was his idea. Better pretend I haven't put my foot in it. He's planning a barbecue for Saturday night for everyone."

Fiona laughs. "Perhaps he's changed his mind about asking me. I wouldn't blame him. But I'll come anyway, if I may, and stay at the pub as usual. Thanks, Charlotte. I really appreciate you inviting me. It's such a short time and you haven't seen Andy for ages."

"Well, neither have you."

They sit together for a moment in silence, staring down at Oliver, who is trying to roll himself over. Charlotte realizes that being a mother has very slightly changed her attitude towards Fiona. She feels less defensive of her position as Andy's wife. This new relaxation within her appears to have struck a chord with Fiona, who seems less determined to fight her corner. Charlotte is almost tempted to tell Fiona how lonely she gets; how difficult, sometimes, it is becoming to remember Andy properly, and that she actually feels quite nervous about seeing him again. It is impossible, however, to frame the words and a part of her shrinks from discussing their intimate and private life with his mother.

"He'll be crawling soon," observes Fiona, leaning to tickle Oliver with one of his soft toys. "Then you'll really have to watch out. He'll be into everything and you won't have a moment's peace. Have you got a playpen?"

Charlotte shakes her head. "Not yet. But I think you're right. Even now, when he's on his front, he can inch his way along like a little seal."

"Perhaps," says Fiona tentatively, "I could buy you one for him. I'd like to do that. We could go off after lunch and have a look for one."

Charlotte is about to say that she'd probably buy one online when she realizes that Fiona would enjoy a little expedition with them both, choosing Oliver's playpen.

"Thanks," she says. "That would be fun."

To her surprise she even believes it.

CHAPTER
TWENTY-EIGHT

Francis waits and watches. He watches Will and Fiona at the Friday night barbecue; he sees Kat sitting on the bench listening to Charlotte, though her expression shows that mentally she is elsewhere, and Charlotte's face as she looks at them all with a trepidation that indicates her anxiety at the prospect of leaving them. Most of all he watches Tim.

He notices how, when Tim has received his blessing at the Mass, he sits down and relaxes; his forearms resting on his thighs, wrists loose between his knees, his eyes closed. He looks totally at peace; he breathes deeply. Francis is more and more convinced that Tim's preoccupation is not simply to do with a tragedy that happened more than a quarter of a century ago and he wonders what it is that hounds him.

He remembers how they exchanged secrets but he guesses that Tim, too, withheld something. Francis is waiting for the right moment to offer his own last secret as a gesture to free Tim from the load he carries. He suspects how it might be done but still he waits.

His opportunity comes after a morning at Buckfast when they arrive home at Brockscombe and Tim is preparing to help him back to his quarters. Francis pauses to stand in the sunshine, watching the house martins swooping in to feed their young in the nests beneath the eaves, and to inhale the heady scent of the sweet williams in the wooden tubs. Nobody is around.

"Do you know," he says, putting a hand on Tim's arm as he takes the wheelchair from the back of the car, "I have such a longing to see Pan one more time. I can't walk that far but how do you feel about attempting it with the wheelchair? It's rough going but I think we might make it."

Tim looks pleased at the idea.

"It'll shake you around a bit," he warns, "but if you're up for it I certainly am."

"Good man," says Francis contentedly. He casts his stick aside and settles himself in the chair.

He wants to be away and out of sight before either Kat or Charlotte comes driving in and offers to accompany them. William is at the office so he has no fear of his arriving. Francis clasps his hands tightly together, praying for guidance and wisdom, and, crucially, that his instincts are reliable. Soon, however, he is overcome by the glory of the day and the splendour of the woods around him. He sees the blue flash of a jay and hears his harsh call; rabbits lollop in and out of the undergrowth, pausing to sit and stare before dashing off with a kick of their hind legs and a scatter of earth. Rhododendrons tall as trees are in flower, pink and white and purple, and, deep in the shadows, the delicate silver birch trees are pale and elegant as ghosts.

226

Tim wheels the chair carefully over the mossy paths and stops beside the little statue. Honeysuckle is draped around Pan's neck and wild roses are thrust between his fingers. On the plinth, beside his small stone toes, a wrapped sweet is lying. Francis stares at it, his heart beating faster, memories jostling and moving him almost to tears. Tim steps forward and picks up the sweet. He examines it, turns it over, passes it to Francis and then wheels him to the wooden seat.

"So who is it," he asks, "who garlands Pan and leaves him chocolates?"

He sits down on the bench and looks at Francis, who sits at an angle beside him so that Tim can see his face. Francis holds the sweet in his fingers and looks back at him.

"It is my son," he answers.

Clearly this is not an answer Tim is expecting and he gives a little start of shock. His brows come together in a frown of disbelief. Francis can almost see him doing the sums in his head.

"Your *son?* But your sons are grown up. They live abroad. Or is there . . .?"

"I have another son. I told you I had an illegitimate child."

"But you said that that was in the early days of your marriage."

"Yes," says Francis. "It was. Maxie is in his late fifties but he has never progressed beyond the mental age of a six- or seven-year-old. Now that his mother is dead he lives at a special home in Exeter and one weekend each month he stays with the couple who look after me. He loves these woods."

Tim stares at him. Instinctively he reaches out his hand and Francis takes it gratefully. It feels strong and warm in his thin, cold one.

"I am so sorry." Tim shakes his head as if knowing no words will be adequate, and tightens his grip. "I brought him a toy car and left it on the arm of the seat."

Francis smiles. "He showed it to me. He was so happy. He said he'd made a smiley face out of stones and cones, and that you'd changed it. He thought it was so funny. He drew it on a piece of paper for me so that I could see."

Tim bites his lips. "It was gone the next time I came back but he left me a sweet like this one as if to thank me for the car."

Francis can see the tears in Tim's eyes and prays silently that this is the moment; that now Tim will speak.

"It was very kind of you," he says gently. "Maxie is a loving person. It gave him great pleasure. He might not live much longer . . ."

Tim's clutch tightens in a kind of spasm and he looks anguished.

"Very few people know about Maxie," Francis goes on steadily, "but I want you to know. I want there to be no secrets between us. You have become very dear to me, Tim."

"I have this disease." Tim speaks quickly as though he is afraid he might lose courage. "It's like MND. It

228

attacks the muscles and then at the end you can't breathe. I don't want anyone to know because then people change towards you. Nothing's normal any more once they know. You get this terrible pity . . ."

So this is it: this is the terror with which Tim lives. His grasp is so tight that Francis feels his bones are being crushed but he makes no move.

"Is that why you came to Brockscombe?"

"Yes. It had been diagnosed but it's a very rare strain and they couldn't quite say how long I might have to live a normal independent life. My grandmother died last year and left me her house in Fulham so I sold it and invested the money and decided to go somewhere where nobody knew me."

"Mattie knows you."

Tim takes a breath and his grip loosens. "Mattie brought me here, yes, but it was far away enough from all my friends for me to feel free."

"She doesn't know?"

Tim shakes his head impatiently. "Can't you see? It would ruin everything. I love her. And she loves me, but we can't . . . I mean, how could we? And don't tell me that medical research is always finding cures. They've asked me to be a guinea pig in some new drug trials but it's so risky. Nobody knows about the side effects and all that stuff. I'm thinking about it."

"So what is your plan?"

Tim is silent for a moment. "I told you I related to those poems of Gerard Manley Hopkins, didn't I? I can relate to his despair. I've made up my mind to end it before it ends me. It's easy enough to do. Not here, of course. I have a plan . . . it's just a case of when."

Francis is filled with horror but he keeps very calm, still holding Tim's hand. Birdsong echoes above them in the canopy; leaves rustle and stir in a current of warm air.

"If you've read his poetry then you might remember these lines of his." Francis pauses, recalling them accurately before he speaks.

I'll . . .
Not untwist . . . these last strands of man
In me or, most weary, cry *I can no more*. I can;
Can something, hope, wish day come, not choose
    not to be.

"'Not choose not to be.'" Tim smiles bleakly at him. "But imagine the waiting all alone for it to come and get you and destroy you and crush you to death."

"You're not alone. You should tell Mattie and give her the choice."

Tim stares at him, shakes his head. "No, no. You're wrong. I couldn't bear it, you see. To see her face change. All that love turning to pity and then fear. What could she say? You won't tell her, will you?"

"Of course not. I shall tell no one."

"And I won't tell anyone about Maxie. Thank you, Francis. I thought it was a child, you see. The child I used to be once. All very fanciful. Did your wife know about him?"

"Oh, no. Liz knew nothing about Nell or Maxie. When Liz died Nell was already a widow and she came to see me, to bring Maxie. We'd lost touch, you see, after Nell married. I arranged a trust for Maxie and then it seemed easier, best for everyone, to stay out of her life with Bill and their new baby." He pauses, as if deciding whether to say something else, but then goes on: "I had no idea about Maxie's lack of progression. It was a terrible shock. I felt, still feel, unbearably guilty. Nell's husband had been so good with Maxie, so understanding, but Maxie should have been my responsibility. He was so happy here. Brack was alive then and he loved playing with him. We agreed, Nell and I, that the secret should still be kept and that I was to be her cousin Francis. We had just a few years together and then Nell died. Rob and Stella agreed to have Maxie to stay on his weekends out. Sometimes he has temper tantrums and I'm too feeble, now, to deal with him. Maxie's very fond of them and Rob's wonderful with him. Maxie's a loving person. A happy person. I try to comfort myself with the fact that, given the choice, he would 'not choose not to be.'"

"I can see why he's so happy here. So am I."

"And will you really go one day, Tim? Just disappear? Without telling us?"

"What else can I do?" Tim looks bleak. "What would you do? Wait until you were helpless and dependent with no family to support you? How can I possibly put such a responsibility on to Mattie?"

Francis sits in silence. He can't promise to be there for Tim: his life is nearly at its end. He lifts the moment

231

up in prayer so that it might be taken out of his hands and limited wisdom.

"Take me back, Tim," he says. "It's been so good to come here again. Forgive me for intruding on your privacy. We old men think we know everything whilst in truth we know nothing. Thank you for being honest with me."

Tim stands up and turns the chair and they go back along the paths together in silence.

Tim pushes the chair carefully, trying to avoid stones and ruts, but it is impossible not to jolt Francis, who steels himself against the rocky ride. It has in one sense been a huge relief to speak out, to tell the truth to someone whom he knows he can trust. At the same time he feels weakened, as if he has allowed himself to give in to something that might now overpower him. Yet, as he looks down at the elderly man in the chair in front him, he thinks of Maxie and his heart is riven with compassion for Francis.

> I can;
> Can something, hope, wish day come, not choose
>   not to be.

He thinks of Hopkins' words and a longing seizes him to make them his own. Yet for what can he hope? A few months with Mattie, tied to him by loyalty and pity?

It's a relief when they reach the courtyard to find that Charlotte has arrived home and is getting Oliver out of the car. Wooster comes to greet them, tail waving.

"I saw Francis' stick lying on the ground," she says, "and wondered what might have happened."

"Tim's given me a little ride in the woods," Francis answers, leaning to pat Wooster.

His voice is quite cheerful, and Tim is relieved. If everyone can be normal for a few moments it will help him to regroup. Charlotte is telling them about her lunch with naval friends and their children.

"It's always good to be with people who are going through the same thing," she says. "People try to understand but you've got to be doing it to know what it's really like. I don't just mean people in my situation but anything: being bereaved, being terminally ill, having no money."

Tim can think of nothing to say and it is Francis who comes to his rescue.

"I wonder if I can be even more of a nuisance, Tim, and ask for a drink of water? It's so hot today, isn't it? Thank you," he adds as Tim gratefully hurries away to let himself into his cottage. "So where did you have lunch?" he hears Francis asking Charlotte, and he stands for a moment to gather himself while they talk.

He feels confused. A part of him dreads the thought of being alone, whilst another part feels quite incapable of holding a conversation with Charlotte, who might notice his distraction and question him. To his immense relief he hears a car engine and, peering through the window, he sees that Aunt Kat is arriving home. He knows what will happen now. This random meeting will

233

morph into a courtyard jolly: tea will be made and brought out into the sunshine and everyone will indulge in an hour of fellowship.

Tim knows that Aunt Kat and Oliver between them will keep everything light-hearted and easy, and he no longer has any fear of joining them. He finds a glass, fills it with water and carries it out to Francis.

"Oh, darling," cries Aunt Kat, just as he guessed she might, "surely we can do better than that? How about some tea? Francis? Charlotte? Would you like some?"

"I'd love some," says Charlotte, subsiding on to the bench with Oliver in her arms. "I'll put him in his buggy. Are you sure you can manage?"

"I think I might just cope," says Aunt Kat. She smiles at Tim, gives him a little wink, and his heart twists with such affection that it makes him feel weepy. "You'll stay, won't you, Francis?"

"Certainly I will," replies the old man. "Never refuse an offer of tea."

Tim pushes the wheelchair towards the benches, positions Francis beside the table, and then erects the umbrella so as to give him a little protection from the sun. He sees that Francis is watching him, and he knows that the old man feels guilty that he has forced the truth from him; fears that he has blundered in where angels fear to tread. Tim gives him a smile to reassure him.

"I'm glad you know," he says softly. "Really, I am."

And then Charlotte is joining them with Oliver, who cries out with the joy of seeing his favourite toy, Wooster flops down in the shade beside Francis, and

234

the tension evaporates. As he sits down next to Charlotte, Tim almost wants to laugh at the normality of the family scene — and suddenly another line of poetry runs in his head:

"For who plans suicide sitting in the sun?"

CHAPTER
TWENTY-NINE

After Kat has gone, Jerry clears up the lunch things and then goes to make the bed. He still is not used to these random acts of lovemaking; this ability to please himself and be responsible to nobody.

"What's your problem?" Kat asks, wrapping her arms around him. "Lock the front door and turn your phone off," and he is delighted to do as she says, though part of him imagines that he can still see Vee's face; her expression as she watches them together.

He goes into the sitting-room, opens a window and picks up the cushion from the floor. It is the cushion that precipitated the lovemaking. When his daughters visited the flat, one of them had come out of the little spare room with it in her hands.

"Where did you get this, Dad?" she asked. "I don't recognize it, do I?"

"It's sweet," said her sister. "I love the little dog. A bit kitsch for you, though, Dad?"

"It was a house-warming present," he said, "from Sandra."

He has no qualms in telling them. Sandra has made a big hit with the family. When he suggested that he'd like to host a lunch for them, and that a friend had offered her house and garden, they'd been enthusiastic. Probably they saw an opportunity to check out their father's "friend" but any suspicions they had would have been immediately set to rest. Sandra behaved impeccably. She helped Jerry prep the lunch he'd brought with him, suggested a few extra treats from her own cupboard as well as a cake she'd made just in case they stayed on until tea time. There was something familiar, rather comforting, about working with her in the big kitchen and he was unexpectedly aware of how much he missed feminine company and the daily round. Once the family arrived, and they'd all been introduced, she effaced herself, making certain that it was Jerry who was running the show; staying in the background but always available to help out. The grandchildren were delighted by the small bedroom full of toys and books and with the swing and the slide in the garden.

When his daughters expressed their pleasure at her kindness, Sandra merely said that her own grandchildren were regular visitors, that she loved having them and that it was great fun to be able to share the toys with Jerry's grandchildren. His daughters relaxed with her and by the end of the afternoon she was one of the party. At one point she even fetched some books and read to the two youngest children when they became overtired so as to give Jerry more freedom and time with his girls.

"What a nice woman, Dad," they said. "This has been such a lovely afternoon."

237

And afterwards, helping her to clear up, he tried to express his gratitude and to pass on his family's pleasure.

"It's difficult for a man on his own," Sandra said, "and I thought it would be nicer for you to see them all in a family setting. I can see why you don't want to keep a big place going just for occasional holidays so I'm very glad it worked out. It's different for me. Two of my sons live locally so I often have the children staying over so that their parents can work, and it makes it all worth it."

"Well, it was really kind of you," he said. "I can't thank you enough," and it seemed appropriate, even necessary, to kiss her cheek. She gave him a hug, quite a serious hug, and he felt a *frisson* of anxiety; he sensed her expectation. This little homely gathering had moved their relationship on to a slightly different level and all his natural caution sent out warnings to him.

To his huge relief her telephone began to ring and she went to answer it. By the time she returned he'd gathered up all his belongings and was ready to leave. He saw her disappointment but pretended to be occupied with getting his things out to the car. Then he drove away, torn with a conflict of emotions.

The cushion was still on the sofa when Kat turned up some days later after the family had left.

"Good grief," she said, picking it up. "What a ghastly thing. Oh!" Her expression of amused disdain froze into horror as she stared at him. "Oh, my God. Did one of your daughters give it to you? I am so sorry."

238

"No," he said, half laughing at her expression. "As a matter of fact they didn't."

He couldn't quite bring himself to mention Sandra but as he took the cushion from her she put her arms around him, and pulled him closely to her.

"I am such a horrid person," she murmured. "I don't mean to be. I just can't help it. You'll simply have to forgive me, darling. You will, won't you?"

He dropped the cushion and began to kiss her; he could feel her chuckling deep inside, which made him laugh, too.

Now, lovemaking over and Kat gone, he turns the cushion in his hands. He seems to be divided between the two women; between Kat and Sandra. Each appeals to different sides of his nature, but how is he to reconcile them? He makes as if to carry the cushion back to the spare room but some lingering memory of Sandra's kindness to his children, the familiarity and warmth of being in a family home again, causes him to hesitate.

He tosses the cushion back on to the sofa and goes to take a shower.

The tea party in the courtyard is still going on when William arrives home. He's glad to see them all, to have a diversion from his thoughts, from the phone call he received earlier from Fiona.

"Are you very busy?" she asked. "Can you spare just a quick moment?"

"Of course," he said, still looking at the columns of figures on his computer, though he pressed the "save" button. "What is it?"

"Well, something rather exciting has turned up and I'd like to talk to you about it."

William was silent: his brain darted to and fro, wondering where this was leading.

"That sounds mysterious," he said after a pause. "So what does 'exciting' mean exactly?"

"I can't tell you on the phone. I thought I might come down this weekend, actually, but I can't get away on Friday," she said casually. "I really do need to talk to you, Wills. Just you and me. Are you OK with that?"

"Yes," he agreed, wondering why he felt nervous. "I suppose so but I can't quite see all the need for this secrecy and silence stuff."

"Just trust me. I'll book myself in at the Cott. Perhaps I could buy you dinner?"

"Well . . . why not?"

"Try not to sound so keen." He could hear her laughing and he tried to pull himself together.

"I'd like that. Sorry, Fi, only I've got a client due and I'm just the least bit preoccupied."

"That's fine," she said at once. "I shouldn't have called you at the office but it's really quite important. Oh, and, Wills, just you and me. Tell the others it's a payback for the barbecues. You can invite them if it makes you feel better, but they won't come."

"How do you know that?" he asked, confused, and heard her laugh.

"Take my word for it."

He was irritated by this smug female response: as if he, a poor simple male, couldn't see what was so obvious to her.

"OK," he said abruptly. "I'll see you on Saturday. I'll be over seven-ish."

He switched off the phone and sat for some moments wondering what this exciting news could possibly be and then put it aside and got back to work.

Now, as he goes to greet his family, he still feels equivocal at the prospect of Fiona arriving quite so soon. He suspects that some emotional crisis is approaching, some change in the dynamic of their relationship, and he can't see how he should handle it.

"What did she mean," he asks Kat later, when they are alone, "that I could invite you all but you wouldn't come?"

Kat's amused, pitying look is almost as irritating as Fiona's remark.

"The fact that she's invited you to dinner at the Cott for the first time since you separated does rather indicate that she's looking forward to a tête-à-tête. To begin with she must know that it's very difficult for Charlotte. She'd have to find a babysitter and you know she only really trusts me and you. So if Charlotte can't go I think Fiona would guess that I wouldn't want to play gooseberry with the two of you and that I'd say that I've got a date with Jerry."

"What about Tim?"

"I don't think Tim would consider supper with Fiona and you and me a big night out. You could try it, of course."

"So why did she even mention it?" he asks irritably.

241

"Just in case you needed a reason to be having dinner with her. In case you didn't want to say that it's just you and her."

"But why take the risk? Any of you might have accepted."

"But we haven't. Charlotte said . . . well, see above. And I'm telling you why I'm refusing. Fiona took a gamble on it. But it's let you off the hook and nobody will be wondering how it went. Except me, of course, now you've told me the truth."

He shrugs: it's all too complicated.

"And have you got a date with Jerry?" he asks.

"I have now," she says.

CHAPTER
THIRTY

"He doesn't usually have dinner on his own with Fiona," Charlotte says to Aunt Kat. "Don't you think it's a bit odd?"

"Not really. I told you that she wanted to do a payback for the barbecues and various other meals she has when she visits us. But I've got a date with Jerry and you can't go because of Oliver, and I think William thought it was a bit churlish to refuse."

Charlotte pushes Oliver a little further along the river bank and then stops so that he can see the ducks. He gazes in silence at a small flotilla of mallards, swimming and diving and paddling in and out of the rushes, and Aunt Kat laughs at his expression. Charlotte watches him, full of protective love, anxious that nothing shall ever harm him; knowing that she is helpless. She feels vulnerable and out of control, which is so unlike her. During the last face-time with Andy it was as if she were talking to a stranger. No, not quite a stranger but a distant friend: someone she'd known quite well once but with whom she's been out of touch. This frightens her. And now William and Fiona seem to be reinstating their relationship. It's not that she doesn't want them to be friends — it would be nicer for Oliver if they are — it's just unsettling.

Aunt Kat is crouching by the buggy, pointing to the ducks and making quacking noises. Oliver chuckles, banging his fists on the bar in front of him, legs kicking.

"I think we can take it that he likes the ducks," she says, straightening up. "Though they don't quite look like the one he has in his bath. So, do you mind Fiona inviting William for dinner à deux at the Cott?"

"No." Charlotte shakes her head. "No, of course not. It's just out of character, isn't it? I know they put up a good exterior for Andy's sake but I've always been under the impression that it costs William rather a lot to sustain it."

"I think it does," answers Aunt Kat as they stroll on. "He was, after all, the injured party. We did discuss this recent approach. I told him that we'd got rather into the habit of treating Fiona as the baddie and she'd begun to live up to it. It would be good all round if the situation were a bit more normal."

"What's normal? Do you mean that they might get back together again?"

"How would you feel if they did?"

Charlotte tries to imagine it but can't find the words to explain her sense of feeling unsettled: out of her depth. It sounds so feeble.

"After all," Aunt Kat is saying, "socially it would make no difference. They've always kept up a good show for Andy's sake. Privately, I think there would still be problems unless Fiona is prepared to give up her job and move back."

"But is that likely?" asks Charlotte disbelievingly. "I mean, that was the whole point, wasn't it? Her taking that job. That's why everything fell apart in the first place. Do you really think Fiona would come back to live here with William?"

Aunt Kat stops to watch a racing eight shooting downstream: eight oars entering the water simultaneously, at precisely the same angle, in a rare and sustained moment of togetherness. The bow lifts from the water as the boat runs forward as though it is speeding across the water rather than through it.

"Beautiful," she says.

Her voice carries over the water and the cox turns his head very briefly to smile at her. Oliver watches, stretching his arms out as if to embrace the shivering reflections, the small boats at anchor, and the gulls that sweep above the fast-flowing tide.

Aunt Kat turns back to her, smiling at her.

"People don't really change," she says. "We adapt, grow — or not — but essentially we remain the same."

Somehow Charlotte feels comforted. They walk on together, pushing Oliver, discussing Mattie's new job at Exeter, and it is only much later that Charlotte realizes that Aunt Kat hasn't answered her question.

Mattie is so happy. She can't quite believe her luck: this job as a research assistant, her own little room — well, living-room, bedroom and shower-room on the campus — and Dartmoor only ten minutes' drive away. She could get there in her lunch-hour and be having a little picnic whilst everyone else is still queuing in the cafeteria. And just down the A38 is Brockscombe with Charlotte and Ollie — and, of course, Tim.

Her quarters aren't quite big enough to hold a party to celebrate her return but it doesn't really matter. Every day seems to be a celebration. Charlotte seems especially pleased to have her back. It's not like Charlotte to be quite so emotional and Mattie is touched by her sister's welcome. She guesses that it has quite a bit to do with Charlotte missing Andy, and getting a bit worked up about the prospect of his next posting, but even so, it's a very nice change to feel that she's appreciated.

Meanwhile, she's taking great care not to crowd Tim. She is certain that he's delighted that she's living so much closer but she needs to give him time to resolve whatever it is in his life that keeps him detached, wary. Her big terror is that he's still in love with someone who's dumped him, yet when they're together she can hardly believe that this is true.

She's trying to give him space but, knowing that he's near, it's so hard not to text him, phone him, make a plan. It's essential to play it cool while showing that she loves him, though she's not certain how it is to be done at such close range. It's lucky that she has Charlotte and Ollie as good reasons to visit Brockscombe, though there are times when she wishes that she and Tim could have more privacy.

It doesn't matter, she tells herself. We have all the time in the world.

She'll go to the gym and work out, have a shower and then maybe text Tim and make a plan for this

246

weekend: perhaps a walk on the moor. He could bring Wooster. Even as she thinks about it a text pings in. It's from Tim.

How about lunch on Saturday at Two Bridges?

Mattie gives a little whoop of delight. She texts back quickly.

Great. Could be there about midday.

She feels relieved, excited: something to look forward to and, more importantly, he has made the first move.

CHAPTER
THIRTY-ONE

Francis stands at his open window. A ghost of a moon is rising in the east above pale fields, ripe with barley, and he can hear the wavering call of an owl down in the copse. He looks out at the familiar landscape, across the carriage drive and the lawn, to the little sunken ha-ha, which divides the garden from the fields beyond, and he breathes in the warm, sweet air, scented with honeysuckle and meadowsweet.

He wonders who will stand here after he is gone, who will watch the changing of the seasons, who will see this valley shining in the sun, sodden with rain, transformed by snow. Who will look for the rabbits playing in the long grasses in the ditch or for the badger clumsily lumbering his way across the field? Even now, at ten o'clock, it isn't dark. The land is washed with a mysterious half-light and the cattle along the river's edge stand knee-deep in mist.

Francis knows that this summer is the last that he will see at Brockscombe: his last hurrah. He is aware of a sense of urgency, to tie up loose ends, to complete his work, yet he cannot quite see his way clear. At least he knows now that neither his boys nor their children will stay here after him.

As he gazes out into the night he thinks of the email from his eldest son, Roger: impossible to think that he is nearly at retirement age and Sebastian not so far behind.

Seb and I have the opportunity of a great investment, Dad. I know this sounds a bit pushy but how would you feel if we were to ask if we could raise a loan against Brockscombe? We'd be talking $400,000 to complete the deal. We could sort out all the nitty-gritty. I'm sending you a link so that you can see what it is we want to get hold of. I think you'll agree it's pretty spectacular. Let me know what you think.

Francis leans from the window and wonders how he will answer his son. Both boys have no doubt that they will inherit Brockscombe, that it will be divided equally between them, and they will certainly have a pretty sound knowledge of its value. He noticed that when Seb was here in February he walked around the grounds, studied the house and the cottages; Francis could almost see him taking notes.

"What about the tenants?" Seb asked. "Shorthold tenancies? Good. That's good."

There is no doubt in Francis' mind that once he is dead and buried Brockscombe will be up for sale and the tenants given notice to quit. Yet these people, William and Kat, Charlotte and her baby, Tim, are almost as dear to him as his own family. And then there is Maxie . . .

"I can't believe you've still got all those toys and books in the playroom, Dad," Seb said on that last visit.

"I didn't take you for a sentimentalist. Once Mum died I thought all that would be gone."

"I have great-grandchildren," Francis answered gently. "I might see them again one of these days."

Seb flushed. "The young are all so busy," he said briefly. "We rarely see them ourselves and it's a long haul to the UK with smalls. Though some of those toys have a rarity value, I shouldn't wonder. But, honestly, Dad, I know you love it here, and all that, but don't you think it's time to be a bit more responsible and move into a smaller, modern place where you can be looked after properly?"

"I'm looked after very well here," he answered, and smiled to himself. He could imagine Seb saying to Roger: "He's just as pig-headed as he ever was. No chance of our getting our hands on Brockscombe just yet."

He could imagine — and sympathize with — their impatience. They were neither of them young men any more: they wanted to retire and enjoy themselves, have a bit of extra money and their ageing father tidied away safely and comfortably. It would be a shock when they realized that there wasn't quite as much money as they'd calculated. Maxie must be cared for; his trust topped up.

Standing at the window, Francis thinks about Nell and those last few years they shared.

"I shall look after him," he promised. "You know I will. He is my son. My first-born."

They stood here at the window, whilst Maxie sat on the floor with some engines and railway track. Her eyes were full of tears.

"I'm glad we kept the toys," he said. "Liz would never throw anything away and the grandchildren loved them. Now Maxie will enjoy them, too."

He held her whilst she wept, kissed her, not knowing what to say. Maxie looked up at them curiously. He clambered up awkwardly and came to them, putting his arms about both of them.

"Mummy," he said. He stroked her head and smiled at her.

"Yes, darling," she said. "And this is Cousin Francis. Do you remember?"

Names had to be repeated several times to help him to grasp them.

"Francis," he said slowly, as if trying it out. "Francis," and then struck his own breast with his hand. "Maxie."

Francis smiled at him and touched his hair lightly. "Maxie."

He had Nell's blue eyes, and her sweet smile, and he was nearly as tall as Francis. They had three happy years together.

The eerie midsummer twilight is deepening into dusk and the moon hangs like a lamp above the bleached fields. Still Francis cannot bear to leave his vigil at the window. He is tired but will not sleep just yet. Pulling the chair a little closer to the open casement, he sinks into it. He can hear the owls hunting over the fields, and the drifting scent of the honeysuckle is all about him. Presently his head slips sideways and he begins to dream.

CHAPTER
THIRTY-TWO

It's the hottest June since records began. Too hot for Kat to do her practice holding the "barre" of the Rayburn so she does her exercises out on the patio instead, using the back of a garden chair. As she works she reruns in her head the meeting she had yesterday with Sandra in Totnes. Sitting, relaxing with her coffee, her mind elsewhere, she was suddenly aware of Sandra approaching. She was smiling, very confident, and without asking sat down in the chair opposite.

Kat was seized with a very childish anger, an indignation that this woman should invade her personal space without asking. It was a moment or two before she could smile back at her, though it was a questioning smile that required a reason for this interruption.

"It's such a treat, isn't it," Sandra began, "to sit in the sun and do nothing? Though I'm not much of a sun person, myself. My skin is so fair and delicate. Anyway, I rarely have the chance, I'm so very busy, but this weather is unusual, isn't it?"

Kat, considering the question too banal to require an answer, continued to look at her interrogatively.

"Let's hope it lasts till the holidays," Sandra continued. "It makes such a difference when you're looking after little ones. Though I don't believe you have that problem, do you? We had such fun when Jerry's family were down. I don't know if he told you?"

Kat was only just able to hide her little shock of surprise. She knew that his family had visited but had no idea that they'd met Sandra. She waited.

"Well, it's so difficult for him in that little flat so we agreed to give a party at my house. It was rather a success. They're lovely children and his girls are delightful. I don't know if you've met them? I think it's a relief for him to know that there's somewhere he can invite them in future."

Kat was only just managing to keep her composure. As Sandra intended, she was angry and hurt that Jerry had mentioned nothing about this party but, to be fair to him, she never encouraged him to talk about his family. She stared at Sandra with dislike, determined to remain cool and say nothing.

"Of course, I know how hard it is to be left on your own. I'm lucky that my family live locally so I have a lot of support but it must be hard for poor Jeremy to lose his wife and to have his family a long way off. I'm so glad I shall be able to help him out."

This time Kat can't resist, though she knows she'll regret it.

"I'm afraid I don't do domestic," she said. "Jerry and I have rather different interests to occupy us. But don't let me keep you sitting in the sun and burning your delicate, fair skin."

She stood up and walked away, still seething, regretting her rather childish remark, and somehow feeling that Sandra was the victor in that little encounter.

Now, as she towels herself down after her exercise, she still feels unreasonably hurt that Jerry never mentioned that he'd taken his family to Sandra's, nor suggested that Kat should meet them. But more importantly, Sandra's gesture puzzles her. This flinging down of the gauntlet indicates that Sandra is very serious about her relationship with Jerry. She's risking Kat telling him about it, being upset, even forcing him to take sides.

Kat throws down the towel and wanders inside. Her mobile begins to ring and she picks it up and looks at it: Miche.

"How are you, darling?" he asks. "And more importantly, when are you coming home?"

Home. Odd how the word wrenches her heart. She remembers Francis' words: "Home is where you live and work and have your being."

"Home?" she asks, trying to laugh.

"Yes, Irina, darling. Home to me and your friends and your work. Don't be foolish. So when? I shall need you very soon."

"I am thinking about it, Miche. Honestly, I am."

"Don't take too long."

He switches off and she stands for a long moment with the phone in her hand and then goes upstairs to shower and change.

When Fiona arrives in the bar just before half past seven she sees that William is already here, with a pint

254

on the bar in front of him, talking to Anton. It's a slight shock to see him so much at home. She feels the Cott is her territory and that meeting him here gives her a slight advantage. She forgets that this is William's local and he is better known here than she is. It also irritates her that he's ordered a pint without waiting to consult her as to what they would like to eat. It establishes further his confidence: his comfortableness.

"It'll be heaving later on," William says, kissing her cheek, "and it's so hot. Would you like to eat outside?"

She thinks about it quickly. It occurs to her that what she has to say to William might be better said outside at a quiet table rather than here in the busy bar amongst local people who know him and Brockscombe.

"That's a good idea. Let's decide what we're going to eat and then we can take our drinks outside. I see you're already organized. In that case I'll have my usual, Anton, please."

William smiles at her unrepentantly and hands her a menu. Presently they go out into the warm evening and climb the steps to the decking where it's cooler. There are several people here and she chooses a table at the far end and sits down. William sits opposite, looking around him and Fiona wonders whether it might be embarrassing for him if his friends should see them having dinner together after all the years apart. She decides she must stop feeling prickly and get him on side.

"This is nice," she says, and grins at him. "So the others couldn't come?"

His eyes wrinkle with reluctant amusement. "It was just as you foretold," he says lightly.

"You mean Charlotte didn't have a baby-sitter and Kat has a date?"

"Something like that. What a master of psychology you are, Fi. So, what's this new exciting plan?"

She is silent for a moment, assembling her thoughts, wondering how best to begin.

"It's about Brockscombe," she says, and sees his eyebrows shoot up. This is clearly not what he is expecting. She leans across the table. "Look, Wills," she says. "It's time to think of the future. You remember what you were saying last time about your cousin Francis not going to last much longer and then what would happen to you? You told me that his boys wouldn't hesitate to sell up round you so I've been thinking about it. Why not do it in your own time with plenty of opportunity to plan?"

William stares at her. "I could leave Brockscombe any time I choose," he says coolly. "I don't quite see your point."

"But you won't go, will you? Not until Kat goes, or Charlotte goes, or Francis dies. But supposing he had an offer that allowed him to sell with no immediate pressure to move until he'd found exactly the right place? That would be the same for all of you. Time to look around rather than staying there like sitting ducks waiting for those boys to give you notice to quit?"

William watches her, puzzled. "We all know the score," he says. "We could all leave at any time. None of us benefits from the sale of Brockscombe."

She frowns. "But surely it would be better for Francis? I can see that the thought of putting the house on the market is horrific for him. At the same time, if he has another stroke he might have to go into some kind of care. Supposing something happened to that woman who looks after him? He's too dependent, Wills. Surely you can see that? He doesn't do anything because he doesn't know what to do and he's too old and weak to take chances. Supposing he were to be given a cash offer with plenty of time to get himself organized, wouldn't that be a good thing?"

Their food arrives at the table and they both sit back. Fiona isn't very hungry but she smiles and says how good it looks and picks up her napkin.

"Can't you see, Wills," she says, when they are alone again, "that you'll be the one losing out here? Andy will almost certainly take the Washington posting and Kat will go back to London, with or without lover-boy."

William picks up his knife and fork. "And Tim?"

"Oh, Tim," says Fiona impatiently, dismissively. "Tim will go as quickly and easily as he came. I've no idea what his plans are but come the winter and the rain, and the long dreary dark evenings, Tim will be out of there before you know it. And that just leaves you."

"But it wasn't so long ago that you wanted to rent his cottage yourself."

"That's because I didn't know about Andy's posting or Kat's opportunity of a West End show."

"So who is this philanthropic entrepreneur who wants to buy Brockscombe on such attractive terms and what do you get out of it? Or is this all hypothesis?"

257

Fiona chooses her words carefully. "It's a friend of a client of mine. He's just sold an internet holiday business for a small fortune and would like to buy a property in Devon. His wife's a local girl and wants to come back to her roots, and he's looking for a little bit of a project. Their children are at various boarding schools so the property needs to have easy access to the M5 and a railway station."

"So you described Brockscombe to them?"

She can feel herself colouring up. "I said that it might, in the not-too-distant future, be coming on the market and they asked me where it was. They were driving down to see her family and did an outside recce."

"You mean they came and had a nosy round?"

"They simply drove past. Probably stopped in the lane and looked over the gate. You can see the house from all sorts of places if you drive in those lanes. They absolutely loved it and are prepared to make an offer assuming that inside is as good as out."

William eats a few forkfuls of his supper and then looks at her. "And what do you get out of it?"

Fiona puts down her fork and picks up her glass. "They've asked me if I'd be prepared to do any of the design work that might come up."

"And you said yes."

"Of course I said yes," she says impatiently. "What do you think? Can't you really see what an opportunity this is, Wills? Oh, yes, for me. But for Francis, too. And for you. If you knew that he was going to be somewhere safe, somewhere of his own choice that he liked, where you could still visit him, wouldn't that be better than everything being taken out of his hands because he's too ill to take decisions for himself?"

William is silent, and she can see that she's made her point; that he's actually considering it. It's a bit of a shock that he has no expectations from Cousin Francis; he's always been so attentive to the old man, popping over to see him from Ashburton, though he never encouraged her to go. Even so, she wants Wills out of there and somewhere she can visit him, and stay with him, once he's on his own again. She asked Kat what her plans were, whether she planned to return to London.

"I don't think I can resist it," Kat answered. "It's such an amazing offer. It's a bit like resurrection, like being born again. I thought I was past it, that my career was over, but Miche has made me believe I can do it."

"And Jerry?"

Kat looked anguished. "I want to keep Jerry, too. I'm hoping we can continue it all with some weekending and more prolonged visiting. I think I can make it work."

Now, Fiona watches William thoughtfully. Once Kat is gone and he is alone maybe they can find some new ground to build on. Like Kat, she thinks she can make it work this time round, keeping her job in London whilst having a base with William in Ashburton: an insurance against a lonely retirement.

Having my cake and eating it, she thinks, and she can't resist a secret chuckle.

William looks up at her as he pushes his plate aside.

"So," he says, "you want me to speak to Francis."

She shrugs. "I think he should make up his own mind. Naturally a valuation would have to be made but this fellow has got a pretty good idea of market prices and he's got cash. That's pretty rare, and Francis should be given the option. What has he got to lose? Why do you have a problem with it, Wills?"

He sits still, staring at his empty glass, thinking about it.

"I don't know," he says at last. "Because it would be the end of an era, I suppose. It's his home, and we've all been very happy there."

She leans forward. "I know all that but it's going to happen. Surely it's better to be in control? Better to jump than be pushed? Can you imagine what would happen if Francis dies? Estate Agents. People crashing in and out, coming round viewing. Strangers goggling all over it and those sons of his giving you notice and breathing down your neck. Tenants are bad news when you're wanting to sell. This man is a very decent guy. He'd give you space and respect. I think you owe it to Francis to tell him what's on the table."

William sighs. "I'm sure you're right. Very well, I'll tell him."

She sinks back, weak with relief. "Fantastic. Thanks, Wills."

He smiles at her. "What for? I'm delighted to know that you have Francis' and my welfare so much at heart."

She decides to ignore his irony and smiles back at him. "So what about another drink? Or a pudding? My treat, remember."

"I won't, thanks. I'll be getting off. Thanks for my supper and I'll let you know Francis' reaction. Charlotte tells me she's invited us all to lunch tomorrow so I'll see you then. Thanks for supper. 'Night, Fi."

He goes out, across the decking and down the steps into the car park. Presently a car engine starts up and she hears him drive away. Just for a moment, as she stares after him, her victory seems to be a defeat.

CHAPTER
THIRTY-THREE

After Sunday lunch is over, Tim leaves them all and goes back to his cottage. He still on occasions feels very slightly an outsider and considers it only right that he should give the others some family time without him around.

He puts Jamie Cullum's *Interlude* on his CD player, stretches out on the sofa and thinks about his lunch yesterday with Mattie: how they'd sat in the sunshine laughing at the geese. She is so easy to be with, so undemanding.

"I'd suggest we go off afterwards and find a picnic spot," she said, "but a Saturday on Dartmoor in the middle of June would defeat even me, I think. The place is heaving."

So they stayed on after lunch, drinking tea, talking about her new job, whilst the minutes flew past. It seemed odd to know that she was now only an hour away and yet still be separated from her. He half wondered if she might suggest coming back to Brockscombe but she told him that she had an end-of-term departmental party later and that the next day she'd been invited to lunch by a colleague.

"Text me," he said in the end, rather lamely. "Let me know when we can meet up or if you're coming down."

He kissed her when they parted, and held her tightly, but all the while his secret lay between them and still he was unable to tell her the truth. He's promised himself that there will be a right moment, as there was with Francis, but each time they meet it becomes more difficult.

He lies on the sofa, with the door open so that he can hear the birds, and is seized with frustration at his cowardice. Abruptly he swings his legs off the seat and stands up, slips out of the front door and sets off for the woods. As usual he feels calmer here, less hopeless, and he begins to form a plan where he might tell Mattie the truth. The place and timing is so important: the words he must say to her.

As he approaches Pan, wondering if there will be flowers, he sees that William is there before him. He seems to be searching for something amongst the dead leaves and woodland detritus and, as Tim comes closer, he sees William pick up a small shiny object.

"Hello," he says, just behind him, and as William gives a little gasp of surprise Tim sees that the object is Maxie's toy car. Just for a moment he doesn't know what to say. William makes as if to conceal the car, then gives a little shrug, as if it doesn't matter that Tim sees, and Tim guesses that William knows that he has been told about Maxie.

William drops down on to the seat and Tim sits beside him. He hesitates, wondering if he should pretend ignorance, but the way that William turns the

263

car, brushing the mud away with one finger, leads Tim almost to suspect that he'd rather be open about it.

And, after all, he tells himself, because I know about Maxie's existence doesn't mean that I know anything more.

"I recognize it," he says, smiling. "I left it here as a present, though I didn't know then who was garlanding Pan with flowers or leaving pictures on the seat here."

"He loves it," William says, not looking at Tim. "He was on his way home when he discovered that he'd lost it. I said I'd come and look for it."

Tim smiles. "You know Maxie well, then?"

There is a little silence. William gives a sigh.

"Yes," he says. "I know him well. Maxie is my brother."

Tim twists on the bench to look at him. "But I thought . . . Your *brother*? Then Francis — "

"No, no," says William quickly. "I should have said my half-brother. Same mother, different fathers. Francis says that he's told you his part so you might as well know the whole truth. My mother and Francis had an affair just after Francis was first married. She became pregnant with Maxie and went with her mother to stay with a relative in Tavistock. A few years later she met my father and they got married. I was born. It was some while before they realized that Maxie wasn't developing as he should. He was eight or nine and I was three years younger, and we'd just got back from a foreign station and started new schools. My father was in the navy and not long after I was born he was posted to Singapore. We all went with him and that is when it

264

was decided that any connection with Francis should be cut. He set up a trust for Maxie and didn't see him again until his wife and my father had died. That's when my mother told me. She insisted that nobody should ever know that Francis was Maxie's father and she made me promise not to tell. Kat knows, though. Her mother and my father were brother and sister and we spent a lot of our childhood holidays together. When she came back from America I knew that it would be difficult to explain why I'd moved here and why Maxie spends so much time with Francis, now that our mother is dead, so I told her the truth. Not even Andy or Charlotte knows. I was surprised that Francis told you but he said he had his reasons."

There is a silence.

"I was very touched by his confidence," Tim says at last. "It was an exchange, you might say."

"Well, there it is," says William. He sounds tired, defeated. "You've been kind to Maxie. Thank you for that."

"When I saw the flowers, and the faces made out of stones and cones on the arm of the seat, I thought it was a child. I'd been remembering my own childhood. Through a stupid act on my part, when I was four, my mother died and I've never really got over it. Being here has helped me. I don't talk about it generally but I did tell Francis."

He knows that he is cheating; that it is not the whole truth that he's told Francis. Yet some instinct tells him that before he tells anyone else that final truth he must tell Mattie.

"I'm so sorry," William is saying. "So very sorry. I'm glad that you've found some kind of solace here." He hesitates, as if he is about to ask a question, and then seems to think better of it. "Thank you for telling me."

An awkwardness falls between them, which Tim does not know how to smooth over.

"I found the dogs' graveyard," he says. "There's a grave there, Brack's grave, which caught my attention. I had a dog just like Brack when I was a child."

William smiles reminiscently. "Maxie loved that little dog. It was so good for him to come here and play in the woods. He was really free for the first time. Rob keeps an eye on him and Stella is lovely with him. Neither of them knows the truth, only that he and I and my mother are Francis' close relations. It will be very sad . . ."

He stops, looking around him, and once again Tim senses defeat and sorrow.

"Very sad . . . ?"

William gives a little shrug. "When Francis dies. Maxie will miss him. He doesn't have a very long life expectancy and any change will be hard for him."

"I suppose, if Francis were to die, then Brockscombe would be sold?" Tim hasn't thought about this before, absorbed as he has been with his own problems. He feels oddly frightened. He's assumed that he is safe here until he chooses to make his move, and suddenly he feels very vulnerable.

"Yes, it would be sold. Neither of his sons will want it." William glances at Tim, frowning, as if he is

266

concerned for the younger man, and then asks the question. "What would you do, Tim, if that happened?"

Tim shakes his head. "Strange though it might seem, I haven't thought about it. I've just felt so secure, so much at peace here, that I hadn't considered living anywhere else."

This at least is true. His plan has always been that he should pick his moment to leave and then make an end to it all.

"I think we've all felt that," William is saying, "but I wonder if we should begin to consider alternatives. Just to be on the safe side."

It sounds like a warning and, remembering how frail Francis is, Tim thinks a very sensible one. William stands up, pocketing the car, and smiles down at him reassuringly.

"No need to start packing yet," he says. "Just give it some thought. Nobody will be going anywhere until after Andy's leave."

He turns and walks away, leaving Tim sitting on the seat.

William walks through the grounds and the garden, lets himself into the house and runs up the stairs. He calls out, to give Francis warning, and when he opens the study door the old man is sitting at his desk and smiling at him.

"Come in, William," he says cheerfully. "Have you found it?"

William takes the car from his pocket, places it on his desk and wanders over to the window.

"Well done," Francis says. "He'll be so pleased. Rob's taking him back but I'll text him so that Maxie knows. Is there anything wrong, my boy? I thought you seemed a little *distrait* this morning when you popped in."

William digs his hands into his pockets and stares out across the carriage drive, across the lawn and the ha-ha, to the fields and the woods. He feels sad and cross and impotent. He hadn't meant to talk to Tim about Francis' death and what would happen afterwards but it had been such a relief to speak out about Maxie and his relationship with him that he'd been slightly weakened by it. It was so important to his mother that the secret was kept for her own and Francis' sake. It was a shock when she told him: he'd always believed that Maxie was his brother, his father's son. Then, when his father died, his mother told him the truth, explained why it would be good for both Maxie and Francis to have some kind of relationship at last, but that there must be absolute secrecy. His sons, she said, must never know. William saw that it was important for her too and agreed to it for her sake. Francis' wife was already dead and for a few years there was a kind of family life between them. To begin with he was angry with Francis that he'd allowed her to bear the pregnancy and Maxie's birth alone, but gradually he grew fond of the old man. Francis was able to do a great deal for Maxie and it was clear that he suffered, and continued to suffer, great guilt about his behaviour.

Gradually a pattern emerged. It was easier not to talk too much about Maxie so as to keep up the fiction that

268

he and Maxie were closely related to Francis. Sometimes he wished he didn't know the truth and wondered why his mother had found it necessary to tell him. It was as if, at the end, she needed to share her burden and tell the truth, as well as making certain that some kind of relationship between Maxie and Francis could continue after her death.

"William?" Francis' voice is concerned. "What is it, William?"

He takes a deep breath and, still staring out of the window, begins to tell Francis about Fiona's plan. When he's finished there is a long silence and he turns round to look at the old man. Francis sits quite still, staring before him, and William has a sudden terror that he might have another stroke. As he starts forward, Francis smiles at him.

"What a redoubtable woman Fiona is," he says, amused. "No wonder she's made such a success. She's a senior partner now, didn't you tell me?" He takes a deep breath. "Well, I'd be a fool not to consider it, wouldn't I?"

"I don't know," says William unhappily, "but I couldn't not tell you."

"Of course you couldn't. And it obviously has great merit. To be able to wind everything up in a calm and civilized way; to make plans. What would you do, William, if I were to sell Brockscombe?"

William sits down in one of the chairs and looks at Francis. Since his conversation with Fiona he's been giving it a great deal of thought.

"I'd look for a house in or near Ashburton. Somewhere I could have Maxie to visit on his weekends out. He's happy with Rob and Stella, and it seemed silly to disrupt that routine when I moved to Brockscombe when I could see him so easily by coming over here, but I should like to have a home for Maxie to come to. And you, too, Francis. It isn't impossible to buy a place with an annexe where you could have your own quarters, with facilities for a wheelchair."

He stops, feeling foolish, wondering whether Francis would consider such an option, but he can see that the old fellow is touched by the offer.

"That is amazingly generous of you, William," Francis says. "Much more than I would have ever dared to suggest or hope for."

My mother loved you, William wants to say, and Maxie loves you. We'd be a kind of family . . . But he says nothing.

"May I think about it?" Francis asks. "It would be such a wrench to leave Brockscombe that I can hardly imagine it."

"Of course," mumbles William. "Just throwing a few ideas about. So what shall I say to Fiona?"

Francis smiles. "Tell her that I'm grateful for her interest and her care and that I'm certainly considering the offer."

William feels rather like a traitor, as if he is somehow forcing Francis out of Brockscombe.

"I couldn't not tell you," he repeats wretchedly.

Francis shakes his head. "I think that this might be an answer to several problems. Please don't feel badly,

William, because you've been the one to deliver the message. Do you think that you could make us some tea?"

William gets up feeling grateful to have something to do, to have a moment to pull himself together, and when he returns with the tray Francis is standing by the window. He turns and walks carefully, with the aid of his stick, to the armchair.

"What a blessing you've been to me, William," he says. "I can't imagine managing without you, now."

William is silent. He feels embarrassed. Francis has always been like this: unafraid of showing emotion, of being slightly dramatic. Perhaps, he thinks, it's to do with being a politician — or a Roman Catholic.

He pours the tea, passes Francis his cup and saucer. He doesn't want Francis to become maudlin, to talk about the past, so he casts about for a safe subject.

"We've been invited to sing at Dartington at the Summer School Music Festival," he says. "With other choirs, of course, and an orchestra. It's a very exciting prospect. It's difficult for us because we sing unaccompanied but we're prepared to give it a go."

Francis asks some questions about his singing group and William answers them, feeling relieved: the awkward moment has passed.

After William has gone, having first removed the tray and washed the tea things, Francis continues to sit alone, thinking about Fiona's bombshell. It is impossible to imagine leaving Brockscombe but he is deeply touched by William's offer. Unwillingly he imagines how it might be if he were unable to manage as he does now; if something were to happen that prevented Stella and Moira being at hand to look after him so that he was obliged to be moved out of his home and into the care of strangers. Suddenly he perfectly understands Tim's need to remain in control of his life — and of his death — and he feels ashamed at the way he tried to influence him.

All my life, thinks Francis, has been spent in trying to manipulate people, governments, policies; all my life I've believed that I've known best. Sitting up here trying to play God to the people around me, imagining that I know what is right for them. And now, having been presented with this offer, I still don't know what to do. Would William really want to live with an old cripple like me or is he just being loyal to his mother? And how would Maxie cope without these occasional weekends of perfect freedom, his visits to Pan and to Brack? And what of Tim?

Francis stands up, picks up his stick and walks slowly to the window. How terrible never to see this view again; never to look out on these familiar and beloved views. He wants to rail and weep but the cool hand of common sense touches his brain and he tries to thinks rationally. He remembers a phrase William used, quoting Fiona: "It's better to jump than to be pushed."

He straightens himself, putting aside sentimentality, reviewing the facts. It seems certain that Kat will return to London, to her work and her friends, and that Andy will be posted to Washington with Charlotte and Oliver to begin a new phase of their lives, and this is how it should be. And once they are gone, and if he, Francis, were to die suddenly or be taken into care, it would be better for William to be back amongst his friends in Ashburton than left alone whilst Brockscombe is sold up around him. Which leaves Tim.

Francis can see no way forward for Tim but he knows what to do. All through his life he has practised mindfulness: a focusing on something that is deeper and bigger than he is. He takes his breviary from his desk, settles himself and begins to read the office of compline.

CHAPTER
THIRTY-FOUR

On the day of Andy's homecoming Charlotte wakens early. For several days she has been preparing for him: the house is clean, special food is cooked, she's had her hair cut. She thinks about what she might wear but keeps changing her mind. It's hot enough for a pretty cotton frock but she's more comfortable in her jeans and it's important that she feels relaxed.

She sorts out some little denim dungarees for Oliver, a T-shirt, and his favourite sunhat, then has another look through her own wardrobe. She knows it's crazy — Andy won't mind what she's wearing — but she can't seem to help herself.

Confiding at last in Aunt Kat doesn't help either.

"I want to look nice for him," she says, "but casual, too, if you see what I mean."

"Oh, darling, it won't matter a bit," says Aunt Kat, true to form. "What ever you're wearing he'll simply be looking forward to taking it off as soon as he can."

Charlotte can't help laughing, though, if she's honest, this is one of the things she's worried about. It seems so long, well, five months, since they were together and she feels very nervous of any kind of intimacy. Perhaps if they'd been married for years it

274

might be different but it's still all rather new and she doesn't know quite how to handle it. The other wives have talked about it. Some say that the children help to normalize things very quickly; others say that it's a good idea to have a bottle of wine open and ready. They all joke about it but Charlotte knows that, in the end, you're on your own.

It would be easier, she thinks, if the ship were actually coming back: all the families down at the dockyard to welcome them home; the sense of achievement and celebration. It's rather different, this flying home just for a week's leave, arriving at Heathrow at ten o'clock, and catching the train that will get him into Totnes just after lunch.

She guesses that everyone will be embarrassingly tactful, keeping out of the way, giving them privacy, and she's beginning to dread the whole thing. Oliver remains delightfully normal, happy and placid, as she dresses him in his dungarees. He looks so sweet, so cute, that she picks him up and hugs him tightly, and has to resist the desire to burst into tears.

Andy sends a text to say that the train has left Exeter and Charlotte puts on her favourite dress — then takes it off again and pulls on her jeans and a shirt. At least this way she feels normal, calm, in charge of things. She picks Oliver up and carries him out to the car. Wooster follows, though she's been in two minds about leaving him at home because it's so hot. Now she decides that she will take him. He'll help to break the ice.

She locks up, climbs into the driving seat and drives slowly out of the courtyard and through the narrow lanes to the station. As she drives she talks to Oliver, and to Wooster, who sits staring out of the back window with his ears pricked as if he guesses something special is happening.

"Daddy's coming home," she says to Oliver, glancing at him in her driving mirror. "We're going to meet Daddy. We'll go for walks, won't we, Wooster? It's going to be fun."

With a thumping heart she parks the car in the station car park. She's early but this gives her time to prepare. She puts Oliver in his buggy, leaves the windows down a bit for Wooster but then, on second thoughts, she lets him out and puts him on his lead. His large comforting presence gives her courage.

Wheeling the buggy, Wooster beside her, she walks slowly through the gate and out on to the station. The voice on the Tannoy is announcing the arrival of the London train and now her heart is beating fit to suffocate her, her legs are trembling, and she holds on to the buggy so as to keep herself upright.

The train snakes round the bend and slows down; doors are flung open and the voice on the Tannoy is still speaking. People are stepping off the train, greeting friends and relatives, hurrying for taxis, and she stands back by the fence watching, looking for Andy amongst the crowds.

And suddenly he is here, coming towards her. He's beaming at them, at her and at Oliver, and at dear old Wooster, with delight and love and absolute confidence. His grin, his stride, his patent love for them, are all so dear and familiar that suddenly her terrors vanish like

276

mist in the sun. He greets her first, hauling her into his arms, saying, "God, it's great to see you, babe," kissing her, and then he's crouching by the buggy, gazing at Oliver, one hand stretched to Wooster, who can barely contain his joy.

As Charlotte watches them the pieces of their life together fall back into place and her anxieties retreat into the shadows. She wonders how she could have feared the future with him, wherever it might take them.

"I'm sure he recognizes me," Andy's saying, and she bursts out laughing.

"Of course he does," she says. "Wooster certainly does."

He puts an arm about her and they go slowly along the platform on their way out to the car and home to Brockscombe.

"I can't go back yet, darling," Kat is saying, after lunch in Jerry's flat. "Andy will only just have arrived and they need a little time to reacquaint with one another. It's tricky to know quite how to play it and poor Charlotte is very nervous. They haven't seen each other for months. 'Home is the sailor, home from the sea,' and all that stuff. Luckily, Oliver likes a nice long nap in the afternoon. The timing will be perfect."

She's keeping it all rather light and bright today. After her run-in with Sandra she doesn't know quite how to play things, and the sight of that cushion, left like a gauge of war flung down upon the sofa, has unsettled her.

"I suppose it could be quite odd, having your father and your aunt living next door," Jerry is saying thoughtfully, "but it won't be for long, will it? Didn't you say that he's being posted abroad?"

"To Washington in the autumn."

Kat would like to leave the table and go to sit on the sofa with him but the cushion is like a warning signal. "Keep Off" it says, and she feels unable to ignore it.

"And you'll be going to London?"

This direct question from him unnerves her further. She's skated round it, laughed about it, discussed the pros and cons, but now the moment has come and she can longer procrastinate.

"I think I shall," she says casually. "It's an offer I can't really refuse but I shall come back quite often. And you'll come up, won't you? We could have a lot of fun."

He smiles at her. "I'd like that."

He stands up to make coffee and she watches him. He's such a nice shape, such a sexy elegance in his old jeans and faded blue cotton shirt, and she feels suddenly terribly sad.

"So how will William feel about it all?" he asks. "You gone. His little family gone. Will he stay there?"

Kat is silent for a moment. William has told her all about Fiona's offer, and how Francis has responded, and this is also contributing to her sense of unease and sadness.

"What William would really like," she says, "is a flat or a small town house in Ashburton, so that he can walk to the office, walk to the pub and walk to his choir group. He'd have his chums in for supper. He's a very sociable chap, William. I don't think he should stay at Brockscombe — even if he could."

"What d'you mean, 'even if he could'?" Jerry puts the coffee pot on the table and sits down. "What would stop him?"

"If Francis dies it will all be sold. It's simply a question of time."

Melancholy overwhelms her: she is unable to keep up her cheerful façade. Jerry watches her compassionately. He stretches out his hand and holds her wrist but he doesn't speak. She knows, then, that he never will. He won't be the one to deal the blow. When the time comes he will simply let the inevitable happen; he will take the easiest and least painful course. But not now, she thinks. Not yet.

She stares at his hand; at the long fingers curled around her wrist.

"You know I don't feel much like coffee," she says, "and the sofa looks unfriendly. Shall we go to bed?"

She'll miss that look of his: that look of gratified, surprised pleasure. She'll miss his tenderness and strength and the fun of it all. He stands up, still holding her wrist, and she smiles at him.

"But remember," she says, "no rushing. We've got to give Charlotte and Andy plenty of time."

In the middle of the week of Andy's leave, Fiona throws caution to the wind and travels down a few days earlier than planned. She can't wait to see Andy.

After all, she tells herself, William and Kat are there, right next door. Why shouldn't I be around?

But she doesn't tell anyone she's coming and she won't ask to stay with William. She books herself in at the Cott, then texts William once she's settled in.

Having a drink in the bar. Come and join me on your way home.

He texts back saying he'll be half an hour and she beams with pleasure. Everything is going her way. First of all, Francis has agreed to consider an offer — though nothing must be mentioned to anyone until after Andy's leave — and secondly, the buyer's wife's mother knew Liz and remembers Brockscombe and is fulsome in her praise of it.

Fiona sips her little special cocktail and broods on the future. She can imagine William alone again, in a comfortable, accessible town house, where she can stay whilst she begins her work on Brockscombe. It will be just like old times. She knows that it's all come as a bit of a shock to William but she's certain that when he's got over it he'll be as excited as she is. This summer, the barbecues, these occasional visits, have been more fun than she's had for a long time and, though she'll miss Andy and Charlotte and Ollie, they'll be back again after two years with Andy probably based in Devonport and all of them living quite close. Meanwhile, she and William could fly out to visit them in Washington. She feels almost drunk with the prospect of it.

Yet when William arrives she can see that he isn't in the same happy mood. He orders a beer, carries it to the table and sits down, looking at her unsmilingly.

280

"I thought you weren't due until the weekend," he says.

"I know," she says, smiling winningly at him, "but I simply couldn't resist. I'm longing to see Andy. Be fair, Wills. You're all here having a great time together, why shouldn't I?"

"Because it's not quite like that," he answers. "We agreed we'd give them this week to themselves. I'm out all day at work and Kat is spending a lot of time with her friends. What will you be doing?"

She stares at him, her smile fading. He looks unfriendly, unwelcoming, and her heart sinks a little but she's determined to win him round.

"I don't plan to be a nuisance," she says, trying to look slightly hurt. "Anyway, I wanted to see you as much as Andy."

He raises his eyebrows. "Really? What about?"

She frowns. "Whatever is the matter with you, Wills? I wanted to ask how things are going. What plans Francis is making, for instance, and what you intend to do now that he's taking the offer so seriously."

"Ah, the offer," says William. "Well, yes, I think he'll go through with it if the price is right."

"And what about you?" She makes certain that she looks concerned for him, caring. "What will you do, Wills?"

He takes a pull at his pint, purses his lips as if he is struggling with some terrible dilemma, and for a moment she feels a flash of irritation with him, but she continues to watch him affectionately and he gives a little shrug.

"Well, I plan to buy a town house in Ashburton," he says.

She gives a silent sigh of relief. "That's a good idea," she says brightly. "I'm glad. I never thought you should have left the dear old Ashbucket. And will there be room for me to stay? While I'm working at Brockscombe?"

His look baffles her. If she didn't know him better she'd say it was a mix of contempt and pity with a dash of amusement.

"I expect we'll probably be able to fit you in," he says affably. "We'll have to see."

"We?" she repeats quickly. "Who's we?"

He looks at her quizzically, as if she's missed a trick.

"Why, me and Francis, of course," he says. "He's got to go somewhere, poor old fellow, and I wouldn't want him to be alone. We'll have to get something sorted out for his wheelchair and all that, of course. But perhaps you might be able to draw up the plans for that as well."

She ignores this little dig whilst she assembles the facts. This is a blow, but of course Francis won't last long and he'll be very generous . . .

"And then there's Maxie," William is saying.

"Maxie?" She frowns, puzzled. "Who on earth is Maxie?"

"You remember, surely? My elder brother, Maxie?"

She stares at him. "But I thought he was just a half or a step, wasn't he? And wasn't he disabled or something and lived in a home? You never encouraged me to visit him with you. I assumed he was dead."

282

"No, no. Not dead. Maxie still lives in a special needs home near Exeter. He has the mental age of six or seven but he's a lovely guy. Francis invites him to Brockscombe for his weekends out but now he'll have to come to me."

She stares at him, her plans slowly crumbling around her. "But why would you do that, Wills? Why make life so difficult for yourself when you could be enjoying yourself?"

He laughs at her. "Why indeed? But why should you think I won't be enjoying myself? I enjoy being with Francis and with Maxie. I enjoy singing and going to the pub with my friends."

"You know very well what I mean," she answers bitterly. "Don't try to be clever. It doesn't suit you."

"No, I know that. You've always made it clear, Fi, that you are the clever one. And yes, I very nearly did fall for it again but you've done me a favour. It is better to jump than to be pushed, and thanks to you I'm sorting out my future. And now," he glances at his watch, "I must be dashing. I'm baby-sitting Ollie whilst Charlotte and Andy go out to dinner." He swallows the last of his pint and stands up. "I'll leave it to you to let them know you're down. Meanwhile you're still welcome to stay at the weekend."

"I'll make my own arrangements, thanks," she answers angrily.

"Suit yourself. See you around."

He goes out and she continues to sit, consumed with rage and humiliation. She tries to see where it all went wrong but it's beyond her. William is impossible; he always was. She wants to scream and break things. Instead, however, she orders another drink and prepares for a long evening alone.

CHAPTER
THIRTY-FIVE

Tim drives slowly up on to the moor, remembering how he drove through that wild spring storm, stopping to phone Mattie to describe it to her. Now they text each other arranging odd, impromptu meetings, relishing these unplanned moments together. Today he is meeting her at the cave but this time he hasn't brought Wooster. Andy and Charlotte have taken Ollie to the beach and Wooster has gone with them.

"He loves a swim," says Andy, "and so do I. I pretend to drown and he tries to rescue me."

Tim likes Andy. It's good to have another bloke around of his own age. They've had a few little chats together and Tim is impressed by Andy's sense of responsibility for his little family, his anxiety lest something should happen to him whilst he is at sea, leaving them alone.

"But in the end, if you think like that, you'd never do anything, would you?" he said. "I could fall under a bus. You have to take risks sometimes."

As he spoke, Tim remembered his mother, the squeal of brakes, and wondered whether, if she'd known, she would never have had him. Now, he parks the car, takes out his rucksack and walks the narrow track over the

285

moor. Sheep huddle for shade under dry-stone walls and small thorn trees, and as he hears the lark winging up and up he thinks of Meredith's poem.

She is waiting for him at the mouth of the cave, sitting with her legs drawn up, arms hugging her knees. The sight of her causes his heart to give that now-familiar flutter and he drops down beside her, putting his rucksack against the rock.

"Can you hear the lark?" she asks, and he puts his arms around her and kisses her.

"I love it here," he says. "It's special, isn't it?"

She holds him a little way away from her, looking at him so searchingly, so anxiously, that he knows, at last, that this is when he must tell her. The moment has come: it is now.

His head is filled with the words that he must say to her but before he can speak she says: "I've got something to tell you. Something really important."

He is taken completely off balance and he can only gaze at her in surprise. She kneels up so that they are face to face and she holds him by his shoulders.

"I'm pregnant, Tim," she says. "I'm expecting our baby."

He is so shocked he can't speak. She still holds him, watching him.

"I'm not sorry," she says. "I can't be. But I'm sorry if you are."

"No," he cries. "No. I'm not sorry. I love you, Mattie. It's just . . ."

"Just what?" she asks, shaking him, gripping him. "Just what, Tim? Please tell me . . ."

And then he does tell her. He explains to her the nature of the disease, that it is a rare strain, and that nobody knows how long it might take to cripple him; to kill him. And all the while she grips his shoulders, staring into his eyes, listening intently. When he's finished she gives a huge sigh.

"And is that it?" she asks.

He looks at her and then begins, incredibly, to laugh. "Isn't that enough?"

She shakes her head quickly. "I'm sorry. Sorry, Tim. I didn't mean it like that. Yes, it's awful. Awful." For a moment she looks stricken but she rallies and reaches out for his hand. "It's just I thought you didn't love me."

He doesn't know what to say. "I couldn't ask you to . . . How could I?"

"But I want to be with you," she says. "And there's the baby. Our baby. You say you don't know how long you might have — well, it might be years. He'll need you. So will I."

"But that's the point," he cries. "Don't you see? I can't say how long it will be before I begin to be . . . useless. Helpless," he adds savagely.

"But we can be together for however long it is," she says.

"But you have no idea," he cries angrily, "no idea what it might involve."

"Neither have you," she says reasonably. "I just know I want to have our baby and be with you. Can we start there?"

He stares at her and he hears Francis' voice uttering Hopkins' words:

> I can;
> Can something, hope, wish day come, not choose
>   not to be.

Still kneeling up, face to face, she pulls him into her arms and rests her head against his shoulder.

"Yes," he says, and at last he is filled with peace. "We can. We'll start there."

As she drives back to Exeter Mattie is in a state of exaltation. Ever since she knew about the baby she's been in such a muddle of emotions: shock, wonder, fear. She can hardly believe it and yet, at some very deep level, she's not surprised. After that first unexpected, unprepared meeting in her cave it was a possibility, but it was as if she was in denial, keeping the thought of it at bay. She still doesn't know whether it was because subconsciously she wanted Tim's child or whether the prospect was too frightening to consider.

And now she has so much to think about. Never will she forget his face when she told him: shock, awe and a kind of odd hopefulness. Once he'd explained his own problem she could guess why he looked like that. He'd considered his life was slowly counting down, running out, and suddenly he was offered an arrow into the future: new life, his own child, something to live for.

All she'd thought about, as he was telling her, was that she wanted to give him this chance. She wanted to

288

be with him, support him. Only now does anxiety kick in; fear of the responsibility of it all. Back then they held each other tightly and after a few moments, knowing that they must now move forward, she leaned back and looked up at him.

"We need tea," she said firmly. "Come on. The hamper's all primed. I've got some biscuits. We'll have our own private little celebration."

To her surprise he was quite ready to join in with her mood. They'd toasted each other and the baby with camomile tea and a brownie, sitting close together on the rug in the sunshine whilst the lark sang and sang. Tim recited Meredith's poem to her.

> And ever winging up and up,
> Our valley is his golden cup.
> And he the wine which overflows
> To lift us with him as he goes . . .

"That's nice," she said, leaning against him. "Who did you say it was?"

"George Meredith."

"Mmm," she said thoughtfully. "I like the name George. We'll call the baby George. Georgina if it's a girl. Then we'll always remember this moment."

She knew that Tim was feeling very emotional and she also knew that she must keep him steady. She would deal with her own fears later.

"So how's it going with Charlotte and Andy?" she asked. "Second honeymoon stuff, is it? I can't wait to see them at the weekend."

"I like him," Tim said. "He's a really nice guy."

The conversation gradually became more general and a little later they were able to make a few plans, as if they were just an ordinary couple planning an ordinary future.

Now, Mattie allows her own anxieties to creep to the forefront of her mind. How will they manage? How long will Tim be strong, viable? What will her parents say when she tells them? And Charlotte? Her heart quails rather at the prospect but she grips the wheel, lifts her chin, and takes a very deep breath. Odd though it might be, it is her father she will talk to first when the time comes to explain about the baby, how that unexpected lovemaking in the cave took her by surprise and unprepared. She'll explain Tim's anxiety, his fears, and that, despite everything, she wants to have his child, to be with him. If she can get her father on side then somehow everything will be managed. But first: their engagement. She knows that her parents like Tim, and the fact that he can afford to buy a little house and keep something put by for the baby's future will be a good mark in his favour. Second: the baby. For the moment, she and Tim have agreed that this remains a secret between them for a few more weeks and she prays that she has the courage when the time comes to deal with the disclosure.

Mattie shivers with a thrill of joy: her baby. Hers and Tim's. She'll go with him to the hospital to talk about this new drug trialling; they'll find out everything there is to know. They'll do it together and — who knows — maybe a miracle will happen.

290

The sunlit, undulating moor flows away from her. Its impression of the infinite, its sheer size, puts these problems into perspective and brings tranquillity, and she drives on, comforted.

CHAPTER
THIRTY-SIX

This morning, all the tables outside Seeds 2 are full. Kat wanders inside, orders coffee and sits at a corner table. She hadn't meant to come into the town today. She had a date with a friend for lunch but the friend called it off, she isn't well, and Kat is at a loose end. Brockscombe feels unnaturally quiet with Andy and Charlotte and Ollie spending the day with her parents, Tim driving off, probably to see Mattie, and William at the office. So here she is, wondering whether to text Jerry, to tell him her date's cancelled and suggest he comes to join her. Perhaps they will discuss the future in more detail.

"Well, what are your plans?" Fiona asked her. "Will you go to London?"

Kat wasn't terribly surprised that Fiona had taken a chance and come down midweek to see Andy and the family. She arrived in the early evening and invited William for a drink and, when she phoned the next morning, Kat was unable to resist her plea.

"I'm in the doghouse, Kat," Fiona said. "Wills is cross with me. How about lunch? Any chance?"

Kat knew all about it. William had come home from the pub in a strop, furious with Fiona for arriving unannounced and for assuming that everyone was as delighted as she was about the sale of Brockscombe.

"It's none of her business," he fumed. "And she has no right to butt in on Andy's leave. We'd made the arrangements and it was all planned."

Kat watched him, wondering what was at the root of his anger.

"I expect she's been feeling like one of the family again," she ventured. "After all, there's been a bit of a change this summer, wouldn't you say?"

William stood at the open door staring out, his hands in his pockets jingling his loose change.

"I was a fool," he admitted at last. "I suppose I did, just for a while there, begin to think we might try again. It was crazy, of course."

"But when did you realize that?"

"When she came down unexpectedly before, and invited me for supper at the pub and told me about the offer on Brockscombe. I began to see that it's just the same old, same old. She'd want everything on her terms and I'd always be watching and waiting and wondering. She doesn't really give a damn about Francis or Tim. She just wants me there, available, and meanwhile she's got a very nice project redesigning Brockscombe, thank you very much."

"But you could say," Kat said cautiously, "that it might be exactly the right thing all round."

William snorted. "You think that makes me feel any better?"

When Fiona phoned the next morning, Kat agreed to meet her for lunch. She picked her up and drove her to Turtley Corn Mill, where they sat in the sun, watching the antics of the peahens and the pretty chickens.

"I cocked up," Fiona said gloomily. "I was so sure it was going well between me and Wills. What went wrong?"

"I think he felt that you were out of order, arranging to sell Brockscombe without asking first," answered Kat wryly.

"It wasn't like that," Fiona said crossly. "It just happened that this guy is looking for a place . . . Well, he clearly told you all about it?"

Kat nodded. "He did."

Fiona turned her glass of wine round and round, staring down at it. "I thought it would be right for everyone. Andy and Charlotte will be going to Washington, anyway, and William could buy a nice little house in Ashburton. He should never have left Ashburton. I could come down and stay with him . . ."

"And Tim?"

"Oh, well, Tim." Fiona shrugged. "Tim will be off whenever it suits him, you just wait and see."

"And Francis?"

Fiona was silent for a moment, then she made a face. "Well, I doubt he'll be around much longer, and I thought it would probably be better if he were in some kind of home with proper care than stuck in that old house with a couple of old women looking after him." She shook her head, baffled. "And then Wills tells me that he's going to take him to Ashburton with him along with that weird half-brother of his. I mean, why would he do that? I tell you, Kat, my plan for our future didn't include an old cripple and a halfwit."

"Honestly, Fiona . . . "

"Oh, I'm sorry. I'm sorry. But for God's sake, Kat . . . "

"And what about me?" asked Kat idly.

And that's when Fiona said: "Well, what are your plans? Will you be going back to London?"

Now, Kat sits watching the morning shoppers, people drinking coffee, knowing that she must make her decision. It's not much of a decision after all: she knows in her heart that she will go to London. The question is how it is to be organized; whether she will accept Miche's offer of a room in his house or get her own place where she can have Jerry to stay.

Even as she thinks about him she spots him through the plate-glass window. She feels the usual gut-twisting lurch of pleasure at seeing him and is making to rise, to wave to him, when she sees that he is not alone.

Sandra precedes him into the café. She looks happy, confident, glancing around and then greeting some friends at another table, who move bags and belongings so that she and Jerry can sit down. Kat watches them with a growing disbelief. Jerry has abandoned his jeans and his old cotton shirt and his rucksack. He wears smartly ironed chinos, with a short-sleeved polo shirt, and he is carrying bags of shopping. Sandra directs where they should be put and he obeys her with an anxiously smiling, almost uxorious, air. He looks domestic, even very slightly henpecked. They sit together in their foursome, one of them is showing a travel catalogue and, just for a moment, Kat remembers how it was at the Cott and she wishes that Fiona would come stalking in.

"Cruises and Saga holidays?" she'd probably cry. "Good grief, darling, whatever next?"

"We'll get together, won't we?" she said to Kat. "When you're back in London? We'll do some shows and have some fun. Promise?"

Kat finishes her coffee and stands up. The movement catches Jerry's eye and he stares at her almost in horror. Sandra is too busy with the catalogue to notice Jerry's distraction and Kat smiles at him. He gives her such an anguished look that Kat feels a flash of pity for him: he is afraid. This knowledge swamps her with jealousy, disappointment and even contempt, so that she has no desire to pause beside the table to make some clever quip.

She nods to him as if to say she understands, raises her hand in a kind of valediction, and slips away unnoticed by the others. Outside she stands for a moment, wondering where to go and what to do. Then she takes out her mobile phone and sends a text to Miche: quite a short text but he will understand it. Just two words: *Coming home.*

Jerry twists round to watch her go; that casually elegant walk in her old jeans and a loose white cotton shirt. His first reaction is huge relief that she hasn't stopped to make a wisecrack; his second is a piercing sense of loss, as if he has rejected something very precious that he will always regret.

296

It was such a shock to see her, he'd been unable to disguise his horror. She told him she was out with a friend for lunch so when Sandra asked if he would help her with the supermarket run he'd been happy enough to agree. Kat would never have asked him such a favour. A weekly shop was beyond her comprehension.

"But why would you do that?" she might ask. "I never know what I might want to eat for supper tonight, let alone in six days' time."

It would be a typical Kat remark: intended to make him laugh but with a big grain of truth in it. He'll miss that laughter. It's no good kidding himself: he saw her look at him with a kind of terrible pity and he recognized that farewell wave. There was a finality in it. The very fact that she hasn't stopped to make some comment to irritate Sandra shows that she's ceded the battle. The war is over.

He turns back to look at the catalogue, which is all about cruises in the Norwegian fjords, and tries to show an interest. Sandra smiles at him proprietorially; they are an item. He looks at her pretty, round, ordinary face and his heart twists with pain, but he smiles just the same.

He glances round again, hoping to glimpse Kat one more time, but she has gone.

All through the evening of Andy's party in the courtyard Tim is aware that something is missing. This has always been the plan — that they would gather for one of William's barbecues on the last Saturday of Andy's leave — and this time everyone is here. Yet as he

297

moves about amongst them, Tim feels a slightly different atmosphere from at those other gatherings. It's not just the knowledge that Andy will be leaving tomorrow — there's more to it than that: there are undercurrents of emotion, tensions beneath the surface gaiety.

Tim wonders how they would all react if he were to suddenly announce his and Mattie's engagement.

"I wish we could," she said when she arrived earlier, Charlotte having agreed that it would be better if Mattie could stay with Tim on this occasion. "But I think we should tell Mum and Dad first, don't you?"

He agreed with her but it would have been good to do it, with all these people he loves best gathered together. Now that the decision has been taken he wants everyone to know. Mattie and the baby have focused his thoughts away from himself and he feels as if he is free from a terrible weight that has shackled his mind to a treadmill of despair. At least, though, Mattie is making no attempt to hide the fact that she and Tim are in love. Her gestures, her glances, her outward shows of affection, all proclaim it and he allows himself to respond. Nobody comments but he can see by Charlotte's quizzically lifted brows she is aware of it. William seems rather too preoccupied with his cooking to take much notice. Aunt Kat just smiles at them both with approval — though she appears to be distracted, even sad — whilst deep in conversation with Fiona, who is being rather brittle and drinking quite a lot. Francis and Andy, sitting together talking quietly, seem to take it for granted and at one point, when Francis smilingly lifts his glass, Tim can't help beaming back at him.

Yet he is still conscious of something missing; something that has been present through this spring and early summer. Soon, he thinks, everything will change. Charlotte and Ollie will be off to Washington with Andy, and Wooster will go to Tavistock. Aunt Kat will go back to London. He and Mattie have decided to look for a small house or cottage on the edge of Exeter near the university. This leaves just William and Francis.

Watching William busy with the sausages and steaks, chatting to Mattie, Tim feels a sense of disloyalty, as if he is abandoning the people who have been so good to him.

"It was always on the cards," Mattie said consolingly, when he said this to her earlier. "We all knew Andy has been given a foreign posting, and it was only a matter of time before Aunt Kat went back to London."

"What will happen?" he asked. "Will they just get new tenants?"

"Probably." She smiled at him. "We could always stay here if it really worries you. It's only an hour's drive from Exeter."

But he shook his head. "You need to be close to the university. I'd hate to think of you driving up and down each day. No, I was just wondering what would happen here with everyone gone. We'll come and visit them. And William can bring Francis to see us. Anyway, it won't be quite yet. We've got to find somewhere to live first."

Although he feels excited at the prospect of this future that has suddenly expanded before him, Tim feels sad, too. He'll miss this small extended family, the walks to see Pan and Brack, the midweek Mass with Francis at Buckfast. And as he thinks of these last months here at Brockscombe, the cold, sweet spring and the warm summer days, he suddenly realizes what is missing. He can no longer hear the thrush singing in the ash tree. Tim experiences an odd and unexpectedly poignant sense of loss. The thrush has claimed his territory, attracted a mate, and now his fledglings have flown the nest and he, too, has gone.

CHAPTER
THIRTY-SEVEN

Francis stands at his window. It is high summer and in the newly harvested fields the gulls look as if they are floating on a pale golden sea. Nearer at hand, the mower stands idle on the lawn where Rob has abandoned it. Two canvas garden chairs have been put on to the gravel carriage drive, where they have fallen forward on their knees as if they are praying.

Soon, Brockscombe will be empty. Contracts have been exchanged and completion will take place within a few weeks, though there is no pressure being exerted. Francis feels quite calm: he is certain now that all will be well. His sons will be able to have the money for their retirement investment and his little family is preparing to move on. Charlotte and Oliver, with Wooster, are going to her parents in Tavistock until Andy arrives home from sea. Charlotte has lost her fear of going to Washington; Andy has restored her confidence and their love is renewed and confirmed. Kat will soon be leaving for London, excited by the prospect of the work that lies ahead. William has made an offer on a town house in Ashburton that looks over the green and has a little courtyard garden. The ground floor, which used to be a shop, is to be Francis' new quarters.

"You'll be able to see people coming and going," William says, anxiously, knowing that nothing will make up for what Francis is leaving behind him. "And you'll have direct access out into the courtyard. I've got great plans for the courtyard, I can tell you."

Francis smiles at him and agrees that he'll enjoy the change of scene and trips to the pub with William. Neither of them is fooled but it's a very fair compromise. There's a big spare bedroom for guests and a smaller one for Maxie with room for the toys and books to be stored. It's a pretty, elegant house and Francis is grateful. He's offered to contribute towards its cost but William won't hear of it. He's made some good investments with the money from his former house, he says, and Francis respects this. He insists on paying for the necessary conversion of the ground floor, however, and William has given in over this one.

There seems to be no mention of Fiona having any part to play in the purchase of the new property. Since Andy's leave she hasn't been down, and Francis suspects that the brief flowering of the old affection between her and William, back in the early summer, has died a natural death. Francis is glad of it. He can't believe that Fiona would ever settle happily again in Ashburton and he thinks that it's better for William to pursue his own friends and occupations without tensions and regrets.

As for Tim . . . Francis smiles when he thinks of Tim and Mattie, house-hunting in Exeter.

"We're having a baby," Tim said to him, "but it's a secret just for the moment. We're going to get engaged, find a little house — thank God I've got Gran's money — and then take it from there. I feel that I should tell Mattie's parents the truth but she wants me to wait and I shall trust her to know when the time is right. I wanted you to know, though, that in the end I decided that I *can* choose. And I've chosen life."

"A baby," Francis said. "How wonderful."

"Yes." Tim looked dazed, awed. "So I shall be a father. It's odd, isn't it, when only days ago I believed I had no future?"

Francis could see that he was full of joy and fear; of pride and doubts.

"Congratulations," Francis said. "Let me know when it's appropriate to celebrate more publicly," and Tim beamed at him, happy suddenly, optimistic, and said, "You'll be the first to know."

Francis longs for his happiness; for the wellbeing of Mattie and the child. He is overcome with emotion for this boy whom he looks upon as his son, along with William and Maxie, as well as his own boys: all his sons. How dear and precious they are to him.

The sudden pain in his heart is sharp and he catches his breath. He turns away from the window with short fumbling steps and collapses into his chair, his stick falling to the floor. He can hear someone moving in the house, on the landing, and he calls out weakly, hoping it is Stella.

But it is Maxie who comes in to him, though Francis hasn't the strength to speak to him. It is Maxie who

303

kneels down beside him, and strokes his hair and croons to him, as if he knows that Francis is falling asleep. He takes his father's cold hand in his large warm one and covers it with kisses and leans against him as though to keep him warm. With an enormous effort Francis raises his other hand and lays it on Maxie's head, and then gives way to the pain. But it is not of Maxie that he thinks now, nor of Nell nor Liz nor of his boys. His last thought is of Father Theo, his intent look of compassionate love, and of his prayer . . .

. . . so I shall rejoice:
you will not delay, if I do not fail to hope.

SUMMER ON THE RIVER

Marcia Willett

As summertime beckons, Evie's family gathers once more at the beautiful old riverside house they all adore. But when Evie discovers a secret that threatens their future, a shadow falls over them all: this summer by the river could be their last together . . . For Charlie, a visit home to see his step-mother Evie is an escape from his unhappy marriage in London — until a chance encounter changes everything. In the space of a moment he meets a woman by the river and falls in love, and his two worlds collide. As Evie and Charlie struggle to keep their secrets safe, they long for the summer to never end. Can the happiness of one summer last for ever?

INDIAN SUMMER

Marcia Willett

For renowned actor Mungo, his quiet home village in Devon provides the perfect retreat. Close by are his brother and his wife, and the rural location makes his home the ideal getaway for his old friends in London. Among those is Kit, who comes to stay for the summer, bringing with her a letter from her first and only love, Jake, as well as a heart in turmoil. Years have passed since Kit and Jake last saw each other, and now he has written to Kit asking to meet again. As the summer unfolds, secrets are uncovered that will shatter the sleepy community, and even tear a family apart. But those involved soon realize that the only way to move forward might be to confront the past . . .

WILD LIFE

Liam Brown

When a troubled advertising salesman loses his job, the fragile wall between his public and private personas comes tumbling down. Fleeing his debtors, Adam abandons his family and takes to sleeping rough in a local park, where a fraternity of homeless men befriend him. As the months pass, Adam gradually learns to appreciate the tough new regime — until winter arrives early, threatening to turn his paradise into a nightmare. Starving, exhausted and sick of the constant infighting, Adam decides to return to his family. The men, however, have other plans for him. With time running out, and the stakes raised unbearably high, Adam is forced to question whether any of us can truly escape the wilderness within.

POSTCARDS FROM THE PAST

Marcia Willett

Can you ever escape your family ties?

Siblings Billa and Ed share their beautiful, grand old childhood home in rural Cornwall. Their lives are uncomplicated. With family and friends nearby and their free and easy living arrangements, life seems as content as can be. But when postcards start arriving from a sinister figure they thought belonged well and truly in their pasts, old memories are stirred. Why is he contacting them now? And what has he been hiding all these years?